ARROWS HISSED PAST MARTIN'S EAR...

One thunked into a tree near him. Phronsie cried out in alarm as a rain-glistened brave pinioned Martin's arms and threw him to the ground.

Then an iron-hard forearm locked around Martin's throat. Desperately he struggled, hands ineffectually clawing at the stranglehold. Gradually he slumped, his body limp. For a brief moment the Sioux relaxed. With the last of his strength, Martin dropped to his knees, pulling down hard. The Sioux rolled across his back, toppled, and sprawled in the pine needles. With a screech Martin flung himself atop the slippery body, his hands seeking his enemy's throat....

THE
SANTEE
MASSACRE

Robert Steelman

A DELL BOOK

Published by
Dell Publishing Co., Inc.
1 Dag Hammarskjold Plaza
New York, New York 10017

Copyright © 1982 by Robert Steelman

All rights reserved. No part of this book may be reproduced or transmitted in any form or by any means, electronic or mechanical, including photocopying, recording or by any information storage and retrieval system, without the written permission of the Publisher, except where permitted by law.

Dell ® TM 681510, Dell Publishing Co., Inc.

ISBN: 0-440-17967-X

Printed in the United States of America

First printing—March 1982

My reason teaches me that land cannot be sold. The Great Spirit gave it to his children to live upon and use so far as is necessary for their subsistence, and so long as they occupy and use it, they have the right to the soil. Nothing can be sold except such things as can be carried away.

> Black Hawk, of the
> Sac and Fox tribes

THE
SANTEE
MASSACRE

CHAPTER ONE

At the outskirts of New Ulm the stage passed several brick houses. Oddly, each had an Indian tipi pitched in the front yard. Blanketed Sioux lounged about, some smoking, others squatting to stare at the distant hills. The whiskered driver, noting Martin's puzzled gaze, spat a gout of juice over the side.

"Government built houses for the pesky rascals, but they won't live in 'em. Keep their ponies in the parlor, store their corn and beans and issue beef in the bedchambers, and that's a fact!"

The Indians looked so indolent and peaceful that Martin was puzzled. "They don't look like they'd scalp anyone!"

"Ho! That's a rich one!" The driver pulled the reins and eased on the brake; the wheels of the stage ground to a halt on the graveled main street of the town. "These are what Governor Ramsey likes to call his 'civilized Indians.' They ain't but a small part of old Shakopee's Santee Sioux. The rest—the wild and woolly ones—are still out in the brush, ready to lift any white man's hair that comes near!" Climbing down, he helped Martin with his valise. "Me—I don't trust the civilized ones, and I'd advise you to keep an eye out yourself! Indians are savage critters, no matter if they do get a house and a plow and mule!"

New Ulm was at the confluence of the Minnesota and Cottonwood rivers, a formless settlement of wide streets, newly carpentered houses, and bustling activity, serving as a market town for hardworking German and Scandinavian farmers. On this spring Saturday the streets were filled with traps, buggies, and spring wagons. Martin, making his way through the crowds, with his valise, heard little English; it was almost as if he were in a foreign country. Trappers in buckskins trudged half bent under the weight of baled pelts brought in for sale. Blanketed Indians stood impassively against storefronts of new lumber. A few bluecoated soldiers from Fort Ridgely came out of a saloon, laughing raucously. Martin crossed to the other side of the street.

Under the roofed walk hung a sign that said North Star Eating House. For a moment Martin paused, looking through the fly-specked window at people eating pork chops and fried potatoes, cream gravy, apple pie. He was hungry, but had little money. Turning away, he searched for a general store. Levi Zook, a scrawled sign said, General Merchandise—Furs Bought At Highest Prices—Land Information—Notary Public. Zook's place was a sprawling huddle of structures: sheds, lean-tos, and canvas-roofed outbuildings, some old and weathered, others of new-sawn boards. The establishment was a busy one. Customers hurried in and out. A press of wagons was unloading, with draymen carrying boxes and barrels and cartons into the store.

There were as many people inside, he judged, as outside. The air smelled of sweat, of plug tobacco, of boots and belts, and of fresh-ground coffee. He sniffed appreciatively; it had been a long time since he had enjoyed a cup of good coffee. At home, the Colonel always insisted on the black Brazilian beans that cost a dollar a pound; the Sayre's cook ground it fresh each morning. In the Army, of course, someone boiled old grounds and the brew tasted like dishwater.

"Excuse me," he said, as a roughly dressed man bumped him. The man scowled, muttered under his breath, and went back to his pint of cider.

From the ceiling hung hams and slabs of bacon. On Levi Zook's shelves were flatirons, musty-smelling bolts of fabric, boxes of dried fish, stocking caps, glass jars of jawbreakers and peppermint sticks. A display case with a glass front was filled with nostrums: Dr. Kilmer's Female Tonic, Oriental Wart Destroyer, Electric Rheumatism Syrup, Stockman's Glanders Cure, Prickly Ash Bitters. Leaning on an anvil, Martin waited to be served, but none of the clerks paid him any attention.

"Excuse me . . ." he said again.

"What?" From behind the counter a beetle-browed man in a flowered waistcoat glowered at him around a cigar.

"I only wanted one of your clerks to sell me some crackers and cheese. Then I'll get out and make room for others."

"Wait your turn," Mr. Zook growled, chewing wetly on the stogie. "Aha, there!" Rushing from behind the counter, he collared an Indian female in a ragged calico dress. "What did I tell you, now! Get out!"

Imploringly the old woman, face crazed and fissured with age, held out a packet of rabbit pelts. "You buy? Please buy?"

"Out!" Zook roared. He took her by the arm and spun her toward the door. "And stay out!" Dusting his hands, he watched the woman flee. Then he picked up the packet of furs she had dropped and handed them to a clerk. "Ain't worth a damn, anyway, but put 'em in the back room."

There was general approval of the action. "Vermin!" the cider drinker said. "Dirty savages," a lady buying gingham sniffed. "There should be a law," someone else declaimed.

Martin was distressed at what he saw. Females, even Indian squaws, should not be treated roughly. The Colonel was polite to scrubwomen, and demanded his sons do the same. But Martin was a mild-mannered young man; besides, he did not want to attract attention. He finally managed to buy a wedge of cheese and a sack of crackers, along with a bottle of cider. The price astounded him, but the clerk shrugged. "If you can do better anyplace else, go there!"

The cider drinker guffawed.

"Ain't any other place! It's Zook's or go to hell, ain't it, fellers?"

It seemed to be a joke; everyone laughed. Martin took his food outside, eating in the shade of a newly leafed cottonwood. Around him wagons rumbled; from an earthen dugout ice from the river was dispensed at ten cents a pound; a drover rolled beer kegs down one plank and up another into the Farmer's Rest Saloon. There was no stage to Pipestone Lake, he found out from a blacksmith pounding cherry-red horseshoes. He tried without success to get a ride on an outbound farm wagon. The farmer didn't speak any English, and looked at him with suspicious eyes. In his Eastern clothing, Martin suspected he didn't look like a native Minnesotan. Well, Uncle Alonzo's farm was only ten or twelve miles beyond New Ulm, near Pipestone Lake. In that insane squadron called Lew Wallace's division, Martin had walked a lot farther than that loaded with rifle, forage bag, canteen, cap box and cartridge box, poncho-wrapped blanket, bayonet and scabbard—the military hardware he hated. He had never fired the rifle; the thought gave him a melancholy satisfaction.

In Minnesota spring weather was uncertain. He had not gone more than a mile, walking through grassy meadows near the river, when clouds formed and rain began to fall. He took shelter under a spread of sycamores along the rain-speckled river and watched the busy traffic: a paddle-wheeler breasting the current; a keelboat slogging downward with a load of kegs, bales, and boxes; a skiff with blue-coated soldiers, one of whom peered through a surveyor's transit and waved his hands. Engineers, probably; this far away, they did not worry him. The rain became heavier and he was soon soaked to the skin. Resigned, he stepped again into the open. It must be two in the afternoon and he still had several miles to go.

The narrow road turned to mud. Pulling the coat collar around his neck, he paused at a fork in the road. A sign said Pipestone. Far down the narrow trail was a small lake, glittering for a moment in a shaft of sunlight. Then the lake disappeared in the rain. He took the turn, not sure he was on the right road. But as he slogged around a bend, he came on an infantry outpost, two sodden soldiers, wrapped in shelter halves, muskets askew like misplaced tent poles. It was too late to evade them. He cursed himself for trudging along with his head down, unseeing. Infantry outposts were common in the farmlands around Washington. After Bull Run McDowell had pulled his frightened army back, and it was suspected that rebels lurked just across the Chain Bridge. But in Minnesota?

"Where you goin', sonny?" the taller of the two demanded.

The shorter man demurred. "First you got to say 'Who goes there,' Casey."

"Advance and be recognized," Casey conceded.

Reluctantly Martin shambled forward, his boots clumps of sticky mud and felt hat drooping. From their unmilitary appearance he decided the two were only militia, from Fort Ridgely, across the river. Still, even militia were now under Federal command.

"Where you goin'?" Casey repeated.

Martin put down the valise, heavier with its weight of water. "To—to Mr. Alonzo Tarrant's farm at Pipestone Lake.

"What's *your* name then?"

He considered lying but abandoned the idea. Who in frontier Minnesota could know Martin Sayre, late of Jamaica Plain, near Boston?

"Sayre. Martin Sayre."

"What you doin' out here?"

"Well, Alonzo Tarrant is my mother's brother. When his wife died—Aunt Flossie—he came out here to farm. He was born here, and when she died and they didn't have any children, there wasn't anything to hold him back East anymore so—"

"Hold on!" Casey commanded, holding up a magisterial hand. "Now just a minute, while I ponder this!"

The small man was impatient. "Hell, Casey, he ain't no Indian—look at that shock of whitey-lookin' hair! Major Keefe said we was to keep an eye out for Santee Sioux!"

Two bumbling fools, but with guns! Martin thought without amusement.

Casey was unsatisfied. "Why ain't you in the Army, a young feller like you—answer me that!"

An idea came to Martin.

"The reason," he explained, "well, I've got to admit it—I've caught the consumption."

They drew back, scowling. Coughing once or twice, not a difficult feat in the chill rain, Martin felt he had already contracted a catarrh. The small man was nervous. He drew out a dirty handkerchief, through which he spoke.

"Hell, he ain't noways fitten for no Army anyway, Casey, a beanpole like him! For Christ's sake—let him go before we get lung fever ourselves!"

When Martin coughed again, heavily, clutching the coat about his narrow chest, Casey gave in. "All right, you, on your way!" he grumbled.

Martin picked up his valise. "Thank you, gentlemen."

In May the sun was already far north, but with the rain clouds twilight came early. For a moment a slit of orange sun appeared in the west and the drizzle ceased. A deer crossed the road ahead of him, turning to watch him with bright soft eyes. Then a flash of lightning lit the dark sky, thunder boomed, and the deer bounded into the brush. Rain came down in sheets. Coughing genuinely, and sneezing, Martin wiped his eyes to peer at a roughly lettered board where the road, at this point little more than a path, was joined by a treelined lane. A. Tarrant, the sign read.

At the far end of the lane was a glimmer of yellow in a window. Gratefully he hurried toward the small house. For a moment he stood before the door, listening to water draining from his garments. Uncle Lon and Aunt Flossie always had nice things. When she died, and Lon went west, his uncle had taken most of the pieces with him. It would not do to ruin a good rug.

"Uncle Lon?" He knocked. Silence, except for the drumming of the rain, then the lamp winked out.

"Uncle Lon?" he called again. He knocked, this time harder. "It's—"

The door flew open and he almost fell into the parlor. His uncle stood in the doorway, a shotgun leveled.

"Who are you?"

"It's me, Uncle! Martin Sayre!"

"Martin?" Alonzo Tarrant stared. "Martin?"

Martin turned sideways so the scanty light better illuminated his features. "Don't you recognize me?"

"But you were in the Army—"

"I know," Martin said. "May I—may I come in?"

His uncle threw arms about him. "Martin! I—I couldn't believe my eyes! Come in, come in, and take off those wet clothes! I'll put on some tea!" He leaned the shotgun in a corner near the door. "I'm sorry about that, but with Shakopee and his braves running loose a man can't be too careful. Why, only last week—" He broke off. "Good Lord, here I am jabbering like an old fool!" Rummaging in a clothespress, he drew out pants and a shirt. "You and I are about the same size. You're a Tarrant, not a Sayre. Change in the bedchamber over there!"

Grateful for dry clothes, Martin sat down at the kitchen table. His uncle cut slabs of bread, sliced ham, and dropped it in a skillet. "There's fresh milk in that jug, and I've learned to bake cookies." Sitting across from Martin, he watched him eat. Martin was famished. At last he pushed his chair back.

"More ham?" Alonzo asked. "Won't take a minute to fry it."

Martin shook his head, feeling strength return to his slight frame.

"No, thank you, sir."

Alonzo leaned forward. Now it was full dark. The light from the Argand lamp lay in yellow pools on the tablecloth.

"Maybe you can tell me what in tarnation you're doing out in Minnesota, two thousand miles from home!"

Martin looked for a long time at the glowing circular wick.

"The Colonel wrote and said you'd enlisted in Lew Wallace's division," his uncle prompted.

"I did, Uncle Lon."

"But what—"

Martin could not look him in the eye. Instead, he folded his arms on the table and laid his head on them. For a long time he couldn't talk.

"What's wrong?"

Head still on arms, Martin asked, "Have you heard anything from home? I mean . . . from Mother?"

"No. But then you know the mails are slow coming all the way out here. Sometimes it's a month. Once it was nearly two."

"I guess they haven't heard—yet."

His uncle was silent, stubby fingers stroking the pepper and salt beard. "You deserted, then?"

Wordlessly Martin nodded, tightened his clasped hands.

"Well, they'll surely take it hard, you know that. Your pa—and your brother Lucas."

"I know. The Colonel—he'll die of it."

His uncle's voice was gentle. "Tell me about it, Martin."

After weeks of flight, deception, hiding, it was a relief to put it into words. Slowly Martin straightened, staring at the flame of the lamp as if it could warm the chill in his heart.

"It was at Shiloh, in what they called the Peach Orchard. It *was* a peach orchard, too, but there weren't any peaches yet. I guess maybe there won't ever be, the way the trees were shot to pieces. Right nearby was a little pond, and the Rebs sneaked down there for water. We rushed them—" He paused, swallowed hard. "I mean . . . the rest of our company rushed them. I kind of lagged behind, a little. Anyway, there was a fight and the pond turned bloody, with men lying half in and half out of the water, screaming—"

"Take your time, boy! Here, have some more tea!"

"One of the Rebs had been shot in the hip. He was lying there, in the water. My sergeant saw the Reb had a map in his breast pocket. He told me to cover him, and he splashed in to get the map. But then—" Martin breathed a shuddering sigh. "The Reb had a pistol in his belt. He—he pulled it out and shot Sergeant Dobbs!"

Uncle Lon made a sympathetic sound, patted Martin's hand.

"Dobbs depended on me to cover him! But I couldn't pull the trigger!" Martin rocked in an agony of remembrance. "I—I couldn't, Uncle! I couldn't shoot that wounded Reb! I couldn't kill anybody! God, I tried! I pulled up my piece and sighted right down the barrel at his face! But I couldn't shoot! Do you know what I'm saying?" He rose, spilling his tea.

"Hush, now," Uncle Lon took his arm, pulled him down. "Hush, Martin. It's all over now, boy."

It was almost like the time Martin had been ten and was climbing an apple tree at Uncle Lon's and Aunt Flossie's big house in Braintree. The Tarrants had no children and were fond of Martin and Lucas. The Colonel and his mother had been sitting on the veranda drinking lemonade when Martin fell and broke his arm. Martin had wept, and the Colonel and Martin's brother were ashamed when he cried out while the doctor was putting on the splints and patching the bloody gouge on his forehead. Uncle Alonzo saw him to bed. "Martin," he comforted, "don't feel bad. Some men cry, some don't. I cry myself when I feel bad." He pulled the sheet up around Martin. "You see, the Colonel and your brother are true Sayres. They're soldiers born. Lucas will go to West Point, like his pa. You're different. But that don't mean you're not as good. After all, you can paint and draw and play the violin, and they can't. So you see, we do the best we can with what we've got." Still, Martin thought miserably, he was no longer ten years old and could not take comfort from that.

"I'm sorry," he said at last. "I didn't mean to take on like that, sir. Anyway . . ." He held the cup in a shaking hand while his uncle poured tea. "Some of the men saw what happened. They told the captain, and they came for me to put me in the stockade. But I heard them and I—I ran away. There was money left from what the Colonel gave me when I enlisted so I bought some clothes from a colored woman and finally got to Louisville and across the river. Then I—well, I bought a ticket on the cars and finally reached New Ulm this morning."

"Does the Colonel—does anybody—know where you are?"

"No!"

"Not even Lavinia? Lavinia Greene, wasn't it—the young lady from Dedham you were engaged to marry?"

"Especially not Lavinia. No, no one knows, though I don't doubt they already got word at home that their son is a—a coward, a deserter!"

Uncle Lon patted his arm. "What you need, boy, is a good night's sleep." Taking a brown bottle from a cupboard, he poured rum into Martin's tea. "Makes for good sleep, I've found." He opened the door to an adjacent room. "Make yourself to home, just like it was our old place in Braintree! That's the old walnut bed you and your brother used to sleep in when you came to visit. Cost me a pretty penny to have it shipped out here on the cars, but it was Flossie's pride and I couldn't leave it. Tomorrow we'll talk things over."

All night long rain pattered on the roof, matching Martin's mood. He slept fitfully. Waking in gray dawn, he listened to rivulets of water splashing from the roof to the sodden earth below. Throwing back the sheet, he rose and went in the borrowed nightshirt to the window. Far down the lane, ghostlike in mists from the lake, something moved. He rubbed sleep-bleared eyes, and squinted again. It was gone; perhaps another deer.

Knowing he would not be able to sleep again, he wandered into the parlor. Gray light shone dully on Aunt Flossie's sideboard, lingered on frames of ancestor Tarrants. Uncle Lon sat by the window dozing, shotgun on his lap.

"Uncle Lon?"

His uncle started, jumped up. Embarrassed, he blurted, "Must have dropped off!" Pulling aside the lace curtains, he looked down the lane. "They're gone, I guess."

"Who?"

Uncle Lon put the shotgun back in its corner. "The Sioux. They're restless these days. Wander around a lot, especially at night. A body's got to keep a sharp eye out."

Martin felt guilty. If he had known, he could have spelled his uncle during the night. He was about to say something when he realized the awkwardness of his position. In the Army he had never fired his gun. Uncle Lon must have been thinking the same thing.

"That's all right, Martin," he said cheerfully. "Let's make breakfast and see what the Lord's new day brings!"

Morning dawned wet but clear. Jeweled spiderwebs hung in the tall grasses of the pasture where Uncle Lon's cows grazed, and a rooster greeted the sun with triumphant crows. Uncle Lon baked biscuits, pouring gravy over them from fried ham of the night before. "When Flossie passed over," he said, "I had to learn a lot of things I never bothered about before. There's nothing like a good woman to ease a man's life."

Dully Martin thought of Lavinia Greene. Condemned to the life of a fugitive, he would probably never know the ease of a good woman. Lavinia was good—and pretty.

"I've been thinking," his uncle mused, sipping coffee. "Certainly no one out here knows you, Martin. And I do need help on the place." He smiled, sheepishly. "Farming was always my dream, you know! But maybe I bit off more than I can chew—alone, anyway." Pushing the last bit of biscuit about his plate, he sopped up gravy. "You're certainly not one of the husky farm lads they raise around here, but you'll get on to mowing and haying and milking. I'm an old man and my time is short. Maybe the whole farm will be your's anyway, some day. What do you say?"

Uncle Lon's place had been a welcome haven. For the first time in months Martin felt some small security. But in his mind he had thought of his uncle's farm as a place to hide. Now to emerge into the bright sun of summer, to abandon a safe haven?

"Uncle Lon, I—I don't think it would work. I mean—after all—people will see me, be curious, want to know who I am."

His uncle gathered the dirty dishes, placed them near the pump.

"Nothing in this life is sure, Martin. But things have a way of working themselves out. You need time to think things over, get a perspective on your life, make some important decisions. You can't hide forever. A boy—excuse me, I mean a *man*—a man with your talents, holing up like a coon in a hollow log. Why, Martin, that'd curdle your very soul! What kind of a life would that be? No, you've got to take a chance, and let the future work itself out as it will."

Martin felt a chill wash his stomach.

"Anyway, there are no neighbors nigh. Nearest is old Kurt Sigafoos, a mile and a half upriver. And few come by here, especially since the Sioux scare. What say, Martin?"

Uncle Lon was right. Martin drank the rest of his coffee, wiped his lips with one of Aunt Flossie's monogrammed napkins; during her life she must have embroidered thousands.

"All right," he agreed. "If you'll teach me, sir, I'll try to help you. I'll try hard."

During the next few days he learned more than he cared to about farm chores. With blistering hands he hauled and tugged at worn plow handles while his uncle's mules looked back in mulish amusement. He shelled corn, cut wood for the cookstove, milked awkwardly but thoroughly, fed the chickens, and gathered eggs. At night he fell into bed exhausted, too weary to fear being discovered. Anyway, Uncle Lon's farm was off the beaten path to New Ulm and there were few passersby. However, they did have one visitor. Martin, washing up for supper, looked nervously down the lane as a rider jogged toward the house. For a moment he froze. The rider passed behind the screen of trees bordering the lane, and he wondered who the man was. When he cantered up to the water trough Martin saw he was a minister of some kind, a tall, angular-faced man in sober black. One hand was on the reins and the other held a Bible.

"Well," the stranger said, swinging down. "And who are you, young man?"

Martin hesitated. Finally he said, "I—I'm working for Mr. Tarrant, sir."

The cleric came beside him, washing his hands also, drying them on the coarse cloth that hung by the pump.

"Alonzo about, is he?"

"Yes, sir." Martin gestured. "He's cooking supper." Raising his voice, he called, "Mr. Tarrant? You have a visitor!"

Hands dusted with flour, Lon came to the lean-to door.

"My goodness, this *is* a pleasure!" Hastily wiping palms on his trousers, he hurried to shake hands. "Guess you don't know this young man, Bishop! He's . . ." Alonzo paused for a moment. "This is Martin, a

young man I hired to help me with the chores. He's
. . . from back east, near my old home in Braintree,
and came out for a visit."

Martin shook hands with the bishop, admiring the
delicate way his uncle had safeguarded him yet not
told a lie. The Tarrants had a reputation for probity.

"Reverend Whipple is bishop of the Protestant Episcopal Church," Uncle explained. He held open the
door. "Come right in, Bishop. I've got supper on the
table, and you're a welcome guest!"

Tucking a napkin into his collar, Bishop Whipple
smiled.

"Martin," he said, "I've been trying to get Alonzo to
call me Henry for a long time, but somehow or other I
can't succeed!"

Uncle Alonzo handed the bishop a bowl of bean
soup flecked with ham and onion, urged cornbread on
him, poured warm milk into the bishop's glass.

"Henry, then. I'll try."

After supper they sat in the parlor, dimly lit with
twilight. Outside, birds chirped drowsy calls. Crickets
sawed various tunes, the lace curtains swayed in an
evening breeze. Martin sat apart, listening to the two
men talk about the Indian troubles.

"The main problem," the bishop said, "is the way
the Santee Sioux have been treated by our white men.
The record doesn't bear too close examination. We've
helped ourselves to their lands, sometimes paying ten
cents an acre, sometimes just appropriating it. Indian
women are violated by white ruffians every day, and
people like that rascally trader Levi Zook victimize
them at his store. I can't say as I blame Shakopee and
the younger braves for keeping to themselves in the
hills and refusing to have anything to do with the government's houses and hoes!"

"Respectfully—Henry—they're still a menace to Minnesota folk. A man can't sleep nights when they come down and prowl around the way they do! I'm sure they've been stealing eggs at night."

Bishop Whipple sighed. "It's a serious problem. I'm not proud that all I've been able to do is pray for a solution, something fair and decent for both sides. I sent a letter to Governor Ramsey but so far I haven't gotten a reply."

"In New Ulm," Martin ventured, "I heard something about an annuity they get."

"I guess you could call it a kind of a bribe. One of the treaties requires the Indian Bureau to give the Sioux an allowance of flour, sugar, beef, tobacco, things like that, each year. But Congress has been so busy with the war they haven't even appropriated funds. That's one of the things that's currently riling our Indian brothers. The 'civilized' ones are getting as feisty as Shakopee and his—I guess you could say 'wild' Indians." The bishop sighed again and rubbed the worn leather cover of the Bible that was always near to hand. "I look for *real* trouble soon."

Whipple stayed the night; Martin gave up his bed to roll himself in a blanket in the lean-to kitchen. He had a bad dream. He was running somewhere, floundering in a sticky morass. Lights followed him, flaming torches. Hounds bayed. Finally he could no longer lift his boots from the mire. Helpless, he fell back, caught in the adhesive grip. A white face loomed above him, burning eyes stared down the barrel of a rifle. The face, he realized, was the face of his brother, Lucas. "No!" Martin shouted, putting up his hand. "No—please, Lucas! Don't!"

Sweating, heart pounding, he woke. Had he cried out, waked his uncle or the bishop? Sitting upright, he heard only night sounds: a metallic *clink* as the stove cooled, the rustling of curtains, a faint *whoooo* from a distant owl. Finally, he lay down again, sleeping until dawn came.

After breakfast the bishop left, riding to Lac Qui Parle to see an ailing parishioner.

"I liked the bishop," Martin said, putting on his tattered straw hat and preparing to harness the mules. "He seems a good and decent man."

Uncle Lon, wiping breakfast dishes, shook his head. "I give you that, Martin. Still, a lot of folks think he's too easy on the Sioux. Always excusing them, say, and taking their side."

"Well, maybe someone's *got* to take their side, Uncle. According to the bishop, they're getting the worse of it."

"Maybe." Carefully his uncle put the Limoges on a shelf. Martin remembered that china from long ago when Father and Mother and Lucas and he went to Braintree for Sunday dinner. Lavinia would often be at table, too. The memory was painful.

"Maybe," Uncle Lon repeated. "But I sure wish they'd get things settled! I don't raise my chickens for the damned Indians to steal the eggs!"

Martin was shocked; he had never heard his uncle use profanity.

Uncle Lon was quickly embarrassed. "Don't usually use words like that, Martin," he muttered, hanging up the towel. "Since Flossie's gone, I kind of slipped a little. Excuse me."

That day the sun was hot, and the air still. Martin jerked at the plow, trying to make the straight furrow Uncle Alonzo demanded. Sweating, he stopped from time to time to take a drink of what Uncle Alonzo called switchel, a concoction of vinegar, sugar, and water from a jug covered with a cool wet rag. Overhead, a hawk wheeled against the cloudless blue. In the distance, trees and rocks wavered in a heat mirage. Letting part of the liquid drain pleasantly down his shirt, he listened to busy hammering from the henhouse. Uncle Lon was replacing broken roosts.

Anxious to finish the field, he plodded on till the sun was low in the west. Pausing at the rail fence, he wiped his brow. The hammering in the henhouse had stopped. In the still of late afternoon the world seemed deserted except for the wheeling hawk.

"Martin!"

He laid down the jug.

"Martin!" There was alarm in his uncle's call. "Come quick!" The mules pricked up their ears. Silently the hawk slid down the west toward a promising target.

"I'm coming!"

Wondering, he started toward the henhouse. Then he broke into a run, loping awkwardly across the new-plowed furrows as he heard the squawk of chickens.

"I'm coming! What is it?"

Anxious, he clambered over the barnyard fence, hurried to the freshly painted henhouse. As he approached the open door he sensed, rather than saw, alien presences. Sunset red splashed inside as panicky fowls scattered about, wings flapping.

"Uncle, where are you?"

In the fury of feathers he could not see his uncle. Turning quickly, he ran outside, toward the back of the structure. As he did so he caught a glimpse of hurrying figures at the edge of the woods. The figures moved quickly, with purposeful grace. As he watched, they slid into the trees and were gone.

He called again, voice panicky. "Uncle Lon?"

Back of the henhouse, he found his uncle. Alonzo Tarrant sprawled like a rag doll across the woodpile, egg bucket clasped in his hands. A Sioux arrow was in his back and the bald poll split like a ripe Persian melon, white outside and pink within. Martin cried out. With a chill feeling he realized the meaning of those swift graceful figures sinking deep within the woods. They were Indians, Santee Sioux Indians. They had wanted eggs. When his uncle surprised the intruders in the henhouse, they had turned and killed him.

CHAPTER TWO

His first reaction was to flee—run headlong, screaming with terror. Trembling, he stared at his uncle, trying not to believe. Someone was talking. *"Uncle Lon. Uncle Lon."* Dazed, he realized it was his own voice, repeating the name over and over. *Uncle Lon!*

As if a candle had winked out, the sun disappeared behind the trees. The world turned dark. One of the cows—Adelaide, probably—mooed in discomfort; she needed milking. It was a curiously domestic sound, at odds with tragedy. Martin sat down on a stump, pulse heavy and drumlike in his temples. *Uncle Lon!* And he had not been able to help. "God!" he muttered. He did not know whether it was a prayer or a curse.

Wetting his lips, he looked around at the barnyard. It would do no good to flee. After all, the Sioux had seen him plowing. They could have killed him while he plodded behind the mules. But all they wanted was eggs. Now they had them, and were gone.

New Ulm was twelve miles away, through the oncoming night. He ought to go there quickly, tell them of the attack, alarm the town. He would be safe in New Ulm. But what about Uncle Lon? He could not leave him sprawled on the woodpile, staring up at the rising moon. He remembered lurid novels about Red Indians, and how the squaws multilated their husbands' victims. Suppose the women came and— Quickly he rose to reach for a shovel. Adelaide mooed and switched her tail. "I'm sorry," he said, and jammed the shovel into loamy soil near the kitchen door.

The night grew. Stars stitched the sky. Sweating, he dug deeper and deeper. Six feet, he thought, was the custom, but he ran into hard clay and decided three feet was enough. After all, it was only a temporary grave. As soon as possible, he would return to see that Uncle Lon had a proper grave and service, along with a headstone.

After taking the coverlet from the old man's bed, he broke off the arrow and managed to wind the quilt about the stiffening form. Alonzo Tarrant was slight and small boned. Martin was similarly small, a Tarrant, in contrast to the Colonel and brother Lucas. Tugging and hauling, Martin finally dragged the body to the grave, Alonzo's heels scoring dark traces in the dew-wet grass.

For a moment he stood at the edge of the grave, looking at the shrouded body. He did not know what to say, although as a child he had always gone to the Congregational church with his parents. Finally, clasping his hands, he found a few words. "Lord, he was a good old man. Be merciful to him, and remember we all loved him. Amen!" Then he went into the house.

Fearing to light a candle, he filled his pockets with oatmeal cookies. Uncle Lon kept what he called his "ready money" in a tin box on his bureau. Martin almost guiltily took the small roll of greenbacks; his uncle would not need them anymore. Into his battered valise he stuffed a few items of clothing. Standing for a long moment at the parlor door, he looked around at the homely furnishings: his uncle's rocker, the mahogany table bearing the Argand lamp, Uncle Alonzo's spectacles on a folded copy of a month-old Boston *Globe*: JACKSON IN SHENANDOAH VALLEY!

In chill moonlight he hurried down the cottonwood lane to the road. The way to New Ulm lay ahead, a ghostly ribbon narrow and winding, little more, really, than a footpath. Leaving the familiar farm, he tasted fear sour in his throat. Behind every maple, every oak, every sycamore could lurk a red assassin. Still, there was no other way. The night was cool, and he buttoned the coat about his neck and started off.

Near him an owl hooted. Something fluttered in the branches of the trees that overhung the road, making of it a dark tunnel. Flinching, he hurried on. In the distance an animal howled, a wavering cry that set his teeth on edge. Uncle Alonzo said it was a myth that wolves ate people. Still, the sound was not reassuring. By the time he had gone a mile his heart was pounding and he felt panic in his belly. Suddenly he noticed he was not walking any longer; he was trotting. Finally he broke into a run, blundering into sumac and scrub oak.

Catching his boot on a root, he fell, heavily. For a while he lay in forest debris, trying to catch his breath. Moonlight filtered through the trees. *Pull yourself together!* he told himself. *Don't be a child frightened of the dark! Indians probably sleep at night just like folks in Braintree!* Sheepishly he got up. The cookies in his pocket were ground to dust.

Suddenly he realized he was not on the road. Where *was* the damned goat path? Frantically he peered through moon-washed trees. Somehow in his panic he must have wandered away from the pale, dusty ribbon. Carefully he walked this way and that, like old Caesar at home when the beagle was on the trail of a rabbit. Surely it was in this direction. No, this! He laid down his valise, walking a few yards north; at least he thought it was north. New Ulm was east of Alonzo Tarrant's farm, though. Uncertain, he turned, squinting up at what he thought was the Dipper, faintly seen through a leafy ceiling. The road, then, ought to be—

He was lost, he finally realized. Lost in the Minnesota woods! Retracing his steps, he found he had misplaced his valise. Cursing, he sat on a hummock, angry and confused. Where in damnation *was* he? He took out a handful of cookie crumbs and ate them, licking his palm. Then he was thirsty. Getting to his feet, he felt a boot squish in a dank pool. He sprawled on hands and knees, drinking gratefully of dead-tasting water.

Refreshed, he abandoned his search for the valise and wandered on, hoping sooner or later to reach the river. Then all he had to do was follow the course of the Minnesota until he reached New Ulm. But as the moon dropped lower and lower, the river eluded him. He was panting for breath now, dank with perspiration in spite of the cool, hands torn with fending off vines and clinging branches. His knees, he suspected, were bleeding. They hurt abominably, and then he realized it was because he was climbing, going higher and higher on a rocky slope. He felt the way a frightened cat feels skinning up a tree to escape pursuit. At any rate, he was now high enough to get a good view of the Big Dipper. Puzzled, he stared at the diamond-bright configuration. If *that* was north, then he had been traveling in a direction opposite from where he should have been! Discouraged and hopeless, he sank down on a boulder. What use to struggle on in this savage wilderness, so different from the well-mannered woods country around Jamaica Plain? After a while he sagged back against a ledge, closing his eyes.

Uncle Lon. Uncle Lon was dead! Drugged with fatigue, he dreamed. The Colonel, Braintree, Lew Wallace's insane brigands. *Don't shoot. Please don't shoot!* The sooty railroad station in Louisville, where he had run out of money and sketched the stationmaster for a fee of two dollars. *Uncle Lon.* Lon was dead. His white beard grew in the ground, tendrils weaving their way among moles and earthworms. Hairy roots twined and burgeoned; finally the white creeping things reached Martin and snaked into his hair, wound about his arms and legs. *No!* he cried. *Please, don't! Oh, God!*

Dazed, he sat up, rubbing his eyes. Where was he? His muscles were streaks of fire, and his joints made of rusty iron. Licking his lips, he felt the tongue strange in his mouth, seemingly overgrown with moss. Blinking, he opened his eyes to see morning sun combing the trees. Quickly he closed them, feeling a lance of pain stab his brain. In that brief flash of light there had been something strange, something alien. Cautiously he opened one eye again, and sprang to his feet in alarm. Cross-legged on a boulder, musket across leathern knees, a hawk-faced savage watched him. The Sioux wore a long-tailed fur cap, and a beaded necklace encircled the lean neck.

Martin backed away in dismay to find himself cornered in a rocky cleft. He pressed against the cool flat rock, paralyzed. It was like the Peach Orchard all over again; he couldn't move. At long last Martin Sayre had come to his end, a proper and deserved end. He had betrayed his family, he had betrayed his country. Closing his eyes, he waited for the merciful bullet. He hoped it would be the bullet, not the scalping knife.

When nothing happened he opened his eyes. The Sioux stirred, stretched long legs. The savage had a hatchet, he saw. Perhaps the grim-visaged warrior would use that to split Martin Sayre's head, like Uncle Alonzo's, and save a precious bullet.

"Hello, pilgrim," the Sioux drawled, uncoiling lazily from the rock and sliding down to stand spraddle-legged, propped on the musket. "Who the hell *are* you, now?"

The Sioux had spoken perfect, if somewhat crude, English. Not only that, the Sioux was a woman, or more exactly a girl. Cradling the musket in the crook of her arm, the squaw prowled toward Martin in an animallike way that made him uneasy. Goggle-eyed, he stared.

"I said hello!"

Sioux, Martin knew, had long black hair. How to account for straggly red hair and hard, china-blue eyes?

"I—I know," he quavered. "I mean—I know you said hello. I—who are you?"

"I asked you first, didn't I?"

Lank and unkempt, clad in greasy buckskins, there was a definite odor to her. Accustomed to Lavinia Greene's French scents, he drew away. Still and all, the smell was not unpleasant. The strange girl smelled of woodsmoke and sweet grass—and blood. There were bloody stains on her hands, and on the bosom of the buckskin shirt.

"Yes. I—I guess you did." Cautiously he left the rocky cleft to circle her, wary. "My name is Sayre. Martin Sayre."

Calculating, she eyed him. "Looks like you had a brush with a catamount. Your shirt's all tore and them pants is ripped down the side."

Modestly he tried to pull together the rent in his trousers. "I—I've had a bad experience." Relieved of his fear, he started to tell her about the horror, voice racing nervously ahead of his brain. "They killed him! They killed him and I had to bury him and I started out for New Ulm but I got lost and missed the road and—"

"Stop gabbling like a turkey hen and slow down!" the girl commanded. She pushed him down on a ledge. Folding her long legs, she squatted beside him and scrubbed her dank locks with her knuckles. "Jesus, I got them bugs in my hair again!"

In spite of his disgust he kept his place beside her and started a more coherent account of the happenings of the day before—and the night, the horrible night. After all, she appeared to be civilized, or at least semicivilized; perhaps she would lead him to New Ulm. Gradually calming, he told her the story of his uncle's death at the hands of the marauding Sioux, burying the old man, the subsequent flight, and getting lost. Arms locked around her buckskin knees, the girl made sympathetic noises as he talked.

"My, you *are* a greenie! You surely need someone to wash your didies. How in hell could anyone miss that road? It's the only goddamn road *around* here!"

"It was night," he said stiffly.

She wiggled her toes in the beaded moccasins, fingered the odd bone whistle hanging about her neck. "Old Mr. Tarrant! Lordy, lordy, lordy! Why, I was by there only last week, and he give me some eggs and an onion. He was a fine old man, only he didn't belong out here. Didn't know beans about farming."

"It was murder!" Martin cried. "Plain murder! He never hurt anyone!"

"I don't hold with killing. Still and all, Sioux has been killed, too, and cheated and hornswoggled. They got a grievance."

"How can you take their side? You're white, I can see now!"

"I don't take sides. I try to stay in the goddamn middle, but it ain't easy."

"What's a white girl doing up here on the mountain, dressed like a savage? I couldn't believe my eyes!"

"Name's Phronsie. Short for Sophronia, which is what my pa named me." She giggled, tossed the mop of dirty hair. "Ain't that a hell of a name—Sophronia? Anyway, I trap for a living. Wolf, bear, beaver, fox—whatever I find. Old Zook down in New Ulm is a skinflint, but he generally gives me fair price. Pa—Jake Bettencourt was his name, before he cashed in his chips—when Ma died, Pa took me up in the hills and taught me how to get along." Her face saddened. "Pa died of the apoplexies last winter."

"You mean you—you *live* up here, all alone?"

She nodded toward the rising sun. "Up the crick, there. That's my diggings. I just took me a little stroll whilst the coffee was boiling and come on you."

"I'm sorry about your father," Martin said. He got to his feet, dusting dirt and twigs from his jeans.

"Now I want you to guide me to New Ulm. I've got to get there in a hurry and warn them!"

Phronsie leaned back against the ledge, crossed her legs comfortably. Tipping the fur hat over her eyes, she yawned. "Can't."

"What?"

"I said I can't. I got a packet of hides that's got to be fleshed and cured or they'll go bad in the heat."

The stony slope warmed as the sun rose. Martin wiped his forehead, annoyed.

"Look here—I'm lost already, and I'm sure I can't find the way by myself! These woods are thick. I wouldn't know what direction to start off in!"

"What's your hurry?"

"Why—why—I've got to warn them, do something! It's not right for me just to stand here while white people are in danger!"

She pulled a blade of coarse grass, chewed on it.

"Won't you help me, damn it?"

When she did not answer, he stamped angrily off. He did not know where he was going but at least it was downhill. The river ought to be in that direction. "All right!" he grumbled. "I'll go by myself!"

Pushing the fur cap back from her eyes, she looked at him, standing hot and impatient in the sunlight.

"I wouldn't advise it."

"Why not?"

"No way can you help your uncle now, and the folks down there surely know Shakopee's braves is restless. Anyway, old General Sibley is down there bawling for help and collecting cannon to fight the Sioux. They don't hardly need you. Better lay up with me a spell, 'less'n you want to lose that fine shock of yaller hair."

At the gruesome thought, he stopped in his tracks. Still and all, he had an obligation. "I'm going anyway. It's my—well, it's a duty."

Shrugging, she got lankily to her feet, picked up the ancient musket. "It's your funeral," she announced over her shoulder. "The woods is probably smokin' with mad Injuns this fine morning."

He hurried after her. "As soon as we can, then? I mean—take me to New Ulm?"

"Guess so."

"Here!" he said in contrition. "Let me carry that old blunderbuss! It must be heavy."

She gave him an icy stare. "Been doin' for myself for years, pilgrim! Don't need no help. Besides, you got all you can do to take care of yourself."

She did not speak again, only loped easily into the brush. Martin shook his head. Phronsie Bettencourt! What a strange wild girl!

Major Lucas Sayre, United States Army (retired), waited at the gate for the postman. Caesar, the gray-muzzled beagle, sat patiently at his feet. Lucas, propped on his cane, looked far down the street and cursed the dawdling of the Post Office.

"One month, exactly!" he growled to Caesar. "Kit Burke has had plenty of time to answer my letter! Probably exchanging lies with the rest of the coffee coolers at the War Department!"

Seeing nothing down the street but old Mrs. Buckley watering her iris, he limped back into the house. His bad leg was hurting.

In the sunroom of the big white house the Colonel was reading the *Globe* and smoking his morning cigar. Lucas's mother knit socks for Martin while the maid cleared the breakfast table.

"No mail yet, eh?" the Colonel asked, invisible behind his paper.

"No, Father. Damn it all, there's been plenty of time for an answer!"

Mrs. Sayre smiled, sweetly. "Now, Lucas, you're always so impatient! What with the war and all, I'm sure Captain Burke is very busy!"

The Colonel emerged from his cover, ruddy countenance and woolly white eyebrows wreathed in Havana cigar smoke. "I've told you all along, Lucas. Don't depend on the damned War Department for anything. When I was in the field with my regiment in Mexico, we had to do for ourselves. The damned shoulder-straps in Washington sent us oilskin slickers at Cerro Gordo when we needed calomel, water buckets when we needed gun oil and cleaning patches! They're a marvel of stupidity, so don't put your hopes in them."

"Besides," Mrs. Sayre added, "you've done enough for your country already. Your poor leg—and how many Congressional Medals have been awarded to Massachusetts boys? Not many! Yours is certainly proof enough that you've done your duty. Why don't you sit down and have that last cruller and some coffee instead of pacing so?"

"That reminds me," the Colonel said. "We haven't heard a word from your brother Alonzo for a month of Sundays, Mary."

"I know." Mrs. Sayre let the knitting fall into her lap and stared out the window. "I'm worried. It's not like him to miss writing."

"I wouldn't concern myself about Uncle Alonzo," Lucas said, patting her hand. "He was no farmer, you know. With that place he bought out in Minnesota he's probably got his hands full, and is too busy to write." His lean face wrinkled in an unfamiliar grin. "I remember how he was all thumbs when he tried to fix something. Aunt Flossie always used to have to rescue him. Remember the time Alonzo fell in the well when he was trying to fix the pulley?"

The Colonel chuckled. "The Tarrants were never what I'd call practical people! Wrote poems, played the harp, things like that."

Mrs. Sayre was indignant. "Now it's not nice to laugh at Alonzo! He's one of the nicest men on this earth! Besides, what's wrong with poetry and music? All you Sayres know is war and battles and such!"

The Colonel leaned from his paper and kissed her. "Just funning, Mary. We wouldn't change you for a prime coonhound, would we, Lucas?"

"Martin, too," Mrs. Sayre murmured.

"Eh?"

"Martin. His letters have been getting fewer and fewer." From her bosom she took a folded paper, put on her spectacles. "Let me see . . . this last one, why, it was six or seven weeks ago! Something must have happened to him!"

"Now don't worry so," the Colonel cautioned. "You know how you get worked up about things. Wallace's division has been in reserve for months and Martin can't be in much danger. Probably they've got him busy peeling potatoes and carrots. Might have cut his thumb, but that's about all that could happen to the boy."

"Lavinia, too," Mrs. Sayre mused. "Lavinia hasn't heard from him either. I was over there the other day and Mrs. Greene says Lavinia is awfully worried."

"Women!" the Colonel grumbled, returning to the *Globe*. "Always fussing about something!"

Lucas's face was somber. "For men must fight, and

women weep." He stared down at the stiff leg. "One thing I know for sure. No female is going to want a cripple like me!"

Mrs. Sayre rose quickly, went to him. "Now don't talk that way, son! It's not true!" She put her cheek against his. "You're a hero, and women are always thrilled by a hero."

"Listen!" Lucas held a finger in the air.

"What, son?"

"I think I heard him whistle!" Awkwardly Lucas reeled to his feet, hurried to the door, letting himself carefully down the steps.

The postman stood at the whitewashed gate. "Letter for you, sir."

"About time, damn it!" Without thanks Lucas took the letter and limped back up the graveled path. War Department, the envelope said in the corner.

"It's here!" he announced, dropping into a chair, cane clattering to the floor. "Yes, it's from Kit Burke, all right! Got his initials right here in the corner!" Eagerly he tore open the envelope and spread it on the breakfast table.

"What does it say, dear?"

Lips working, Lucas scanned the letter. His face fell. With an oath he crumpled the letter and flung it from him.

"Bad news, eh?" the Colonel asked, folding the *Globe*.

Lucas gnawed at a knuckle, stared at the floor where the cat was batting the crumpled letter with its paw.

"The worst. Kit says they're topheavy with brass right now. They—they can't use me."

"Oh, that's too bad," his mother said. "I was so hoping—for you, I mean."

"I know how you feel, Lucas," the Colonel sighed, reaching for a fresh cigar from the mahogany box. "Of course, I feel the same way. It's hard on a soldier, any soldier—especially an old relic like me—to sit in a corner." Leaning over, he retrieved the crumpled letter, smoothed it with the flat of his hand. His eyes were still good. He read Kit Burke's copper-plate script, lips moving silently.

"God damn it!" Agitated, Lucas rose to his feet, bracing a hand on the table. "Excuse me, Mother, but I wanted that job! Christ, I can sit at a desk as well as any man! And I know supply! I got the best marks in my class at the Point in supply and logistics! Why don't they send some of that fat-butted brass to McClellan and make room for me?"

"Wait a minute," the Colonel said.

Mrs. Sayre leaned forward, concerned.

"There's more, Lucas," the Colonel said in a tight voice. "You—you didn't read the rest."

"You mean there's a chance—"

The Colonel shook his head. "No. Not that, but—" He broke off. Slumped in his chair, he looked very tired. "You read it, son. I—I can't."

Lucas took the letter and held it close to the window for better light. "Topheavy with brass . . . no chance . . ." His face paled as he reached the unread portion of Kit Burke's letter.

> But beyond that, old comrade, there's something else I should tell you. I particularly wanted you to know before the official word got to you. Your brother Martin deserted under fire at Shiloh. I haven't got all the facts yet but will inform you as I learn them. He refused to use his rifle under

direct orders from his sergeant. When the smoke cleared the provost went to arrest him, but he had fled.

The Colonel rubbed his forehead, stared at the floor. Mrs. Sayre's hand went to her throat. Lucas swallowed hard; the lean Adam's apple moved up and down under the stiff collar of his blue uniform:
"I know this will be hard on—"
Lucas stopped reading.
"Read the whole thing, son," Mary Sayre said quietly. She put her hand on the Colonel's. "We want to know."
Lucas started again:

I know this will be hard on the Colonel and you. The Sayres have always been military men of the highest caliber, honorable and valiant. But I hope you won't be too discouraged. There may be circumstances—

"Jesus!" Lucas cried. "*What* circumstances? Here I am a damned cripple, wanting to fight, and that brother of mine is able-bodied, and *refuses*! What circumstances could there possibly be, tell me that!"
"Please!" Mrs. Sayre begged. "Lucas, don't talk that way! We don't know yet what happed. Kit seems to say that all the facts aren't known."
"A deserter!" The Colonel's face was ashen. "Martin Sayre. A Sayre, from Jamaica Plain! Deserting at Shiloh!" Wearily he got to his feet, laid down the half-smoked cigar. "Mary . . . Lucas . . . I've got to excuse myself. I'm going in to the library and lie down on the couch for a while. I've got to think about this."

Ceasar strolled through the door from the garden, looked inquiringly about. Sensing trouble, he sprawled on the floor, head between paws, looking up at his master. Lucas reached down and scratched the long mottled ears; Caesar whined, licked his hand.

"Lucas," Mrs. Sayre pleaded, "don't take on so, son! You know, Martin was always . . . well, different. It's not up to us to judge. The Lord saith—"

Awkwardly Lucas rose, propped himself on the cane. "The Lord also saith, 'An eye for an eye, a tooth for a tooth'!"

"Whatever do you mean, son?"

Lucas didn't answer. Instead, he hobbled down the hall into the dim leather-smelling library. The Colonel lay on the sofa, staring at the ceiling.

"Father," Lucas blurted, "we've got to do something about this!"

Lucas wondered if his father had heard him. Then the old man sat up, clasped hands between his knees.

"Did you hear me, sir?"

"I heard you." The Colonel reached for the bourbon decanter, poured himself a drink. "Do something? What, God damn it all? Do *what*?"

Lucas helped himself to the bourbon. The cane fell clattering to the floor, and he cursed. Without its support, he collapsed on the leather sofa. Together he and the Colonel sat for a long time, companions in shame. Finally Lucas tossed off the drink and set his glass on the table.

"I don't know," he admitted. "I don't know what we can do. But I'll think of something." He glared balefully at the cane. "By God, I'll think of *something*!"

CHAPTER THREE

The trapper female's camp was deep in the forest, approached by a winding trail that was little more than a narrow trace through brush and vines. Martin, scrambling on rocky slopes and gasping for breath, caught only glimpses of her buckskin back.

"Wait!" he called, collapsing on a fallen log.

She turned, peering back at him through the willows bordering a stream. "What's the matter?"

He had to wait before replying. "I'm not used to this."

Something approaching contempt was in her voice. "Damn it, I got work to do! You done rested enough. *Hopo!*"

Hopo was a word strange to him, but there was no mistaking its meaning: *let's go*. Unhappily he got up, trotted after her.

At last they came to a clearing. The stream they had followed splashed happily through a meadow, foaming into a deep pool. A fire still smoldered. Over it, on a tripod of saplings, hung an iron pot. Martin smelled coffee boiling in a tin panikin. On a stick stuck into the earth a strange flat slab of meat was broiling. Piles of iron-jawed traps lay about, and furry pelts in profusion, some piled high, others stretched on circular frames of bent branches, laced to the frames with rawhide. Wolf, some looked to be; others might be fox, beaver. One particularly shaggy pelt, he was sure, was bear. Other pelts were baled, and tied with more rawhide strings. All stank. At the edge of the clearing stood a rude shelter, a lean-to of saplings roofed with pine boughs laid up like shingles to shed the rain. Nearby was a rude cross of peeled branches over a grassy mound, with a bunch of withered wildflowers in a glass jar.

"Sit," Phronsie invited, pointing to a stump.

Exhausted, Martin sat. Sniffing, he asked, "What's that?"

"What's what?"

"The meat. Smells like—well, roast pork."

Phronsie squatted before the fire, pulled out the stick on which the flounderlike thing had been roasting, and laid the meat on a flat rock. Taking out her sheath knife, she cut off a piece, peeled it, and handed it to Martin on the end of the knife.

"What is it?" he demanded.

"Beaver."

She cut herself a slab. Grasping it in strong white teeth, she tugged on the other end with one hand, at the same time snicking off a mouthful. The knife narrowly missed her lips. "Beaver. Beaver tail." Reddish juice ran down her chin. She wiped it with the sleeve of the buckskin shirt. "This here is a nice fat one!"

He felt queasy.

"Ain't you hungry?"

"Beaver," he said. "Well, beaver is—beavers look like some kind of a big rat."

"Probably are," she agreed.

"Have you got anything else? I mean—bacon, or maybe bread and butter?"

Tugging on the meat in her teeth, she stared in disbelief. "You funnin' me? Now where in damnation you expect me to bake bread? Or raise pigs? Or milk cows?"

"I just thought—"

"Lordy, lordy!" She was disgusted. "You *are* a greenie! Well, let me tell you there ain't nothing better than meat, wild meat. Pa and I lived on it for years."

Martin was famished. Still, the image of the rodent-like beaver would not leave his mind. Phronsie paid him no more attention, only continued her pulling and snicking and chewing. After a while he muttered, "Well, maybe I'll try it."

She handed him another chunk on the point of the murderous-looking knife. Gingerly he bit, let a small piece roll around in his mouth. The image of the whiskered beaver began to fade. It wasn't *too* bad, something like beef, with a dark aftertaste.

"Could I have another piece?"

"Like it?" she asked, cutting off a bigger chunk.

"Well, it's a little strange."

"Filling, though, and healthy, real healthy."

He ate that, then another chunk, and finally finished a large part of the tail himself.

"Damn me!" Phronsie said. "I never see anyone eat like you. You must have a tapeworm, pilgrim."

Martin wiped hands on his shirt, and restrained a belch. "It was good. Rich, though." He staggered to his feet, feeling his stomach. "Oh, am I full!"

Phronsie dragged a raccoon skin from a pile, squatted in the sun, and picked up a bone scraper. "Got to get busy," she said. Holding the tool in both hands, she worked the scraper all over the carcass, getting as much meat as she could. Out of the corner of her eye, she saw Martin staggering to the woods, his face green. She started laughing. Finally, white and shaken, he tottered back to sit again on the stump.

"It's hardly funny!" he grumbled, wiping his mouth.

"I'm sorry I laughed! But you looked so comical!" Still scraping, she added, "Wild meat takes a little getting on to. And beaver tail *is* fatty."

Martin was still bilious. Watching him, Phronsie finally laid down her scraper, went to the lean-to, rummaged in a leather bag. Coming back, she poured a handful of brown powder into a cup of water, mixing it with a twig until it was a greenish-yellow liquid. "Here," she said, handing the tin cup to Martin. "Drink this. It'll soothe up your gut."

He was wary. "What is it?"

"Don't you trust me?"

"What is it?" he insisted.

"*Wi tan ots.*"

He was puzzled.

"*Wi tan ots!* Anyways, that's what the Sioux calls it. Cattail roots. Dry 'em in the sun, grind 'em up. I always keep some on hand. Good for bellyache, loose bowels, all kinds of things."

He tilted the cup, tasted.

"Drink it all," she urged. "You'll feel better."

He drank, and felt better. The gaseous billowing in his stomach subsided. Feeling better, he offered to help.

He knelt beside her and she handed him another

scraper. "Push hard—" She stared at him. "What is your name again?"

Knees on the hide, pushing hard on the fleshing tool, his stomach began to feel uncomfortable.

"Martin," he answered.

"Martin what?"

"Martin Sayre. Alonzo Tarrant was my uncle, my mother's brother."

She sagged back on her haunches. "You must be from back east, too."

Swallowing hard, he stopped scraping. There was a sour taste in the back of his throat, and his stomach rumbled.

"From back east? Why?"

"Well, you wasn't birthed out here, I know *that*. Couldn't no one from out this way be innocent as you are." She squinted at him. "Scrawny, too—kind of measly looking."

Martin hiccuped, put a precautionary hand to his mouth.

"What's the matter—Martin? You look kind of green."

The image of the beaver, a huge whiskered rat, overwhelmed him. Staggering to his feet, he fled to the cover of the surrounding trees. In a sunlit glade he gave back all the rich beaver meat. Discomfited, he thought he heard her yawn, stretch.

"You sleepy?"

He blinked. "Well, it's been—let's see—yesterday morning I woke when it was still dark, and I haven't slept much since."

Phronsie took off the fur cap, wiped beads of perspiration from her brow. "Bed down over there, then, in my place."

He shook his head. "As long as I'm here, I want to help."

Mischief in blue eyes, she grinned, stuck the cap back on at a rakish angle. "Guess I got to give you credit for trying, pilgrim—"

"Martin."

"Martin, then. But you ain't no help." She picked up the skin he had been working on, held it to the light. "You don't need to push so damned hard as all that." The skin side of the hide glowed with tiny sparks where sun shone through. "No, it takes a touch, Martin, and you ain't got it." She nodded toward the lean-to. "Go rest!"

Gratefully he rose on legs that seemed to be melting, like a candle left too long in the sun.

"All right," he agreed, "but I want to do my part. Is that understood?"

She grinned again. "*Compris*, like the Frenchies say."

Falling into the lean-to on a soft pile of furs he knew nothing more. When he woke it was late afternoon; sun lit the clearing with a golden glow. Passive, he lay in the lean-to, staring listlessly. His glazed eyes picked out bales of fur, the dead fire, a battered coffeepot, a tin that said Mohav Coffee. Then, suddenly, recollection flooded back: Uncle Lon, his mad flight through the night, the wild girl. Sitting up, he rubbed sore arms, sore calves, sore shoulders. His mouth tasted dark and mysterious, but the cramps and gas had disappeared.

The girl! Phronsie! Where was she? Without her he felt alone, defenseless, in a hostile forest. Scrambling to his feet, he searched the clearing.

"Phronsie!"

Nothing. No answer.

Ashamed of his fright, he called again anxiously. "Phronsie!"

Indians might be lurking about. Too, he remembered the blue-coated militiamen; they might be out on scout and discover him.

"Phronsie! Damn it, where are you?"

He heard a distant voice, then saw a commotion in the willows along the stream. A moment later she emerged, dragging a limp doe. Puffing with effort, she dug in her moccasined feet and dumped the animal beside the fire. "What in hell you yelling about, anyway?"

He swallowed, hard. "I—I didn't know where you were."

"Well, *I* knew!" she said. "Lordy, Martin, you spook easy."

"But—Indians—"

Rolling the animal over on its furry side, she gutted it with one long easy slash.

"They ain't like to bother us."

Seeing insides spill out in a bloody torrent, he was sick again, and turned aside.

"Thought a little venison might be nice for supper," she said cheerfully. Hoisting the doe, she wrestled it high to hang on the stub of a limb. In spite of nausea he forced himself to approach.

"Can I help?"

She shook her head. "Don't need no help."

Again he smelled that odd mixture of woodsmoke, sweat, blood, woman. Martin was a healthy young man, with a young man's appetites. For a long time he had been without a woman. The Colonel had taken him early to a refined house, advising the merit of periodic visits until he married Lavinia Greene. In the Army, too, there had been brothels available. Naked harlotry disgusted him, and so he had been continent. Now, however, he felt an uncomfortable stirring in his loins. Phronsie was a woman, though hardly in Lavinia Greene's image. Lavinia was all laces and French scent and giggles.

"All right," he grumbled, and again knelt to flesh the pelts. This time he was more careful. When she had dismembered the deer carcass and cut off some choice chops, she nodded, approvingly.

"Pilgrim—"

"Martin!" he insisted. "Pilgrim sounds like you're making fun of me."

"Martin, then! I'll try to remember. But what I wanted to say—you ain't doing a half-bad job. You might be a help to me after all, and maybe learn something whilst you're about it."

"I'm glad to help," he said, "but I don't intend to stay around here very long. I want to get to New Ulm as soon as I can."

She spitted the chops on green twigs. Poking the ends of the twigs in the ground, she adjusted the meat over the glowing coals. "Ain't nothing in New Ulm for a man to pine for. It's an ugly little town. Full of farmers."

She was right, of course. Again he thought of the soldiers. With the military telegraph, word of his defection might quickly travel even to Minnesota. What about California, then? He could get there. He had Uncle Lon's money, and it was a long way from Shiloh. He doubted they had even heard about the war out in California.

"But," she agreed, handing him a chop, "I'll take you down there when I pack my furs in to Zook's, if you want."

The outside of the meat was crackly brown, the inside a delicate pink. Martin ate ravenously, licking his fingers. This was different from beaver tail; it was like something from the grill of the Parker House in Boston, where Uncle Lon always took him on his birthday. They ate clams there, too, and vanilla ice cream. He felt a pang of nostalgia.

"Is your chop all right?"

Lost in reverie, he started. "Yes. I guess so."

She was close, looking intently into his face as if anxious to please. He did not intend to offend her, but the strange woodsy odor made him draw back, chop poised. Instantly her face changed, becoming set and hard. Slowly she rose. Perhaps she blushed, he thought, though her skin was so brown and weathered he was not sure.

Contrite, he reached out, but she drew away. "I—I didn't mean to—"

"I know what you mean, pilgrim!" Snatching off the tattered fur cap, she knuckled her scalp defiantly. "Bugs again!" she said, with forced gaiety. "Lordy, they purely love me, don't they?"

"But—"

"For all I care, Martin whatever-your-name-is, you can go to New Ulm right now if you want, or for that matter, plumb to Hell!"

Now I've done it! he thought miserably. *I need her, and I've hurt her!*

"Phronsie! I—I—"

Giving him a withering look, she said something short, hard, and bitter in a gruff tongue that must have been Sioux. Kicking the fire into a shower of sparks, she ground the rest of the meat into the ashes.

Angry, and still hungry, he blurted, "Now that was a silly thing to do! Just because I—"

"You're a prig!"

"Well, I'm a gentleman, and you're surely no lady."

She faced him, her eyes hot, fists on buckskin hips. "Never said I was, did I?"

"What was that you called me a minute ago?"

She grinned, malevolently. "That's for me to know and you to find out."

"It was Sioux, wasn't it? Sioux talk! You're a savage! Like those murderous scoundrels that killed my uncle! I don't trust you any more than I would them!"

She tossed her head. "What if I was a Sioux, greenie? I'd be proud of it."

Baffled, he could only shake his head and mutter. Phronsie, satisfied with victory, made an obscene sign, probably Sioux also, but unmistakable in its meaning—thumb thrust between first and second fingers. "Get the hell out of my camp!" she spat, and strode into the willows.

Martin was penitent, not only from compassion but from necessity; he needed Phronsie. That night he slept again in the lean-to and was afraid. Owls hooted, a wolf howled from a far-off ridge. Martin was sure he heard a bear sniffing about the camp. After a while he slept, tired in mind and body. When morning came, Phronsie was already broiling deer liver and making coffee from the diminishing Mohav can. Uncertain, he splashed water on his face from the tin basin and raked fingers through his hair. He was a fine one to talk about others; his own blond locks were stringy and dirty, and maybe—just maybe—he had bugs himself. Sheepishly he approached.

"Good morning."

She didn't look up.

"I—I'm sorry about last night."

She shrugged. "Don't make me no never mind."

"I'm really sorry, Phronsie. You're right; I am a bit

of a prig." With muttered thanks he took the chunk of liver she handed him. "You gave me hospitality when I needed it, and I'm grateful. I'll try hard to make it up to you, believe me."

He worked hard. There seemed an endless supply of fresh pelts: beaver, mink, fox, wolf, even three glossy black ones from bear. When he thought he had completed the last pile Phronsie disappeared and brought from a cache more bundles. His hands grew sore, then blistered, formed callouses. He grew accustomed to the kneeling posture, the stretching forward and back, fingers numb from the bone scraper.

Working, he thought of home and family—the Colonel, mother, Lucas, Lavinia. What were they doing at this moment? The Colonel was surely smoking a cigar. Mother would be knitting, Lavinia writing her soldier boy a letter never to be delivered. Lucas, bold Lucas, was in Virginia with his regiment, confounding the enemy and winning medals. So many years Martin Sayre lived in his brother's shadow. Still, he was not resentful. That was, he had long ago decided, the way things were. *Karma,* they called it in India, he remembered from Oriental Philosophy under Dr. Biddle at Harvard College.

They ate well, very well; venison steaks, deer liver, fish from the stream. Phronsie snared young rabbits and fried the best of the tender flesh. Martin recognized some familiar things like lamb's quarters and wild onions, gooseberries and currants. But there were strange edibles that Phronsie, now somewhat mollified, identified.

Stirring a stew in her iron pot, she held up a peeled tuber. "The Sioux call these bear roots. They're a kind of wild turnip." Chopping greens on a board, she explained, "This here is wild spinach." Martin enjoyed the tart red berries she gathered and asked, "What are these? I like them."

"*He tan i mins.*"

Seeing her in a good mood, he gibed, "I wish you wouldn't talk that Sioux gabble."

"Sarvisberries, then."

When he craved sweets, there was a stone crock of box-elder sap, boiled till thick and treacly, eaten by dipping a finger into the crock and licking it. It was gross manners, but Phronsie had no spoons. "Anyway," she assured him, "fingers was made before spoons."

"*Were* made."

Licking the peeled stick with which she was stirring the stew, she squinted. "Eh?"

"Fingers *were* made. That's better than saying fingers *was* made."

For a moment there was hostility in her eyes. "I don't hold overmuch with grammar. It ain't never brought me a dollar."

Days passed; he became strangely content. Phronsie, working at her own fleshing board, watched him closely. "With the grain, Martin. Always with the grain." At times she even nodded approval. One day she startled him by saying, "God damn me, you final turned out to be a help instead of a hindrance!" Almost shyly she put out a brown paw. "Thanks, Martin. I—I'm grateful, too. We're partners, eh?"

He smiled. "Partners, Phronsie."

She was an amazing creature. He began to see depths in her he had not suspected. At night, after chanting some Sioux gibberish, she rolled herself in a blanket and slept near the forest pool at the edge of camp, leaving the lean-to to Martin. When he protested she only shrugged. "I like it better outside."

The lean-to, of course, was "outside" to Martin, who was accustomed to sleeping in a proper bed. Still, he was so steeped in the belief that females needed shelter and comfort more than men that he insisted, thinking it a kind of gallantry that had been lacking in his relationship to her. She gave him a quick answer that injured his pride.

"Stop jawing, will you? City folk ain't used to the wilderness and has got to be cosseted." Malice in the blue eyes, she grinned. "Someday, when you get to know your way in the woods, I'll let you sleep out in the air, too."

"*Let* me?" he fumed. "I guess I can sleep anywhere I want to!"

Amused, she only tossed her head, stalking away to the pool with her ragged Hudson Bay blanket.

At times she could be strikingly feminine in spite of the wild appearance. Her fingers were dextrous at sewing and patching. With scraps of gingham from her "possibles" bag she mended Martin's ragged jeans. From her excellent cooking Martin gained weight. He had always been a finicky eater, but the hard work—scraping skins, chopping wood, hauling water, doing the many chores—began to toughen him. He grew almost comfortable in their relationship.

To entertain him, she sang songs in a clear sweet soprano, old ballads like "The Turtle Dove," "The Maid of Amsterdam," and "Lydia, My Love." There were comic songs, too. When he thought about home and was sad, she cheered him with "The Gray Goose" and "Miss Bailey's Ghost." Sometimes, merely to pique him, he was sure, she sang an unfamiliar song titled "My Days Have Been So Wondrous Free." It seemed to Martin she compared her own wild existence to his civilized upbringing:

> My days have been so wondrous free!
> The little birds that fly
> With careless ease from tree to tree
> Are not so blest as I!

Still, his guilt would not die. The burden of the flight from Wallace's division lay heavy. One night he woke in alarm, bathed with sweat, crying out. They were after him, the bluecoats! Blindly he scrambled from the lean-to, blundering about in utter panic. Then he realized Phronsic was beside him, a strong hand gripping his arm.

"What the hell's the matter?" she demanded.

Dazed, he stood in the moonlight, body trembling. "I—I—"

"You see a ghost?"

Gradually he calmed. "In a way, I guess. I just ran. Really, I didn't know what I was doing."

"A nightmare, then."

He swallowed, wrapping arms about him against the night chill. "I guess so."

In spite of his insistence that he was all right she made him a hot drink with another of her heathenish Sioux herbs. Wrapped in her blanket, she squatted at his feet and watched him. "Drink it all. That's the way. Damn it, it ain't going to hurt you! Drink up!"

He downed the bitter stuff and felt better.

"Martin, you got something on your mind. You want to talk about it?"

He stared into the red eye of the fire. Maybe that was what he needed, to talk to someone, in talking somehow to explain to himself. Finally he decided. Perhaps it was the Indian brew she had made, perhaps it was only his own feeling of helplessness.

"It's something personal," he told her. "It's very important to me. I want you to understand. Good Lord, I want *me* to understand! It seems I don't remember exactly what happened or how it happened. Maybe if I go over it again it'll come clear."

She was silent, watching.

"I'm a deserter, Phronsie."

"A what?"

"A deserter. I deserted from the Army. From the war. From Wallace's division, at a place called Shiloh."

She seemed unimpressed, which annoyed him. "I heard about the war. It ain't come out here yet."

"Don't you understand? I'm a deserter, a traitor! When I came out here to my uncle's farm, I was running away! The Army was after me, to court-martial me!"

She looked puzzled.

"A trial! A court-martial is what they call it in the Army. If they ever find me, they'll shoot me! Sometimes when I wake up so wild and crazy, I am dreaming they found me, the bluecoats, and they are going to shoot me!"

She adjusted the folds of the blanket against the chill. The moon was gibbous, a silver bowl high in the sky; the forest murmured night sounds. In the distance something crashed through the brush. There was silence again except for the dying rustle of embers, a feathery brush as an owl soared against the moon, the burble of the creek.

"What did you do then, that you had to run away?"

He told her.

"So you wasn't a very good soldier. I guess I wouldn't be either. I don't mind killing animals. They expect it, and I do it quick so they don't suffer. But I don't reckon I could kill a human, either, unless he was after my own scalp."

He sighed. "Not even then, I guess. I mean—not even then could I kill. I'd probably be like a damned sheep, just standing there, ready to die!"

She shook her head. "Anyone can kill when they're threatened. A body can kill if someone dear to him is in danger, too. You could, Martin. You ain't so damned different, after all."

"I don't know."

"Look here." She got to her feet and poked a stick at the fire. It flared up, briefly and she examined his face. "It ain't like you was afraid of the enemy, was it? You just didn't want to kill another human."

"The Army won't see it that way. I'm a deserter, and they've got to make an example out of me." He watched the flames die again, only a bluish glow.

"Well, you're safe here, ain't you?"

His voice was harsh. "I don't want to be safe anymore!" He remembered Uncle Alonzo's words. *You can't hide forever. A man with your talents, holing up like a coon in a hollow log! Why, Martin, that'll curdle your very soul!* Maybe that was what was the matter with him; his soul, his immortal soul, was curdling. "I want to go to New Ulm, Phronsie! Will you at least set me off on the right track in the morning?"

She considered this, standing motionless in the moonlight, arms crossed on her breast, shifting from one bare foot to the other. "If you're bounden to go, I guess you can go. But look at it this way, Martin. You ain't about to shoot anybody, like you said. So they don't hardly need anyone like you down there. What they need is people that ain't afraid to kill. Kill Indians!" Her voice grew angry. "Kill 'em all! Kill the Sioux! Get the bastards off'n our land! That's what them damned farmers are saying!"

When she saw the dismal look on his face she paused, contrite. For the first time she touched him, almost timidly.

"God damn me, Martin, I didn't mean—"

"I know what you mean," he said heavily. "You're right. Nobody needs a coward. I wouldn't be any use to them."

"Jesus Christ, Martin—I didn't *mean* it that way!"

He got to his feet. His stomach churned, and he felt confused and distraught. "I'll stay, of course. But when your pelts are all fleshed and dried and packed, I want to go to New Ulm, Phronsie, if you'll take me. I'm a white man, and I belong with white people, no matter what they do to me. I'm tired of running away. What will come—will come."

One day at noon, the sun overhead so that the trees cast almost no shadow, he and Phronsie rested from their labors, eating more of the deer liver he favored. It was pink inside and tasted fresh and delicate, not at all like odorous liver and fried onions back home. Realizing the sun was near the zenith, Martin wondered how long he had been in Phronsie Bettencourt's camp.

"Penny for your thoughts!" she joked. Replete, she sprawled on the new grass, carving an Indian flute from a green stick of willow. "God damn!" Quickly she licked her thumb where the knife had slipped and cut her. "Now how come me to do that?"

"A penny?" he murmured. "Is that all?"

She was annoyed at her awkwardness, and drove the blade of the offending knife into the ground. "Probably all they're worth!" Holding up the flute, she squinted through it. "Looks pretty fair, anyways." Putting it to her lips, she blew, uncertainly. "It pleasures me to make these things but I ain't—I'm not—

much of a musician! Guess I got a tin ear, like Pa did. He liked music, though. I do too, though I don't hear much anymore."

He took the flute from her. "Let me try." He blew a few notes. Some were off key, but on the whole the crude instrument did very well. Then too, he had not practiced for a long time. In the Army he had had an ocarina—what the Johnnie Rebs called a "sweet potato"—but he did not want to think about the Army. "Wait a minute. I can do better than that." Moderating his breath, he finally managed a mellower tone. Encouraged, he blew a few notes of Bach.

Phronsie's eyes widened. "Damn me, that's pretty! How did you do that?"

He played a little more as he remembered it—awkwardly, and with a few false notes, but ending with a passable trill.

"You musical, ain't you? I can tell."

Properly handled, the Indian flute was capable of a sweet and appealing tone. Phronsie was awed. She sat wide-eyed, hands on knees. After a while she said, "How about something lively?"

Pondering a selection suited to primitive tastes, he tried "Yankee Doodle." But she shook her head. "Guess I liked that first tune the best. That kind of . . . well, it was sort of up and down and back and forth, like a—a hummingbird, skipping round from flower to flower."

He smiled. "*De gustibus non est disputandum.*".

She frowned. "What was that?"

"Just a little Latin. It means—well, like 'everyone to his own taste.' We all have different likes and dislikes. In music, as in other things."

"You speak Latin, then?"

He liked the smooth slippery feeling of the peeled

willow in his fingers and he stroked it, almost sensually. "Italian, too. Maybe a little German."

She wriggled closer. He felt the warmth of her buckskin thigh against his own.

"By God, you're eddicated, ain't you? Quality, I'd say!"

It was not often he impressed her, and he savored the moment. "Yes," he admitted, "I've been to college. Harvard College."

He had not known this tall lean girl could be soft and yielding. Her pressing against him made him suddenly uneasy. For distraction he picked up a scrap of sun-dried hide and took charcoal from the fire. Idly he began to draw. "At the conservatory I had one course in sketching. I was never very good, but—" Turning his head, he peered at her from a corner of his eye. "Stay like that for a minute, will you, Phronsie?"

"Why?"

"You'll see."

He drew rapidly, fingers awkward at first but little by little regaining their old fluency. Actually, he had been rather good at it in those untroubled student days before the war.

"What *are* you doing?"

"Your picture. Sit still and don't move! I'll be finished in a minute."

Professor Rigney, he thought, would have been proud of him; Martin was elated at the knowledge he had not lost the knack. Of course, it could hardly be called a portrait. It was more caricature, emphasizing the strong lines of the face, the wide eyes, the firm jut of the chin, the hair just washed and glinting in the sun. Finally he was done.

"I'm sorry I didn't have colored crayon," he apologized, holding up the boardlike hide. "It would have come out much better."

For a moment she stared. Then she got up, gracefully, like a young animal, moving to a place where the full blaze of sun illumined the sketch.

"Oh, Martin!"

He dusted his hands, satisfied.

"You made me look pretty!"

He did not remember making her look pretty. When she returned to kneel beside him, he took another look. She was not a beauty. Her rough look and even rougher ways hardly brought out any residual pulchritude. Yet he had to admit that, somehow or other, and he did not understand how, he had made Phronsie look—well, at least, appealing.

"You made me look pretty," she repeated. Rising, she touched his cheek in a quick gesture that seemed to embarrass her as much as it did him. Then, almost gruffly, she said words he had never expected. "Thank you, Martin."

That night, after a long day, he prepared for bed. The last thing he remembered was hearing Phronsie move about the camp, and the sound that meant she was grinding more sunflower seeds to have them ready for their morning "coffee." They had run out of Mohav. She was singing, too. Drowsily he realized the melody was Bach, pure Bach, though he could not make out the words. Sioux gibberish, probably; he was amused at the thought of Papa Bach hearing his melody sung to Indian words. Then he drifted off, but did not sleep well. For a long time he lay quietly, hands clasped behind his head. Well, maybe she *was* pretty, in a savage way. Or she *could* be pretty, laundered and scented and put into civilized clothing. He heard a splashing mingled with the clear flutelike voice; what was she doing?

Moonlight lay on the camp like a fall of new snow. Curious, clad only in ragged drawers, he got to his feet and emerged from the lean-to. *Mirabile dictu*— Phronsie was bathing in the pool at the edge of camp! Though Martin himself frequently washed from the tin basin, using Sioux soapweed and modestly screened behind the willows, he had never been quite sure that Phronsie even took off the greasy buckskins. They seemed integral as her skin.

Moving silently, he approached the stand of willows bordering the rocky pool. "The little birds that fly with careless ease from tree to tree"— Parting the willows, he saw a slender form washed in moonlight— "are not so blessed as I!" Unaware, she soaped her arms, her shoulders, her breasts. He had never seen a woman naked like that, except, of course, for prostitutes. Lavinia Greene—of course he had never seen Lavinia's body, and probably never would. Even when they were married it was customary, he understood, for females to disrobe privately, slipping only then into an unrevealing nightgown. But Phronsie Bettencourt now looked so appealing, so vulnerable, that a new dimension to his sexual awareness was established. Not knowing what he was going to do, and yet knowing perfectly well, he slipped into the cool pond. Slowly, his chin just above water like a swimming beaver, he approached. Still she sang, cupping hands to pour water over her body, white as alabaster. The only thing Phronsie Bettencourt wore was the eagle-bone whistle about her neck.

Putting his head under, he reached out to grasp the firm young legs. Amused at how he would startle her, he rose, dripping. But he was unprepared for the reception. With a warwhoop Phronsie twisted free. A fist driven like a piston smashed into his mouth; her knee found his groin. Quickly ill, he bent over. Like a wildcat she was on his back, viselike arm about his neck, her weight bearing him down. Spluttering and choking, he sank to the sandy bottom, a bare foot planted firmly on his back. Wriggle and flail as he would, he could not free himself. It was true, he realized, that as a man drowns his life flashes in serial form before his eyes. Martin was a child again, at Uncle Alonzo's in Braintree, drinking lemonade on the green lawn. He was a young boy at school, and a promising student at college. He saw himself playing the violin at the conservatory, and then he joined the Army and quickly ran away. There was Uncle Alonzo's pale face as he lay dead, murdered. Then Martin was through the night, on his way to warn the burghers of New Ulm. He had met the wild girl on the mountain, and now she was drowning him. Trying to scream, water filled his mouth. *Dying! Dying! Dead!* Almost casually he stopped breathing, and was still.

The pinioning foot must have released him because he floated slowly to the surface. Phronsie had him by the shoulders, staring.

"Martin! Was that *you*?"

He was too spent to do more than nod.

"God damn it, why did you do that?"

He belched. A great deal of water ran out. He could only wag his head foolishly.

"Don't you *never* do that again!"

Legs rubbery, he started to sag again into the pool. She grabbed the waistband of his drawers to haul him upright.

"That was a greenie trick if I ever saw one. Out here, pilgrim, when someone sneaks up behind you and puts their hands on you, a body protects himself first and asks questions afterwards!"

He found his voice, weakly. "You—you didn't have to practically"—he belched again—"practically *drown* me!"

"How did I know who the goddamn hell you was? You might of been some rascally breed after my honor!"

Bedraggled, he stumbled to shore and sat down, trying to get his breath. "I—I'm sorry. I just thought—"

Belligerent, she stood spraddle-legged in the middle of the pool, fists doubled on bare hips. "You thought what?"

He blinked, seeing in moonlight the darkness of her forearms against the pale boyish hips.

"I thought we were friends, you see, and I—"

"Friends? Was that friendly?" She snorted, an animallike sound. "If'n I want to be mauled by a man, I damn well intend to give him permission first! And I don't recollect giving you permission to do anything, Martin Sayre, except to live in my camp whilst you're hiding out. Is that clear, pilgrim?"

Of late she called him pilgrim only when she was put out.

"Yes," he said meekly, and added, "ma'am."

CHAPTER FOUR

Early summer had come to Minnesota. On the meadows lay a blanket of yellow daisies and deep mauve hyacinths. There was the carmine of clustering vetch, and in the swampy areas around their creek the waxen blooms of mariposa lilies. Martin recognized many of the flowers; his mother had been an avid botanist. The others Phronsie identified for him, though she usually called them by some tongue-twisting Sioux name.

Neither mentioned his escapade in the forest pool. Phronsie, he had learned, took things as they came, day by day, and did not harbor grudges. Martin, however, his manliness challenged by her putting him down so easily, was made more uncomfortable by the fact that he still yearned for her. Watching her go about the camp, long-legged and lithe, small compact breasts barely showing under the supple deerskin shirt and the copper-tinged hair shining in the sun, he struggled with his urge, trying to rationalize himself out of the predicament. Ridiculous—it was ridiculous for a Jamaica Plain Sayre to harbor such thoughts about a crude frontier Amazon, a woods creature who was almost an Indian herself! Circumstances being different, how Lucas and the Colonel would have jeered at him. Lavinia would have smiled with pity, and tried to understand. Yet, there it was. He wanted her, and tried to suppress his passion by working harder and longer, keeping an eye on the business at hand.

Otherwise the wilderness life agreed with him. What the plowing on Uncle Alonzo's farm had started, the rough life had accelerated. He ate well, slept well, and became wiry and tough. With hair long and uncut and a straggly beard on his chin, he looked like a trapper himself in the leather shirt and moccasins Phronsie had made for him. Gradually his status as a fugitive left his tortured mind. Even the image of his murdered uncle began to fade in a new and healthy life. No longer did he have nightmares, but was able to discuss his situation with a certain casualness. In the lengthening days of early summer he found comfort talking with Phronsie as they baled and packed the last of the pelts.

"You been in big cities, Martin. What are they like?"

He shrugged. "Smoky. Crowded. Horsecars. Too many people. Wagons rumbling, whistles blowing."

A rawhide thong in her teeth, she paused. Her hair was neatly combed, fastened back by a scrap of red ribbon. Though she still smelled of smoke and sweet grass, the aroma had become more pleasant.

"Horsecars? What in hell are they?" When she saw the shadow of a frown on his face, she added, quickly, "I guess that don't sound so good, does it? I'm just purely used to talking so. Pa did, and he learned me."

"Horsecars," he said reminiscing. "Well, they're nothing special. Just public conveyances that—"

"What?"

"They're cars with iron wheels, drawn by a team of horses. They run on iron tracks right down the main streets and carry passengers. They're dangerous, though. In Louisville, when I was coming out here, a man was run over by a horsecar. They come down the street pretty fast, clanging their bell, and this man was deaf and didn't hear the bell. The car cut his leg off."

She grimaced, then asked, "Where is Louisville?"

He told her. She had no idea of geography.

"Well, is it near Mankato?"

He laughed. "Heavens, no! It's a long way off!" He pulled hard on a rawhide thong and turned his own bale over to cinch it on the other side. "I was glad to know how to draw, there in Louisville. I didn't have any money, and the station agent paid me two dollars to sketch his likeness. If it wasn't for that, I wouldn't have eaten. Fact is, I financed most of the trip that way, painting and sketching—prize heifers, barns, family groups, whatever people wanted." The memory stirred others. Before long he was telling the details of his flight, and then about the Colonel and Lucas and Lavinia Greene.

"We were going to be married," he mourned, stacking the baled pelt on the others. "But I guess now—" He broke off with a sigh, looking down at his hands, brown and hard, fingers calloused. The violin would be difficult.

Phronsie did not seem interested in Lavinia Greene. She got up and hoisted her pack experimentally. "If you was to go down by the little waterfall and dig some bear roots, I'd cook a mess with venison ribs for a meal."

He was on his knees, prying the tubers from damp earth with Phronsie's skinning knife, when he heard the strange whistle. He stopped, looking up, turning his head this way and that. Birds had been singing, and this shrill sound might have been a new species, winging north for the summer. Still, it did not sound quite birdlike. It was not any of the familiar bird songs Phronsie had identified for him—loon, junco, redwing blackbird, magpie, the drowsy twittering of quail.

A moment later he heard the shrill music again, this time in a descending musical figure. Uneasy, he got to his feet, shading eyes with a hand as he stared into the forest around the sunlit glade. Again, silence; nothing but the rushing of the creek, a hum of insects. Scooping up the roots in his arm, he turned to hurry back to camp. It was then that the willows along the creek parted. A paint-smeared face, topped by an eagle feather, watched him. In panic he ran, dropping the bear roots.

"Phronsie!"

Tripping on a rock, he scrambled up, looking over his shoulder. "Phronsie!"

The whistle pursued him. When he dashed into camp, breathless and bruised, Phronsie was standing at the ready, musket cocked.

"What in hell—"

"Indians!" he cried, pointing back along the trail. "Sioux Indians!" Out of breath, he could only gasp and hold his heaving sides. "They—they—"

"Shut up!" Phronsie snapped. "Leave me listen for a minute, will you?"

"There!" he cried. "Hear that?"

She put down the musket. "I damn near didn't, you was blowing so hard!" Lifting the eagle-bone whistle from her breast, she blew a similar note, falling and rising in a throaty tremolo.

"Friends," she said calmly. "Old friends. Guess we got to put some water in the stew."

Stolidly the Sioux emerged from the forest, faces grave as carved idols. They were six, tall, and broad shouldered; the sun lit them in bronze magnificence. They wore shirts of skin decorated with tufts of hair that Martin suspected were human, and bright with row on row of dyed porcupine quills. Eagle feathers fluttered from long hair or stuck upright from shaved scalplocks. Some wore necklaces of curved animal claws; the braids of others were wrapped in sleek black fur.

"*Hau!*" Phronsie greeted them, raising her hand, serious in manner as the Sioux.

"*Hau!*" repeated the tallest, a brave with a bladelike nose twisted askew. They paid Martin no attention.

One of the band appeared to be of some importance. He was the shortest one, with muscular bowed legs. His face was so knobby and seamed it looked like the carved head on the Colonel's walking stick back in Jamaica Plain. On his head he wore a stuffed birdskin fastened to a band of black fur. The face was painted blue, with a white moon on the forehead and a star straggling across the beaked nose. Standing somewhat apart from the others, he waved a ribboned wand at the black flies that this morning were mercilessly biting.

Reaching out, Skew-Nose picked up the Mohav Coffee can, shook it, and looked disappointed. Phronsie laughed and said something in the guttural Sioux tongue. Skew-Nose shrugged and squatted beside the fire; the others followed suit.

"Martin," Phronsie ordered, "go away someplace and sit. We got palavering to do, and they don't know you."

He hesitated, uncertain about leaving her. Still, she seemed quite composed, even serene, almost like Lavinia Greene welcoming members of her Dorcas Society of a Wednesday.

"Git!" she urged, an edge to her voice. Cautiously he complied, sitting on a rock at the edge of the camp and wondering how quickly he could reach the loaded musket if need be.

For a long time Phronsie sat in silence with her visitors. Finally she took from what she called her "possibles bag" a stained corncob pipe and pouch of tobacco. Gravely she passed around the tobacco, finally filling her own corncob as the Sioux tamped down stone pipes. Handing around a brand from the fire, they all lit pipes and smoked in silence. Time passed. A fly bit Martin on the neck and he swatted impatiently. The sun climbed higher. Rivulets of sweat rolled down his neck and into the bosom of his shirt. Still nothing happened; only the interminable puffing of pipes, streamers of blue-gray smoke rising to twist and curl in the sunlit air.

Finally Skew-Nose got up. His hair was fashioned into a topknot and he wore a red blanket around his thighs, held like a kilt by a cartridge belt. He spoke in a deep voice, supplementing his words by motions of his hands. Martin understood nothing of the talk but was intrigued by the graceful flow of sign-talk.

Skew-Nose was an accomplished orator. His voice grew deeper, more compelling, while his hands flashed in intricate maneuvers like the flight of birds.

Finally he held out a brown arm, corded with sinews, and drew the other back.

"*Tccchk!*" he hissed.

There was no mistaking the gesture. It was an arrow sent in deadly flight.

"*Sha!*" the other braves muttered in chorus. "*Sha, sha!*" It seemed to be an approval of Skew-Nose's words.

One by one others rose to make their speeches. Phronsie sat impassive, puffing the corncob. He had never seen her smoke before and disliked it. It reminded him of toothless hill-country grandmothers in Virginia, rocking on the front stoop and pausing only to spit into the yard.

"*Sha!*" Phronsie said, joining the others in approval.

The shaman, or whatever he was, was last to speak. He was more eloquent than the others punctuating his words and signs with slashes of the ribboned wand. Finally, in a dramatic gesture, he flung aside his blanket and displayed his genitals in impassioned contempt of something, or somebody. Martin drew in his breath sharply at such immodesty. Phronsie only continued to puff on the pipe as if such a display were a matter of course.

The speeches completed, she laid down her pipe, got to her feet. Talking in a high, clear voice, she also signed, expertly. Martin saw in her gestures a perhaps feminine delicacy of movement not apparent in the signs of the others. Reluctantly, too, he was forced to admire the way she dominated the meeting, a conclave of fierce and hard-bitten warriors. The Sioux watched intently, moving only to take a coal in horny fingers for relighting a pipe.

Somehow or other Phronsie seemed to be making

an important point. Her voice was eager, anxious, and her fingers flew in arabesques. Overall there was a consistent pattern: a graceful gesture repeated, words that appeared in the monologue and then reappeared with emphasis.

He did not know how long she spoke but it was a long time. Finally, making a flat-handed gesture that must have meant, "I am finished," she sat down.

Again there was long silence, broken only by the bubbling of the stewpot, the gurgle of pipes sucked dry. Then Skew-Nose rose; a grin split his leathery visage. Playfully he gave Phronsie a shove, and she shoved him back, giggling. Looking down his nose at puppy play, the shaman drew a hand across his bare stomach in a gesture which plainly said, "I am hungry," and stuck a finger into the stewpot.

"Martin," Phronsie called. "Take that deer haunch down out of the tree and bring it here. Company's come for dinner, and we need more meat."

Resentfully he pulled down the smoked meat and carried it to the fire where Phronsie was dishing up their stew for her guests. These were Indians, Sioux Indians, murderers, and they had killed Martin Sayre's Uncle Alonzo, cruelly and unnecessarily! Phronsie must have noticed his displeasure because she said from the corner of her mouth, "Don't look so damned grim! Indians catch on fast, even if they don't speak English!"

"I catch on too," he muttered, "even if I don't speak Sioux! You're friends with them!"

"What if I am?" She pushed him aside to hack chunks from the leathery haunch. "We're here on their sufferance. If you can't look less like a thundercloud, go take a pee or something!"

Rebuffed, he stalked back to his rock. Eating with murderers, sharing food with killers!

Phronsie and Skew-Nose appeared to be especially good friends. The tall brave dropped a wad of grass into her bosom and she retaliated by retrieving it and scrubbing his face. The rest howled in laughter. Martin had never thought of Indians as having a sense of humor. To hear them giggle and joke made him even more distrustful. Most of his knowledge of Indians came from Mr. Fenimore Cooper's novels. Cooper's red men were uniformly grave and ponderous. These Santee Sioux, with their quick changes of mood, could obviously not be trusted. They were like dangerous children, children playing with guns and knives. And in their unpredictability they had killed Alonzo Tarrant. Even now, New Ulm was preparing for an attack by these same savage children.

The afternoon wore on. Martin's hunger grew, and his thirst, but he did not move from his rock. Anyway, the visitors had by now eaten almost all their food. The Sioux sat idly about, lolling in the sunshine, exchanging remarks, gossiping. Finally Skew-Nose rose, followed by the others, and went to the cross marking the grave of Jake Bettencourt. They gathered silently about the grassy mound with its glass jar of wildflowers wilting in the sun. Phronsie stood at the head of the grave, hands clasped, speaking in sibilant Sioux what must have been a memorial to her father. Except for the wild and colorful dress of the Sioux, it might have been a Methodist service at the Jamaica Plain cemetery. When she finished they all remained still, Sioux with their heads bowed.

Finally she took a deep breath. From the distance Martin thought the sun touched a sparkle of tears. Then there were brisk farewells, the Sioux all shaking hands with her. "*Hopo!*" Skew-Nose barked. Martin remembered that word: *let's go!* Almost as if by magic, the band melted into the forest greenery, and were gone.

Slowly Phronsie walked back to the camp. Martin sat stubbornly on his rock. Somehow she ought to rationalize her conduct, even apologize for having been so friendly and gracious, but she paid him no mind, seeming in a brown study. Finally hunger overcame him. Sullenly he picked up the leg bone and gnawed at the few threads of meat left by the ravenous Sioux.

"They ate like they were starved," he grumbled.

Still she did not speak, seeming deep in thought. It was near dark when she picked up her blanket and said, "Guess we can walk down toward New Ulm tomorrow. You better get a good night's sleep, Martin. Them packs is heavy."

He was annoyed at her coolness. "Is that all you've got to say?"

"What else should I say, then, pilgrim?"

"Nothing!" If she didn't know, he wasn't going to tell her. Angrily he strode to his own bed in the lean-to, lying awake a long time after hearing her say her scurrilous Sioux prayer in that high clear voice. Shameful, absolutely shameful! How could she be redeemed? Did he even want to?

Next morning Phronsie roused him early. "Traveling time! We got a long way to go today, and a heavy load!"

With sleep-dimmed eyes Martin stumbled from the lean-to. She was already frying deer steaks, and handed him a bowl of freshly gathered sarvisberries. "No coffee," she sighed. "Guess we'll have to do with

Adam's ale. That's what pa called it. Nothing better in the world to drink, he always said, than good cold water!"

Martin was in a truculent mood. From time to time Phronsie glanced at him as they ate, but he avoided her eyes. Consorting with Sioux! Defending them, as she had done from time to time, was one thing. But breaking bread, joking and giggling with red killers?

When it came time to leave she loaded him up like a pack horse. Baled pelts towered above his head, secured by a lashing of leather straps around his shoulders and hips and a tumpline across the forehead.

"Too much for you?" she grinned.

With difficulty he shook his head, restrained by the tumpline.

"I can take some off if you want!"

"No," he growled. "I'm all right!"

"Well, then—" She handed him the staff she had whittled. "This'll help. And when you get tired, we'll stop. All right?"

"All right."

Lithely she got into her own harness, adjusted the straps, stood wide-legged before him, propped on the musket, her own cargo of pelts higher than his. It irked him.

"Ready?"

He gestured at the camp; the lean-to, blankets, pots and pans, cracked mirror hanging from a limb. "What about this stuff?"

"Ain't no one going to bother it. Out here folks is honest, not rascally like they are in the city!"

Was she trying to annoy him? After all, he was a product of the city. Before he could decide, she was moving.

"*Hopo!*" she called back, gaily.

Planting his feet with care, he trudged after her, leaning on the staff, determined to walk to New Ulm without stopping or complaining unless she did first. Almost immediately, however, he lost sight of her as she swung around a leafy bend. He quickened his pace, listening to her sing:

> . . . the little birds that fly
> With careless ease from tree to tree
> Are not so blest as I!

They had started when the sun was hidden by boughs that overhung the trail and struck through only in patches. After a while they emerged on a rocky escarpment. Martin slipped and scrabbled in the rubble, keeping upright only with the aid of the staff. He sweated and toiled after Phronsie, inwardly cursing, more and more annoyed at her goatlike manner as she picked her way through the boulders.

"You all right, Martin?"

Out of breath, he could not answer. Sweat dripped into his eyes. His backbone seemed permanently twisted awry. She paused, solicitous, but with mischief in her eyes.

"Want me to carry your pack too?"

Grimly he waved her on.

In midmorning, the path dipped again into the trees. He was grateful for the shade. His throat was dry and parched, his stomach began to growl from hunger. What he would give for a drink of cool water! Eagerly he looked for a spring, a watercourse of some sort. There was only the green gloom of the forest, the mocking cry of a jay, an oppressive heat as the sun rose higher. Good Lord—would she never stop her headlong pace?

With the sun almost directly overhead, Phronsie finally paused and dumped her pack on a mossy flat rock in the shade of a giant cedar. "Nooning, I guess."

Gratefully he slipped out of his own pack, staggering in the process. His leg muscles burned like fire and his lungs labored. Phronsie, however, looked casual and cool.

"You sure you're all right?"

"I told you I was all right!" he wheezed.

"Well, you don't need to be so goddamned snippy about it!"

Hungry and thirsty, he was ashamed to see that in addition to the heavy musket and a sack of cap and ball, Phronsie had also borne the burden of a leather water bottle and a packet of dried meat and johnnycakes, small flat slabs of dried and ground turnips mixed with water and then fried. She poured him water and handed him a cake first, which annoyed him further. He was so grim and silent that she stopped chewing the mealy cake and stared at him.

"What in hell is gnawing your belly now, pilgrim?"

Martin had always had in his mind an idealized image of woman, eternal woman, and respected that image. Phronsie in no way conformed; she was not only heretical, but profane. As for her affection for the people that had murdered his uncle . . .

"I wish I'd known you were an Indian lover when I first saw you, back on the mountain there!" He gestured.

She picked up the johnnycake, bit out a piece. "What would you have done, then, if I hadn't rescued you from the bogeyman?" The words were joking but her voice was ominously casual.

"I don't know," he muttered. "Maybe I'd have been

murdered by those same Indians you were so friendly with! Maybe it would have been better that way!"

With an oath she rose, crumbling the cake in her fist, and threw it violently away. "Why, you cussed hypocrite! Here I come on you bawling in the woods, I take you to my camp and change your didies, I feed you and cosset you, and this is the thanks I get! God damn it, I guess maybe it would have been better if Shakopee and his people had skewered you and gutted you and hung you up to bleed!"

"Now just a minute—" Angry himself, he scrambled to his feet.

"Don't 'just a minute' me, you polecat! You been grouchy as a grizzly that sat in a bear trap, and I'm plumb weary of it. I ain't never said anything against your friends, even when you was mooning over that Lavinia Greene or whatever her name was, and weeping crocodile tears about your pa and ma! So don't speak ill of *my* friends! Why, old Wolf Talker and Fool Dog and Shakopee are the finest people I know, and don't you say a word against them!"

Powerless to stem the flow of invective, he could only open his mouth, foolishly, and stare. He had never heard a female erupt so violently.

"With your brains in a jaybird's head, he'd fly backwards, Martin Sayre!"

"Phronsie—"

"Don't even speak my name no more, thank you! It's mine, and I value it, and I damn well don't want any of it on your stupid tongue! No sir and no ma'am—I'd just as soon see you deep in Hell as a pigeon can fly in a week!"

She stamped her foot in a manner so unmistakably feminine that he was struck again by the paradox, but he pressed on.

"You've got mighty fine friends then, that's all I've got to say! Mighty fine, to go around stealing eggs from honest farm folk! Mighty fine, to murder a good old man that never did anyone harm! Mighty fine, so damned fine that every farmer in this valley has got to fort himself up at night so your feathered friends can't sneak in and scalp women and children! God, *my* friends don't do things like that! And if I can't speak your precious name, Phronsie Bettencourt, then don't you mention Lavinia Greene, that's a credit to her gender in a way *you* could never possibly understand!"

Her tanned cheeks turned pale and her eyes narrowed; one hand touched the skinning knife in her belt. "I ain't a proper female, then? Is that what you're saying, Martin Sayre?"

Ashamed of himself, then, and contrite, or cowed, he did not know which, he muttered, "That was unfair of me! I'm sorry, Phronsie. Listen to me—"

"I won't!"

"Remember?" he urged. "Remember the night we sat out under the stars and you made the Indian flute I played?"

Suspicious, she glared at him, "So what if I do?"

"That night you said I was quality because I was educated and knew Latin and how to play the violin and all." Sorry that he had hurt her so, he chose his words carefully. Her ways were different from those of the burghers of Jamaica Plain. According to her lights, she was in the right. He had difficulty with the words, pouring ashes on his own head. "*You're* really quality, Phronsie. Bear with me if at times I don't understand you, just like you don't understand me. But *you're* quality, making your own way in a rough world, and as a female."

She lifted her chin. "What's wrong with being a female?"

"Nothing," he said hastily. "Believe me, nothing! Nothing at all!"

"You ain't just saying that?"

"No. I mean it!"

Somewhat soothed, she said, "Well, then—all right. And maybe, I take back them things I said about you. Not all of them," she hurried to warn him, "but most of them, the worst things. Because you ain't—you're no prize package yourself, Martin!"

"I'm not," he agreed, humbly. "And I'm grateful for what you've done for me, Phronsie."

Together they sat down to the interrupted meal. Martin said, "It was strange to me, of course, to be in the same camp with Sioux Indians, you understand."

"I give you that."

Trying to be agreeable, but curious also, he went on. "I didn't understand what was going on. Would you like to explain it to me?"

For a moment she was silent, tipping the water bottle high. He watched as the whiteness of her neck emerged, from the shirt, pale against the brown of her cheeks. Women did not have an Adam's apple, he remembered; her throat did not bob up and down like in a man's when he swallowed. When she put down the bottle, there was an edge in her voice. "What you watching?"

"You," he said simply.

"Why?"

"I like to, that's all."

She considered this. "Well, all right."

"Who were those people, then?"

She took out the corncob with its tiny encrusted bowl, and a pouch of tobacco.

"I never saw you smoke until yesterday, when the Indians came."

"Pa taught me. I always crave tobacco after a meal. I—I didn't smoke in camp because I was afraid you'd think I wasn't no lady." Tamping down the tobacco with a thumb, she went on. "That was a committee, I guess you'd say, going down to talk to General Sibley. Shakopee sent them. Old Wolf Talker, the one with the star painted on his nose, is Shakopee's big medicine man. The one with the broken nose is head of their Fox Society. Big men, all of them—Fool Dog and Little Elk and the rest."

"Why were they going, when the whites are apt to fire on them at sight?"

She puffed a perfect ring, watching as it drifted upward among the flat-leafed fronds of the cedar. "The Santee Sioux want peace. Their land is gone, most of it, to the plow, and Shakopee wants to keep what's left." She drew deep on the pipe. "They're sorry about your uncle. Seems some young bucks got a hideful of old Zook's rum and went crazy. Shakopee's offering to turn them in for trial if the government will make the farmers stop taking over Sioux land."

"They didn't sound that peaceable to me," Martin said, remembering the sibilant *tccchk*, the gesture of sending an arrow on its flight. He remembered, too, the shaman Wolf Talker, baring his privates in a gesture of contempt.

"Oh, there's differences of opinion among the Sioux, like with the whites! Down there they got that old fire eater General Sibley—they call him the Baron of the Border—on one side, and Bishop Whipple on the other. The Sioux has got their politicians, too. Little Elk is a reasonable cuss, but old Wolf Talker is set in his ways. I hope they can all come to some kind of agreement or there'll be plenty blood on the land. Shakopee and his folks has been pushed around plenty enough. Now there's even talk the government isn't going to give them their due the first of the month."

"Their due?" Martin asked. "What due?"

"In '58 the Santee Sioux and the whites signed a treaty. The settlers got a big passel of Indian land for a measly ten cents an acre. According to treaty—Pa explained all this to me—the government was bound to give the Santee Sioux beef, coffee, flour, sugar, tea, stuff like that, each summer. Well, they done it, so far. But now old Zook's warehouses is crammed to busting with this year's annuity, and the government back in Washington ain't—hasn't come through with the money to pay him."

Now Martin understood the warehouses in New Ulm, the endless wagons discharging their cargo into Levi Zook's establishment.

"Old Zook says, 'No money, no grub. Let 'em eat grass,' he says. Oh, I purely hate that man! I'd admire to jump down his throat and gallop his insides out! Zook and the other rascally traders are one of the things that causes trouble." Her voice shook with emotion; she paused for a moment, knocking the dottle from the pipe. "When Pa was alive he talked to Shakopee and his folks, tried to reason with them, keep the peace. Now that Pa's passed on, they come to me and ask what to do. Hell, I ain't as smart as Pa! But I do the best I can."

"What did you tell them?"

She shook her head. "I didn't know *what* to say. I guess all I did was explain there's two sides to everything—" She put away the pipe and the tobacco. "Like with you and me, I guess! 'Twasn't much. Pa would have done better."

He remembered Skew-Nose's familiarity with her, and was uncomfortable. "The one with the broken nose is a big man," he murmured, thinking of his own slight stature. "A handsome man!"

"That's Yellow Horse, 'cause he had a dream about riding a yellow horse when he went up on a hill once and didn't eat anything for three days." She grinned. "You know how he got that nose?"

"No."

"I broke it for him when we was rassling in Shakopee's camp one day. I wasn't more than fifteen, but I was big for my age. Pa put me up to it."

Wrestling an Indian? Fifteen years old? In a Sioux camp? Martin turned with relief to another matter.

"They had a name for you. I kept hearing it over and over. Sounded like *ya sis to ka—*"

"Iron Girl."

"What?"

"That's what Shakopee and his people call me."

Iron Girl she certainly was. When she got to her feet, lithely and briskly, Martin staggered to his own, wincing. He did not object when she generously swung up his pack and placed it on his aching shoulders. "Off we go!" she said gaily. "If we make a flat shirttail, we'll see the lights of New Ulm before it's clear dark!"

They did indeed catch sight of the yellow wink of New Ulm lamps by dark. By now Martin seemed to have caught a kind of second wind. He was enjoying the vermilion sunset. Skeins of geese winged northward against drifting banners of cloud. His lungs, now accustomed to the effort, drank deep of air fragrant with pine and cedar. Together he and Phronsie stood where the wilderness trail joined the dusty road, the road Martin had lost that frightful night in the forest after Uncle Alonzo died.

"Martin?"

On the evening breeze he smelled woodsmoke from cooking fires. Down there, among the sprinkles of lampglow, was a town; civilization, people, white people. Soldiers, too, perhaps—and the telegraph.

"Yes?"

"You sure you want to go into New Ulm?"

He had come to experience life in a fullness he had never known; a rough life, true, but a hardy and zestful one. Besides, he had lately experienced restless feelings about Phronsie Bettencourt. Did he love her? No, certainly not! Love of a good woman was an exalted passion that hardly applied to this raw and uncultured female. Still and all . . .

"What about it?" she asked. "It isn't too late to turn back."

In his deerskin shirt and moccasins, beard and hair shaggy and unkempt, perhaps he would not be recognized by anyone. On the other hand, if someone did—

She touched his arm, "Well?"

Planting his staff in the dust of the road, he stepped out toward the distant lights.

"Let's go!" he said.

CHAPTER FIVE

Rumors abounded, some possibly true but most just fiction. Sioux scouts, it was said, had been seen on the outskirts of New Ulm. Mankato, a small town nearby, had been besieged by Shakopee's braves, and half the town destroyed. Shakopee and his people intended to break into Zook's warehouses and take for themselves the provisions they had been promised. The President had called off the draft that stripped Minnesota of so many young men and agreed to send Federal troops from the Virginia battlefields to rescue New Ulm and Mankato and Winnebago City from the depredations of the Santee Sioux. New Ulm was fearful.

Martin and Phronsie, laboring under the weight of their packs, paused to watch the awkward squads drilling on the plain formed by the bend of the river. A white-bearded veteran, probably from the Mexican War, waved a rusty saber and shouted commands at a bewildered collection of farm youths, grizzle-bearded merchants, and grandfathers. At the ferry landing an enthusiastic but misguided crew labored to train an ancient fieldpiece.

Phronsie snickered. "They expect Shakopee to come down Front Street in column of fours so's they can mow him down? Lordy, lordy, lordy—what fools!"

One discussion that turned out to be truth, not rumor. Wolf Talker, Yellow Horse, and the rest of the Sioux delegation had been taken prisoner and jailed at Fort Ridgely.

"Why, the bastards!" Phronsie cried upon hearing this. "The everlasting bastards! The Indians was just trying to head off trouble! Now the whites are going to have the whole Sioux nation on the warpath! Did you ever hear of such a—such a—" Words failed her, not a common occurrence.

In spite of his feeling about the death of his uncle, Martin also felt dismay. Seizing the Sioux delegation was certainly an unwise act, one that could only aggravate a delicate situation.

Phronsie yanked the sleeve of the red-faced man who had mentioned the incident. "What did they do that for?"

The man, who had been standing before the Dakota House in conversation with a whiskered farmer, turned truculently.

"Do what—uh—ma'am?"

"Put the Sioux in jail at Fort Ridgely?"

"That's the only place for troublemakers! I wish we had enough jails to put *all* Indians behind bars! It's the only way peaceful folks will be safe on their own land!"

"Their own land?" Phronsie was furious. "Their own land, is it? Well let me tell you, mister! This land has been Sioux land since—"

"Come away," Martin urged. "Please, Phronsie—this is no time to start an argument!"

"But—"

He pinched her arm, hard.

"Ow!"

"Damn it, come *away*, I said!"

Reluctantly she followed him. "What the hell you do that for? I was only—"

"You were spoiling for a fight! You know New Ulm isn't the place to speak up for the Sioux, no matter what the merits of the case!"

Grumbling, she trudged after him toward Zook's place. "That *hurt*!"

"Not near as much," he said acidly, "as if that windbag reported you to the Army. They'd probably put you in jail along with your Sioux friends."

Under a lowering sky, the air fresh and smelling of rain, they walked up Fifth Street and across a meadow that bore a sign: North German Park. Here more volunteers drilled, bearing a motley collection of muskets, shotguns, and cap-and-ball pistols. Several shouldered rudely carved wooden rifles. The drillmaster, a peppery little man wearing an oversize fur shako, ran about them like a terrier at a sheep's heels.

"Straighten up, there, you! Throw your shoulders back! Now—port *arms*! No, no! *Port* arms! Great suffering Jesus Christ! Can't you hay-footed dolts remember *anything*?"

Before Zook's store Martin saw a stack of weeks-old copies of the *Minnesota Republican*. He left a penny on the pile and opened the newspaper. THE BATTLE OF CEDAR MOUNTAIN, GARIBALDI VICTORY IN ITALY, and in smaller headlines, Singing Tour of the World-Renowned Hutchinson Family.

Governor Ramsey had sent a message to President Lincoln asking for help, but there was no reply. "The Sioux," Ramsey complained, "know that many of our young men have gone to fight in Virginia, and will take advantage of our desperate situation." Phronsie, looking over Martin's shoulder, formed letters with her lips. Amused, he watched her.

"Well," she said, "I can read the big letters right enough. Cedar Mountain, see? It's the squiggly little rascals that give me fits."

"You've taught me a lot," he said. "I'm glad I can teach you, now. Soon I'll have you parsing sentences."

"Doing *what*?"

"You'll understand, later."

No sooner had Martin spoken the words than he froze in panic. The tall man approaching in the black coat and clerical collar was Bishop Henry Whipple. He felt sweat break out on his forehead. Afraid the *Republican* would rattle in trembling hands, he stretched it tighter, trying to appear intent on the news, at the same time compelled by dreadful impulse to watch the bishop, to detect a telltale sign of recognition. But Whipple paused only for a moment. Doffing the flat-crowned hat, he bowed.

"Miss Bettencourt."

She ducked her head. "Morning, Bishop."

"How is the fur business?"

"Fair enough, I reckon." She seemed tongue-tied before the cleric.

"Are you getting along all right these days?"

"Yes, sir."

Whipple tipped his hat again, not looking at Martin. "If there's anything I can do for you, Phronsie, anything you need—"

"Thank you, Bishop, but I make out all right."

Martin watched him pass down the street, a tall, handsome man with a kind of grace about him.

"Only damned person around here with a brain in his head," Phronsie muttered, threading her way among the "cracker-and-molasses" Indians congregated before Zook's place.

Martin, however, was elated. Dropping his pack on the porch of the store, he began to whistle.

"What you so chipper about?" Phronsie grumbled.

"I've met the bishop before. He took supper with Uncle Alonzo and me one night, and we talked a long time. Still, he didn't recognize me!"

"Guess he didn't."

"Do you know what that means? Maybe I don't have to give myself up. At least, it's worth a try. Let's see—" Martin rubbed his bearded chin. "From now on, I'll call myself Brown. Yes, that's it! Brown's a common enough name. I can still be Martin. Will you remember that? Martin *Brown*!"

"Of course!" Opening the door, she dragged the bundle of pelts within. "Think I'm a dummy or something? Sometimes you don't give any credit for nothing!"

The interior of the store was more crowded than Martin remembered from his initial visit, weeks before. Farmers, trappers, city officials, laborers, ferry crews all moiled about, haggling, arguing, discussing the Sioux threat in an atmosphere redolent of cigar smoke, millinery, leather boots, and rum dispensed from a barrel on the counter at ten cents a cup. Levi Zook, teeth clenched on a stogie, looked warily at Phronsie.

"Hello, you old skinflint!" she cried. "Brought you the finest pelts that ever growed on an animal!" To

Martin she muttered, "Old scoundrel! Pa hated his guts!"

"Well, let's see what you got," Zook nodded. "Though I can tell you this right now—pelts ain't bringing what they used to!"

Together Martin and Phronsie dragged the bundles into a back room. Taking a gold penknife from his watch chain, the trader cut the rawhide thongs and fanned through the rich pile, puffing on the stogie. "Mmmm," he said. "Well, now—hmmm!"

Phronsie was impatient. "I ain't heard so much humming since the day a nest of mud daubers fell on me out of a sycamore tree! Those is prime skins, Zook! Last winter was hard! Look at how long and shiny the hairs is on that wolfskin!"

The trader opened Martin's bundle, rapidly thumbed through it. "This beaver has got a hole in it!" Clouds of smoke wreathed his head as he chewed on the stogie. "Hmmmm—this here wolfskin looks like the poor critter had the mange!"

"I ain't never heard you talk no different," Phronsie snapped.

Zook tossed down the last skin. "I seen better from your pa."

"You ain't never!"

Zook found a stub of pencil and went to figuring on a shingle. "Mmmmm. Four dollars—two fifty—maybe a dollar apiece for the skunk pelts—say five dollars apiece for the bears—that beaver with the hole in it ain't worth anything, but I'll throw in fifty cents—" He spat on the earthen floor, gnawed a new point on the pencil. "Let's see, that makes a grand total of . . ."

Phronsie waited, impatient.

"Two hundred and forty-nine dollars and fifty cents." He handed Phronsie the shingle. "Tell you what. I'll make it two hundred and fifty dollars! Fair is fair!"

Phronsie stared at the shingle. "Fair? You call that fair? Two hundred and fifty dollars for four hundred worth of prime furs?"

The trader shrugged.

"A whole year's trapping, and you offer me a measly two hundred and fifty dollars? Why, I froze and starved and worked my fingers to stubs for them pelts!"

"If'n you don't like the price," Zook said with an air of finality, "you can take 'em somewheres else."

"Somewheres else?" Phronsie's voice became shrill. "Oh, my suffering stars! You damned robber—you've druv out every other decent trader from Breckenridge to Fairmont with your shady ways!"

From the open door someone chuckled, "Tell him, Phron! Go get him, girl!" Martin turned to see the doorway crowded with grinning onlookers. "Phronsie—" he said, uneasily, but she pulled away from the hand on her sleeve.

"You can't buffalo me, gal!" the trader said nervously. He puffed harder on the stogie. "I give you a price, and I'm gonna stick to it! I know furs, I do, and no one ain't going to bamboozle me into one red cent more! Two hundred and sixty-five is my offer, and that's final!"

"Three hundred and fifty!"

"No ma'am! Two hundred and sixty-five, and that's only because I knew your pa and he was a good old man!"

"Zook, you always cheated him *too*!"

"Make him pay up!" a man yelled in delight. "Go get him, gal!" someone added. Another shouted, "Fight, fellers! Fight!"

Phronsie picked up her musket, stalked out to the store, Zook following behind. Like a lean and hungry panther she prowled along the counter, casting a speculative eye at the shelves with their rich freight.

"What you going to do?" Zook demanded.

A row of glass lamp-chimneys caught her attention: high ones, short ones, curved ones and straight, some with beaded edges and frosted bulbs, others ornamented with gold leaf. Fancy parlor lamps that the few well-off farmers in the area used on Sundays or when the preacher called.

"Two hundred and sixty-five, then," Phronsie announced, "and I'll take the balance out in smashing these here pretty lamp chimblies!"

"No!" the trader cried. "Them is fragile, very fragile!"

She poked a lamp chimney tentatively with the barrel of the musket; it responded with a delicate *ting*. "Three hundred and fifty, Zook?"

"Better give it to her, Levi!" a grizzled boatman urged. "I mind the time she wrecked Ahlstrom's saloon when he was selling that rotgut to the Injuns!"

"All right!" the trader howled, mopping his brow. "All right, then! Only take that damned blunderbuss away from my glassware! Damn it to Hell, take it *away!*"

"Three fifty, then?"

The trader agreed. When she lowered the probing musket, the trader sidled cautiously past her and took a sheaf of greenbacks from the till. Gleefully the spectators crowded around to watch him pay out the notes, counting in unison. "Five, ten, twenty, twenty-five, thirty, thirty-five—"

Zook watched sourly as Phronsie tucked the wad of bills into her bag. "I won't forget this! If'n I wasn't scared you'd bust up my store, I'd of told you to go whistle up a stump! But don't you come in here no more, you female catamount, or I'll have the law on you!"

To a chorus of cheers Martin and Phronsie departed. Martin was troubled. "Why did you have to carry on like that? I had money! I've got over a hundred dollars from Uncle Alonzo's sugar bowl!"

She halted in the street while distant thunder sounded. "Martin, there's one thing you got to get straight. I told you before and I'll tell you again. I been taking care of myself since I was eight years old. I pay my own way, and I don't take nothing from anyone I didn't earn right and proper! There's only one way to deal with that oily rascal, and I learned it from Pa! Besides, Zook got a bargain, and he knows it!"

She was probably right; he gave in. "Anyway, it seems you're kind of a local celebrity."

"I'm Jake Bettencourt's gal, that's all. Everyone knew Pa, and respected him. The only thing I'd want is for them to respect me, too, on my own account." Agreeable again, she strolled by his side. "It pleasures me to stay in town for a day or two—see old friends, buy me thread and needles, a new comb, maybe some licorice or maple-sugar tits for my sweet tooth. Pa and I always stopped at the Widow Cates's boardinghouse up on Center Street, t'other side of the park. She don't charge but two dollars a day for a room and three meals. You coming along?"

He had never given thought to what he would do or where he would stay in New Ulm. Glancing at the thunderheads, seeing a sawlike jag of lightning pierce the sky, he agreed. "All right. Good a place as any, I suppose."

They were crossing North German Park again when

the heavens split. Rain poured down. Though the day had been warm, only slightly overcast, the rain was icy-cold, drenching them. Martin followed Phronsie as she loped across the grass, jumped like a deer over a hedge, and bounded toward Mrs. Cates's house. He was uncomfortable in the rain but Phronsie seemed to be having a fine time. Through the veil of rain delighted laughter drifted back to him. *Free. The little birds that fly with careless ease*—what was the rest of it?

A great flash of light came, a brilliance that made him blink and cower. Thunder rolled, a cannonade that sought to press him into the ground. There never was a storm like this in Massachusetts. Most were mannerly and well behaved, like the citizens of Jamaica Plain, murmuring politely and dropping moisture like a blessing. This prairie storm was the grandfather of storms. At the river's edge a giant oak had been riven by the lightning; smoke curled up from the splintered stump.

"You hear that last bang?" Phronsie yelled against the rain as they stood dripping on the front porch.

He blinked. "My ears are still ringing!"

"He's one of the Sioux gods."

"Who?"

"Why, Thunder, of course." She shook herself like a wet dog and pulled the bell. "Now you *know* why he's a god. Of course, there's Rock and Buffalo and a lot more, but Thunder talks the loudest so you have to listen to him."

Her hair was bedraggled, clothing hung on her like rags, and striving for breath, she stood flat-footed in a puddle of water. He wanted to take her in his arms and kiss her, she looked so fresh and childlike and excited.

"Damn it!" She blew a shrill blast with the eaglebone whistle. "Ain't nobody home?"

Mrs. Cates opened the door.

"Phronsie!" She swept her into motherly arms. "My stars, child, you look like a drowned rat! For all the noise outside, I guess I didn't hear you knock." She turned to Martin. "And who is this . . . gentleman?"

"My friend, ma'am. Martin . . ." Phronsie paused, small pink tongue darting over her lip. "Martin Brown. Yes, Brown! He—he's been helping me up at the camp."

"Come in, come in, the both of you!" Mrs. Cates stepped aside, beaming through steel-rimmed spectacles. "You too, Mr. Brown. Any friend of Phronsie Bettencourt is a friend of mine."

The house was a rambling affair overlooking the river, with a lace-curtained parlor, a large dining room behind a beaded curtain, and a wide staircase leading to an upper story. The hallway was filled with greenery in brass urns. Martin detected the oily smell of furniture polish, diligently and frequently applied.

"Thank you, ma'am," he said.

Unbuttoning her shirt and shaking her curls, Phronsie said, "Me and Martin would like to lay up a spell in New Ulm, if you've got a couple rooms, Mrs. Cates."

"Why, of course! There's the big front room you always liked, and Mr.—Brown, is it?" She looked at him over the spectacles.

"Uh—yes," he admitted. "Martin Brown."

"Thad?" she called.

A young boy, curly headed and apple cheeked, peered through the beaded curtains. "Yes, Grandma?"

"Take this gentleman up to the corner room in back and see he gets made comfortable. Supper's at six, Mr.

Brown." To Phronsie she said, "First thing, we've got to get those wet clothes off you, child, or you'll have a catarrh." With Phronsie protesting that a little rain never hurt anybody, Mrs. Cates drew her away to the kitchen, calling out to Thad to hurry back and pump water for a good hot tub.

At supper Martin was early. He had no fresh clothes to put on, and was forced to make do by rolling them to dry in copies of the German-language daily *Pionier*, which Thad brought him. Around the big table sat a dozen or more boarders, mostly men, along with an elderly female schoolteacher and Mrs. Cates's sister-in-law Emma, "poor dear departed Elmer's sister," Mrs. Cates explained to Martin in introducing him around.

Noisily the boarders helped themselves to soup from a willow-ware tureen. Martin did not see Phronsie, and wondered what was keeping her. He started to ask Mrs. Cates but she had already disappeared into the kitchen, commanding the boy Thad to help with roast and potatoes and apple sauce, the biscuits and the rest of the bountiful meal.

"You in town long, Mr. Brown?"

The sister-in-law looked at him like a small wren, hair buns cocked to one side.

"Ah—I don't know, ma'am."

"What's your trade, then, if I may be so bold?"

He was pondering an answer when he saw the male heads turn as one toward the beaded doorway from the parlor. Phronsie Bettencourt stood there, holding aside the curtain. Martin swallowed hard, hearing the sound of his throat plain in the silence that congealed around the diners.

"Phronsie!" someone muttered. Martin realized it was his own startled voice that had sounded.

Though the silk dress borrowed from Mrs. Cates was too large, it was belted tight at the waist, and the skirt draped around her thighs like a Grecian robe. The gingery hair was swept up and back, molded by a red ribbon. Instead of the Indian moccasins, she stood in proper buttoned shoes. In one hand she carried a lacy handkerchief, holding tightly to it as if uncertain of the effect of her late arrival.

"Phronsie!" Mrs. Cates cried, coming into the dining room bearing a steaming brisket. "My, don't you look nice! Come, dear—supper's set!"

Martin, somewhat dazed, struggled to his feet to offer her a chair. But a stocky gallant in a military jacket was quicker. "Here, ma'am!" he offered, pulling up a chair beside his own. "Sit here! Lieutenant Phipps, ma'am, of the Fifth Minnesota!"

For the rest of the meal the officer monopolized Phronsie, waylaying choice items from passing platters and insisting she try them. Martin finally recognized him. It was the drillmaster of the afternoon, the one with the fur shako. The rest of the boarders alternated bites of beef and potatoes with pleasurable glances at Phronsie Bettencourt. Martin was only amused, he thought, and paid her little attention. Then, when he found he himself was watching between forkfuls of lemon pie, he wondered if he could be jealous. Jealous? Martin Sayre, of Jamaica Plain, near Boston, which was the hub of the universe, to be jealous over a raw untutored frontier girl? Nonsense!

After supper the boarders withdrew to the veranda to smoke stogies. Mrs. Cates and Thad and the sister-in-law cleared the table and washed dishes. Martin wanted to have a word with Phronsie, to tell her at least how pretty she looked in a dress. While she lingered in the hall, reminiscing with a grizzled trapper who had known her father "in the old days, before the country was so danged crowded," he stood patiently aside, feeling awkward and ill at ease. When the ancient shambled away in a cloud of smoke from his corncob, Martin said, "Hello, Phronsie."

"My feet hurt in these damned cast-iron shoes," she complained. Leaning on him, she unbuttoned the tops. The storm had passed; late sun streamed through Mrs. Cates's starched curtains and illumined Phronsie's hair in patches of red and gold. He smelled what must have been perfumed bath soap. Curiously, he missed the old familiar scent—sweet grass and smoke.

"It—it got nice, after all," he stammered, preparatory to asking her to sit with him on the front porch; he needed to talk to her. But at that moment the militiaman joined them, preening his mustaches. "Ma'am?"

Martin turned, annoyed. But Phronsie said, "Lieutenant," and inclined her head toward the interloper.

"I was just wondering if you would do me the favor of a little stroll along the river. It's quite warm, and after such a meal a walk does the digestion wonders!"

Martin scowled, about to call attention to the fact that he had been conversing with Miss Bettencourt, but decided he preferred not to attract undue attention. Phronsie gave him a wry look, a look with a dash of mockery. Her blue eyes danced.

"Lordy, Lieutenant—I'd be mighty pleased!"

Martin glowered as they left arm in arm. Putting on airs like that, coquettish airs! As for the damned Fifth Minnesota or whatever it was . . .

During the evening he sat on the veranda in silence, watching the serene flow of the Minnesota, hearing the creak of rocking chairs and the *splat* of tobacco juice in cuspidors as the boarders talked over the Indian threat. For a time he watched the pair stroll the grassy bank, pausing where a stern-wheeler was unloading. Then they passed under a screen of willows. He watched until quite late, then went in to bed. For a while he lay sleepless in the summer dark. When he found he was waiting to hear the front door open, to hear again Phronsie's voice, he felt like a fool. Resolutely he turned over, and drew the sheet up.

In Washington, Lucas Sayre sat in the War Department building at Seventeenth and F with his old friend Kit Burke. Kit was angry, talking like a Dutch uncle.

"Lucas, you're a damned fool! With that leg of yours, you ought to be back home in bed!"

Lucas, boot off and pants leg rolled up, dabbed at the suppurating wound with a handkerchief. "I can handle this myself, Kit. After all"—there was sarcasm in his voice—"you staff people down here don't need a poor game-legged infantry officer, so it gives me something to do!"

"But—"

"Martin Sayre brought shame on the Sayre name, and has got to be returned to justice! That's the only way the Colonel and I can hold up our heads again!"

Captain Burke sighed, shook his head. Teeth clenched on a cigar, he stared at the document on his desk, reached for a pen.

"Well, if you're so damned pigheaded—"

"I am."

"Then I'll sign the blasted thing! But I don't see what good it'll do for you to hobble down to City Point and talk to people there."

"That's where Wallace's division is right now, isn't it?"

"Yes."

"Then that's where Martin's friends and bunkmates will be. Maybe they can tell me something, tell me if he ever spoke at times of going anyplace."

Shrugging, Burke signed the pass and handed it over. "That'll get you anywhere except into Lee's headquarters."

Lucas struggled to his feet with the aid of the cane. "You don't know what this means to me, Kit." He shook hands. "Unhappy circumstances, to be sure, but at least I feel I'm not useless anymore!"

Kit accompanied him to the door. Outside, messengers hurried through the halls. Blue-clad officers congregated in a sunny alcove, wreathed in tobacco smoke as they conferred. Jackson, it appeared from their conversation, had defeated the Federals at Cross Keys and escaped from the Shenandoah Valley in spite of the trap laid for him.

"Wait a minute," Kit muttered, holding Lucas's arm.

"What?"

"I just had a thought. Come back in while I look into something."

"Kit, I'm in a hurry. There's a steamer going downriver at eight o'clock tonight."

"You've got time." Kit made him sit again on the sofa in his office and left the room. Lucas fidgeted, hands crossed on his cane, watching a bluebottle fly buzz about the room. Finally Kit returned, accompanied by a small, square man in a black nankeen coat and an iron-hard square hat. His black beard was cut square, and he looked boxlike and compact.

"Herman Nally," Kit introduced him. "Nally, this is

my old friend and companion in arms, Major Lucas Sayre."

Mr. Nally nodded, noncommittally.

"Nally is a Pinkerton," Kit explained. "He's leaving Army service because of a certain domestic problem we won't go into. So he's free, or will be, soon as he gets some complications straightened out."

"That's right," Mr. Nally said. "The trouble with duty with the Army—it's too confining. I haven't been home for six months. Wait till I catch the son of a bitch that's been fooling around my wife!"

"What has all this got to do with me?"

"You're in no shape to go gallivanting around on a wild-goose chase, Lucas! I saw the medical report on your wound, didn't I? You'll lose that leg, and maybe your goddamned life if you don't listen to reason! Here's what I had in mind." Burke stubbed out the cigar on the sole of his boot. "You Sayres have got plenty of money." He grinned. "I remember the parties you gave up at Jamaica Plain. Nothing but the best! And that house! Estate, more like! Anyhow, the hire of a good detective won't break you. Why don't you and Nally here go into Rob Fleming's office next door—Rob's home on furlough—and come to terms?"

Lucas frowned. "If you think I can't handle this myself—"

"That's not it at all. It's just . . . well, call it two strings to your bow. You and Nally! Nally's a good man, one of the best, and we hate to lose him. But his wife has been lonely—"

"I'll kill the son of a bitch," Mr. Nally mused.

"Anyway, it's hard these days to lay your hands on a good detective.

"My terms," Mr. Nally offered, "would be reasonable. A decent salary, and traveling expenses."

"What say, Lucas?" Burke asked.

Lucas gnawed the carved handle of his cane. "Might not be such a bad idea, at that." He glanced at Mr. Nally. "We haven't got a whole lot to work on yet."

Briskly Nally nodded. "I once tracked an embezzler to Sacramento and back with nothing to go on but a sample of his handwriting. Don't worry, Major!"

Lucas pursed his lips. The Army employed many Pinkertons in its spy network. Only a year or so ago Allan Pinkerton foiled an attempt in Baltimore to assassinate the president-elect, Mr. Lincoln, and Pinkerton stock was high. Kit was right, of course. Lucas had always respected Kit Burke's judgment. Then too, perhaps he *was* rash in thinking he could find Martin all by himself.

"Agreed." He shook hands with Nally to seal the bargain. "And Kit—thank *you*. Good advice, old friend!"

Together he and Nally went to the office next door and talked a long time. Thanks to Kit Burke's connections, they both left a week later for City Point on the river steamer *Allegheny*, chartered by the Sanitary Commission. In the interval Mr. Nally had gone home to Wilkes-Barre, Pennsylvania, and apparently found the son of a bitch. Lucas did not inquire as to the details.

CHAPTER SIX

Unwillingly in the hospital at City Point, Lucas Sayre waited for detective Nally to return from Louisville, Kentucky. Police there reported a man resembling Martin Sayre had been seen in the railroad station. Lucas's bad leg was swollen with fluid and the Army surgeons had affixed drains. Sitting up in bed, he read the letter from Kip Burke the orderly had just brought:

> Hope you are better, Lucas. Well, sources here say most deserters seem to flee west as quick as they can, hoping to get as far away as possible from the war. What with the recent horrible Federal losses at Mechanicsville and Gaines's Mill, I cannot say I blame them. Sometimes I myself, reading the casualty reports, feel hopeless and discouraged, even at this great remove from battlefields. Of course, I do not mean this as any excuse for Martin. But war must have seemed a horrible thing for a sensitive young man.

Sensitive young man! Lucas thought, chewing on his cigar. *Cowardly!*

> I am enclosing herewith a letter from your father sent care of me. I hope that . . .

Abandoning the rest of Kit's letter, Lucas shook the heavy manila envelope. A smaller white one fluttered out. Tearing it open, he reached for his spectacles and read the small cramped hand.

> . . . terrible news. Your mother's brother, Alonzo, has been killed by the Sioux Indians on the farm in Minnesota where he moved after your Aunt Flossie died. No one seems to know much about it. The only facts are they found him dead, tomahawked, and buried in a shallow grave. The Indians in Minnesota are on a rampage. Of course, your mother grieves terribly. I do all I can to comfort her but she needs more than that. Lucas, I know how you feel about Martin, but can't you come home for a while? It would mean so much to her, and me. I am an old man now, and . . .

Lucas folded the letter, laid it on the table beside his bed. Poor old Alonzo! Alonzo was a typical Tarrant: too gentle by half, impractical, foolish, a dreamer. It was the Tarrant strain that had diluted the blood of the Sayres, the hardheaded no-nonsense Sayres.

"Major?"

The orderly tapped at his door, accompanied by a young doctor, only a lieutenant, with barely a wisp of beard on his chin.

"What in the hell is it now?"

The orderly bore a tray of instruments and a basin. A towel was folded over his arm.

"This here is Lieutenant Culp. He wants to lance that leg, sir."

"Yes, that's right, Major. If you'll just—"

"Wait a minute!" Lucas looked beyond the doctor. "Nally? Come in, come in!"

Nally clumped through the doorway in square-toed boots, paper-wrapped bundle under one arm. "Good news!" he reported.

The doctor was annoyed. "Sir, you'll have to wait outside till I—"

"*You* wait outside, Lieutenant!" Lucas barked.

"But—"

"Out!" Lucas waved his cigar. "This is important business!"

Defeated, Doctor Culp and the orderly retired.

"Sit down, Nally. Good news, you said!"

"Well, it's a start." The Pinkerton unwrapped the package and handed Lucas a picture, a framed crayon portrait. The sketch was expertly done, with style and assurance: head and shoulders of a middle-aged man in a blue official cap.

"Who the hell is this?"

"Station agent at Louisville. Seems a young man needed money for a ticket to Chicago and offered to do his picture. The agent's description tallies with what you told me. Slight of frame, blue eyes and blond hair, v-shaped scar on forehead!"

"That must have been Martin! Yes, the scar where he fell out of the apple tree. Anyway, I'd have known by his style. I mean his painting style. Martin was good at art stuff. You know, music and painting and things like that. Never brought him a dime, but he liked to putter around with it." Carefully he propped the portrait on the table. "Chicago, you say? Wanted money for a ticket to Chicago?"

"Yes, sir."

"Well, what do we do now?"

"First of all, I've got to go home for a day or so and check up on my wife again."

"Damn it all, who are you working for, Nally, me or your wife?"

The Pinkerton was stubborn. "A day more or less isn't going to make any difference, Major. And them was the terms of our agreement. After all, a man's domestic arrangements has got to come first."

Lucas chewed on his cigar. "Well, all right, if you have to. But get back here soon as you can. God damn it, Nally, I'm tied down to this bed and have got to depend on you, at least till my leg mends."

Nally rose, set the hard hat square on his head.

"Here's my bill so far, Major."

Lucas scanned the account. "What's this two-dollar item, for God's sake?"

Nally pointed to the portrait. "I had to give two dollars to the agent for the picture. It's evidence, ain't it?"

Lucas took a wallet from under the pillow and peeled off greenbacks. "Hurry back, you hear me? The scoundrel will be in the Sandwich Islands before we collar him!"

"Yes, sir," Nally agreed.

Nally never returned from Wilkes-Barre. An item in the Harrisburg *Messenger* reported that a Mr. Herman Nally had been found shot to death in his home on West Coal Street in Wilkes-Barre. Though Nally was known to have a wife, her whereabouts were unknown. Lucas's teeth bit all the way through his cigar. *Damned fool!* He knew what had happened; the son of a bitch shot Nally and ran away with Nally's wife!

"Sir?" the orderly inquired.

"Bring me my clothes."

"But—"

"You deaf? Bring me my damned clothes!"

The orderly scuttled out, returned with Doctor Culp.

"Major, you can't—"

"I can do anything I want to!" Lucas growled.

It was true; he was not on active duty. His accommodation in the hospital was a courtesy, granted because of the interest of a War Department staff officer.

He got his clothing, his valise, and his cane. From the valise he took the Root's Patent revolver the Colonel had given him when he graduated from the Point—five shot, with a musket hammer, sheathed trigger, and a six-inch barrel. "Good to see you again, my friend," he muttered. After carefully cleaning it and oiling it, he slipped it back into the valise.

Limping heavily on his cane, he visited the City Point quartermaster. The pass from Kit Burke got him passage on a military train returning to Rock Island, Illinois, only a hundred miles or so from Chicago. Once there, he would find a way to travel the rest of the distance. Until the train switched engines in Cincinnati it did not occur to him that Martin might have fled to Alonzo Tarrant's farm in Minnesota. Yes, that was certainly it! Good old Uncle Alonzo, who had always favored Martin over him! Excited, he banged one fist into the other and stared raptly at the farmland passing the window. Already his leg felt better.

* * *

THE SANTEE MASSACRE

The jailing of the Sioux delegation at Fort Ridgely fanned into flame the anger of the Indians. Though as yet there was no organized hostile action, sporadic raids were reported all along the valley of the Minnesota River. A farmer at St. Pete was slain as he plowed his field. In Renville County a family holed up in a root cellar for three days while Sioux burned their dwelling with fire arrows. A raft loaded with sawn lumber was driven aground by arrows launched from the bank, and then boarded by whooping savages. Three boatmen were killed; the fourth, a Swede named Mansson, escaped by swimming underwater to the far shore. General Sibley visited New Ulm to assure the citizens the state would protect them. The soldiers from Fort Ridgely, he claimed, could travel quickly up the river by steamboat in case New Ulm were attacked in force. No one believed him. "Them soldiers," someone remarked, "are skeered to come outside to pee." There was hope that if Congress ever got around to approving funds for the Indian annuities, this might mollify the more impetuous Sioux. But Congress, occupied with the war, had forgotten the western frontier and its problems.

Before leaving town General Sibley, impressive on his big mare, reviewed the raggle-taggle militia and complimented their warlike appearance. Mrs. Cates, however, voiced the opinion of the townspeople. "Them boobies is more apt to shoot theirselves in the foot than hit an Indian!"

Martin, looking for Phronsie the next morning, could not find her. Mrs. Cates said, "Oh, she got up early and went off to see Sarah Biggs, over on Spring Street. Sarah brought Phronsie into the world. Old Sarah's midwifed a thousand babies in her time."

"Did she say when she'd get back?"

Mrs. Cates, knitting in the parlor, clacked needles steadily. "I daresay it won't be till suppertime, Mr. Brown. She's got a lot of friends among the blanket Sioux in town, and she always visits awhile with them. Of course, I don't hold with her being friendly with Indians, but she's got a mind of her own, has Phronsie!"

"She has," Martin agreed.

"I don't never trust an Indian! They ain't got a speck of pity or compassion. Animals, they are—wild animals, ought to be put in cages!" She dropped a stitch, frowned, pulled out yarn. "Look what they did to poor old Mr. Tarrant, down by Pipestone Lake. Never caused anyone no harm, and they killed him to get eggs, they say! Imagine! Why he'd have *give* them eggs if they'd only asked, nice and polite!"

Martin's voice was cautious. "The Sioux killed him?"

Her needles clacked viciously. "Mr. Sigafoos, down the road, missed him, come by to see if he was sick. Found the poor old man buried by the back stoop, an arrow in his back! They say the red devils got scared about what they'd done and covered him up! There was that nice young man, too!"

Martin's throat seemed dry and parched. He clasped his hands to stop their trembling.

"Bishop Whipple stopped often at Mr. Tarrant's place. This nice young man—blond he was, the bishop said, with blue eyes—come out from the East. Never seen again! They do say the Sioux carry off young people to be slaves."

Martin swallowed, found his voice. "That could be, certainly."

She held up her knitting, peered through her spectacles. "Oh, the bloody times we're in!" Pulling aside the curtain, she looked out through the screen of morning glories at the sun-drenched morning. "Ain't it a shame God made this lovely world, and made Sioux Indians too? Sometimes I wonder." Dropping the curtain, she added, hastily, "Not that I question His will, you understand, Mr. Brown. It's just that His will is hard to understand sometimes."

"I suppose so," Martin murmured. "So many things are hard to understand." Shaken, he rose, stretched, tried to appear casual. "Ma'am, I'm going out for a while, but I'll be back for dinner."

He still had Uncle Alonzo's money, and took off the deerskin shirt and ragged pants to buy civilized clothing: a nankeen coat, woolen jeans, a broadcloth shirt, and a pair of stout boots. Old clothes in a packet under his arm, he strolled down Front Street, uncomfortable in the tight boots and confining coat, but thinking a little wear would soon make them tolerable. No one noticed him or paid him much attention. He was still shaken by Mrs. Cates's story. *But I can pass for Martin Brown,* he thought. *Martin Brown, itinerant painter.* From—where? Illinois? Kentucky? It didn't matter. He was inventive; he could make up something credible. New Ulm was a thriving market town. There were probably people who wanted family portraits, painting of neat barns, pictures of prize bulls and such; he might make a living that way. Stopping by a furniture shop, redolent with the smell of pine shavings, he talked to the proprietor, a burly man in paint-smeared jeans.

"Guess so," the carpenter said. "Sure, I could sell you some paint. But you ain't going to make no money painting houses around *here*. These pinchpenny Dutchmen and squareheads does their own painting."

"I don't paint houses. I do portraits, landscapes—things like that."

"Oh!" The carpenter spat into the sawdust. "An artist feller, hey?"

Before he left, with a box of pigments in jars and an assortment of small brushes under his arm, he had a commission. Mr. Mason wanted a picture of his father. "Ninety-eight years old next month! He ain't going to be with us long, so I thought I'd like to remember the old gentleman with something to hang up in the parlor."

Using scantlings borrowed from the Cates's woodshed, Martin set up an easel in his room. From Zook's store he had bought a yard of canvas. When it had dried sufficiently in the sunlight, he carefully trimmed a brush and sat expectant before the easel. What to paint? The backyard below, with its sagging stable, fringed by marigolds, outlines indistinct under the cascade of climbing morning glories? That would not be satisfying. A face, then. Whose face? Phronsie? No; he found her countenance elusive, contradictory. In camp he had known every feature, the sweep of nose and curve of temple. But since she had come down to supper such a strange and different person, he was confused. What *did* she look like? Who *was* Phronsie Bettencourt?

Perversely, he found himself thinking of Wolf Talker, the medicine man. An old rascal, certainly; a vicious and crafty assassin. Still, there was character in the shaman's withered face. Not civilized character, of course, but still character: lean, hawklike, natural—natural like the woods and the streams and the animals. He would paint Wolf Talker from memory.

Losing track of time he labored at his easel, painting, rubbing out, painting again, impatient at the limited supply of pigments and the awkwardness of big brushes. In his mind he could see the old man with photographic clarity, headband of black fur surmouted by the stuffed bird, blue-painted face with the white star straggling across the beaklike nose, the eagle-feather-tipped flyswatter or whatever it was. Eagerly he worked, disregarding Mrs. Cates's call to dinner. The sunny image of the window frame on the carpet turned long and angular, his fingers cramped. He painted on, feeling he was managing to catch the essence of the man—the wild proud stare of a bird of prey. Satisfied, he leaned back in his chair and examined his work, only then becoming aware it was late.

"Mr. Brown."

Mrs. Cates was ascending the stairs.

"Are you in there?"

Hastily he slipped the portrait of Wolf Talker behind the bureau. Martin certainly did not want to risk being known as an Indian lover.

"Yes, ma'am."

Wheezing, she paused at his door. "My stars—if I climb those stairs once more today I swear I'll die of an apoplexy!" She noticed the easel, the paints. "My goodness, Mr. Brown, you an artist?"

He nodded.

"I knew it! You got long thin fingers, and a kind of a sensitive look about you. Well"—she turned—"supper's set."

"I'm coming," he promised.

Phronsie did not appear at supper. Martin was annoyed. Had she forgotten him totally? It did not seem polite to go gallivanting off with not a word. Eating chicken dumplings and fried potatoes, dried-apple pie afterwards, he decided it was to be expected; Phronsie was her own woman.

The next morning Mrs. Cates reported Phronsie had left very early to visit an old man who had been a friend to her father. Martin became exasperated. "I wish she'd light someplace long enough for me to have a word with her!"

The landlady looked shrewdly at him. "Never knew her to sit still very long, Mr. Brown! Phronsie's got to be moving all the time. She ain't likely to settle down to anything."

Uncomfortable, he shrugged. "Well, it's nothing to me!"

Her rheumy blue eyes twinkled. "Of course not!"

During the day he worked again on the portrait of Wolf Talker, sharpening a detail, painting out a shadow, endlessly refining. Still his attention wandered. Finally he put the portrait away in its hiding place and sat fretting by the window. Perhaps he ought to go out to the Mason place and make a preliminary sketch of the carpenter's antique father. But he was not in the mood. Where in the hell was she? He needed to talk to her, confide in her. Other than Mrs. Cates he knew no one else, and Phronsie was the only one he could trust. Besides, what he wanted to talk about concerned her also. Where in damnation *was* she?

At supper he only played with the fried liver and onions, buttered a piece of Mrs. Cates's cornbread and didn't eat it, pushed away the rhubarb pie with its flaky crust. Muttering an apology, he excused himself from the table and returned to his lonely room. A rising moon shone through the curtains, casting silvery spiderwebs on the carpeting. In the sycamore outside his window a bird called, a mellow plaintive trill. From the distance another answered. *I hope they get together*, he thought, *better than Phronsie and me!*

Everything in the yard below seemed transformed by the moonlight. The sagging stable looked mysterious and romantic, the black hole of the loft perhaps a window where a lovelorn maid watched for the arrival of the young knight who would save her. Martin sighed, noisily.

He did not hear her return. It must have been near midnight when he decided he could bear it no longer. The house was asleep. When he opened his door to peer out, all he could hear was heavy snoring, punctuated by a massive tick from the clock in the parlor below. Silently he padded down the hall in stocking feet toward Phronsie's room at the front of the house. The door was ajar. Uneasy, he dared to peek in. If the landlady knew he was visiting a female guest's room in the night hours he would be instantly expelled; probably Phronsie would, too. Mrs. Cates was a staunch Baptist.

"Phronsie? Are you there?"

In the dim light from the oil lamp in the hallway he saw the bed was still made up. Where could she be? A lone female, running around at such an hour of the night. He despaired of her; not a brain in her head! Suppose Indians were prowling along the riverbank? A clerk in Zook's store had said he came on one as he was returning from a prayer meeting. "Scouting the town!" he reported. "Skulking in the reeds by the ferry landing, and had a bunch of grass and weeds on his head so's he looked just like a bush!"

He was about to give up when he heard faint music. Someone was humming a melody, a familiar melody. His ears strained as he turned his head this way and that to locate the sound. No one was in the room. So where—

Suddenly he recognized the tune. It was the snatch

of Bach he had tried to play on the Indian flute the night he and Phronsie had talked.

"Phronsie?"

Uneasily he entered, eyes searching the gloom. "You here?"

The window overlooking the porch roof was open. Curtains swayed in the night breeze. Looking out, he saw her sitting, knees drawn up and arms locked about them, on the shingled roof.

"What are you doing out there, for Heaven's sake?"

Startled, she looked up. "Martin!"

She wore a thin silk nightgown, probably borrowed from Mrs. Cates, and precious little else. Tightly she wound arms about her body. "What are you doing in my room? Don't you know Mrs. Cates—"

"I know." Gingerly he stepped out on the roof, squatted beside her.

"God damn it, Martin . . ."

Pleased with his stratagem, he said, "Don't talk so loud! Someone will hear us."

"But—"

"I want to talk to you about something important."

"This isn't any place to—"

He put a finger to her lips. "How will I talk to you otherwise? You're always gone someplace!" When she was silent, shaking her head in disbelief, he went on. "Phronsie, I want to marry you."

"What?"

"Be quiet, damn it!" She started to rise but he clutched her arm, forcing her to sit again. "If you don't listen to me, I'll make a ruckus and rouse everybody. You know what will happen then."

Angrily she squatted, muttering under her breath. "Lordy, you are crazy as a loon!"

Quickly he continued. "Phronsie, I can pass here, pass for Martin Brown. I can paint, make a good living for us. Already I've got a commission for a portrait. You and I can get married, rent a little house, be happy together. Phronsie, I want you. I love you! I didn't know it at first, but I know it now. You can have pretty clothes, sleep in a real bed, safe from wild animals and not have to work so hard, scraping those damned skins and getting cheated by that rascally Levi Zook. You can live like a lady, and that's what you are—a lady! Maybe not your usual kind, like back in Jamaica Plain, but a better kind. The *real* kind, not some primped and prissy Boston female! Will you do it?"

She stared at him, eyes dark pools in the moonlight.

"God damn it, Phronsie—speak to me!"

She could only shake her head in wonder.

"I love you, don't you understand that? I love you, Phronsie Bettencourt!"

Her voice trembled as she rose unsteadily. "Oh, Martin! No!"

"But I do!"

Her voice was uncertain. "Nobody ever told me they loved me! Not even Pa. Sometimes he told me I done good—did good. Sometimes he said I wasn't half bad, for a female. But he never said he loved me! And Ma died when I was little—I don't even remember her. No one ever said they loved me!"

He rose also, saying, "*I'm* telling you, Phronsie. I love you!"

Virginal in the white nightgown, she muffled a sob. The sound was so alien that he was touched. He wanted to take her in his arms but she pushed him away, trying to compose herself.

"Martin, this is silly!"

"Why is it silly, pray?"

"I'm no good for you. I can't even sleep in a proper bed! That's why I came out here, where I could breathe good air and look at the stars."

"But you'd learn!"

Shaking her head, she held wound arms about her as if she were cold. "I'm not right for you, Martin. You need some homebody to bear you lots of children and go to church with you of a Sunday."

"But—"

She touched his cheek, a hesitant gesture. "I'm plumb honored, Martin, but you got the wrong woman, believe me! I'll never change. I been brought up in the woods. That's where I belong, with all the wild things."

Still he implored. Finally her voice stopped its trembling, became firm and decisive. "No. I said no and I mean no! For the good of both of us." When he continued to argue, she plucked the Sioux whistle from its cord at her bosom. "I swear, Martin, if you don't stop haggling, I'll blow this whistle and claim you tried to have your pleasure with me, right here on this porch roof!"

It was an ignominious end to his plan. Phronsie Bettencourt was not attainable. In a way he had always known it; now it was certain. Wryly he looked about, thinking how ridiculous it was anyway to propose marriage on a porch roof at midnight.

"Be real quiet when you go in."

"I will," he promised.

That night he slept fitfully. At dawn, the sun barely topping the ridges beyond the town, he woke. Distraught, he slipped into his new clothes, wandered down the stairs. From the front porch he heard voices though the rest of the house seemed wrapped in slumber.

Phronsie stood in the graveled walk between the marigolds chatting with Mrs. Cates. The landlady was wrapped in a cloth coat; the hem of a nightgown showed beneath. Her plump feet were in carpet slippers.

"Mr. Brown! What gets you up at the crack of dawn?"

Unhappily Martin stared at Phronsie Bettencourt. She was dressed as he first saw her—greasy deerskin shirt, moccasins, fur cap sitting jauntily on ruffled locks. She carried her possibles bag over her shoulder and leaned casually on the old musket.

"So you meant to go away, without even saying good-bye?" he demanded.

Mrs. Cates, scenting disagreement, moved diplomatically aside.

"That wasn't a very nice thing to do to me, Phronsie."

She did not meet his eyes. "I've got a bellyful of town," she said in a low voice, moccasined toe scuffing the gravel.

"It's hardly polite, even so."

"There ain't no polite in the woods. What the hell do I keer for polite?" Deliberately she seemed to be trying to be crude, arrogant.

"I guess . . ." He paused, tried again. "I guess you had me fooled. I figured you had possibilities, real possibilities."

If he had thought to hurt her for his rejection at her hands, he did not succeed. Lifting her chin, she said proudly, "I'm what I am, Martin, and I ain't one damned bit ashamed of it! You're what you are too, I guess."

Helpless, he nodded. "I suppose you're right."

From the porch Mrs. Cates called out. "Good-bye, Phronsie! I got to go in and hustle up some biscuits."

Not knowing what else to do, Martin held out his hand. She put her hard brown hand in his.

"Perhaps I'll see you again, sometime, Phronsie. Sometime—someplace."

"Maybe."

Withdrawing her hand, she swung about, hefted the bag, walked quickly down the path, and turned toward the river and the ferry. For a long time he watched her grow smaller and smaller; finally she was gone. *Phronsie* gone! It did not seem real. For a time she had been the furniture of his life—real, solid, reassuring. Now she was not Phronsie Bettencourt; she was Iron Girl again. And both were gone.

"Mr. Brown?"

Dazed, he turned.

"I fried up eggs for you, and there's hot oatmeal. Biscuits, too."

"I'm coming," Martin said, and walked heavily back into the house.

CHAPTER SEVEN

Martin had not known how much he would miss Phronsie Bettencourt. The salt of his life had departed. Always amused by mooning lovers, here he was now, a mooning lover himself, sitting dejected in his room and staring out the window. He hardly heard the clamor and clatter of the militiamen drilling on the green to the shouted commands of Lieutenant Phipps.

Mrs. Cates knew what was the matter. "Phronsie's a wild creature, Mr. Brown—always was—like one of them Canada ducks that passes this way spring and fall." Dusting his room while he slumped in the chair by the window, she went on, "There's lots of nice girls in this town, you know. Now you take the Widow Dietz. Her man got sick and died last winter, and Bertha'd be mighty pleased to have a handsome young fellow come calling." She shook the turkey duster out the window, adding, "Bertha's got twenty acres of prime bottomland along the river, a team and plow, and a red barn that Hans painted just before he was took."

Martin uncrossed his legs, crossed them again, sighed. "Thank you, Mrs. Cates, but I—"

"You *could* do worse," she pointed out, bustling here and there, closing bureau drawers and straightening doilies. "Man was made to live with woman—proper married, that is! Oh, how I miss my man Elmer!"

Wanting solitude, Martin said, "Well, ma'am, I'll think on it."

He had visited Mr. Mason, the carpenter's ninety-eight-year-old father, and made preliminary sketches for his first commission. Listlessly he took out the easel and his canvas and paints and stared for a long time at the sized cloth. From time to time he glanced at the sketches. Wherever he looked, however, he saw the wrong face, Phronsie Bettencourt's. When he closed his eyes, she was still there, the frank and honest gaze, tumbled ginger curls, a spark of mischief in her eyes. Remembering, he saw her also thigh-deep in the forest pool, body slim and pale and virginal, the small breasts round and firm as oranges—or was it apples? Someone in mythology, a Roman or perhaps a Greek, called them golden apples.

Finally, moved by an impulse he did not care to analyze, he put brush to canvas and found himself doing Phronsie Bettencourt's likeness. Rapidly and surely he painted, finding the brush doing his bidding more easily than he had believed. In minutes he had roughed out the head, the neck, and the shoulders and reached for a finer brush to limn the eyes, the nose, the delicate bone structure of her cheeks—high, almost like those of the Indians she consorted with. Suddenly, with a muttered curse, he flung down the brush in a spatter of paint. Resignedly he knelt and tried to wipe it up. "Damned mooncalf!" he muttered between clenched teeth. *Sitting here pining away for a dream, for something you can never have, and probably wouldn't want if you had it!*

Angry with himself, he clattered down the stairs and walked toward the green. The weather was blistering hot; the sun beat oppressively on his bare head. Paying a penny for the *Minnesota Republican,* he learned that Bishop Whipple was soon to leave for the East to discuss the Indian problem with President Lincoln. From the safety of the state capitol General Sibley was still reassuring the settlers along the river that the troops at Fort Ridgely were sufficient to repel any Indian attacks in force that might occur. However, the gossip Martin heard was anxious. There were reports that Shakopee's Sioux were gathering, and that unless his peace delegation was immediately released from custody at Fort Ridgely he would burn and destroy New Ulm as an example. Even the "civilized" Indians, squatting sullenly before the government brick houses, were in a dangerous mood. Cutworms had destroyed most of their corn crop. Levi Zook ignored their entreaties for food, repeating his ultimatum, "Let 'em eat grass!"

Lieutenant Phipps, lounging in the shade of a cottonwood tree while his awkward squads rested, waylaid Martin.

"You look healthy to me," he remarked.

Martin was puzzled. "Tolerable enough, I guess."

Phipps spat. "Better think about it, then. People has been wondering why you ain't volunteered yet."

"People? What people?"

"Oh, people." Phipps spat again, this time closer to Martin's boots, and put on the oversize shako. Moving off, he barked commands. Listlessly the volunteers rose, shambled into a straggling line, muttered to each other.

Volunteer! Martin thought. Volunteer again, as he had at the Colonel's insistence? He had disgraced himself once and did not want to be put to the test again. Of course they were Indians he would be called upon to kill, not fellow humans. Then he was contrite, remembering Yellow Horse and Wolf Talker and the rest. They were, well, *different*, of course. Still, he could never bring himself to kill another man, no matter how different. In an emergency he would stand passively, most likely, a steer in an abattoir, and await death. It was not an agreeable thought. Yet there it was.

Back in the room he counted his money. Only a few dollars were left after his buying clothing, paints, brushes, and canvas and paying room and board. He would have to finish the portrait of old Mr. Mason, then go looking for other commissions. But he was dispirited and sat gloomily staring at the half-finished portrait of Phronsie Bettencourt, while his own mind supplied the absent details. Twilight came, then dark. Not wanting to encounter Lieutenant Phipps, he skipped supper. Night fell. A crescent moon was caught in the branches of the oaks fringing the hills above the town. Night birds called. From the river he heard muffled challenges from sentries stationed in a line between the town and the ridges beyond. At last he threw himself fully clothed on the bed and slept a troubled sleep. Again he was playing on the lawn at Uncle Alonzo's house in Braintree. Lucas jeered at him. "Crybaby! Coward! Martin is a coward! Look at him bawling!"

Crybaby! Coward!

THE SANTEE MASSACRE

"Martin! Look at Martin!"

Uneasily he rolled over, burying his face in the pillow.

"Martin. Martin!"

Lucas was still taunting him. Angry, he sat up, then blinked in the light of a lamp.

"Martin! Wake up!"

Dazed, he rubbed knuckles into his eyes. In the doorway stood his brother, Lucas. It was a dream, surely a dream, yet the lamplight was real.

"Lucas?" he murmured.

"It's me, Martin."

Slowly, unbelieving, he rolled over, sat on the edge of the bed and blinked in the lamplight. Behind Lucas he saw Mrs. Cates's pale, frightened face.

Lucas was propped on a cane. His face was thin and sallow and he looked ill, very ill. Carefully his brother set the lamp on the bureau and unbuttoned his coat. A pistol was stuck in the broad leather belt. Martin recognized the weapon. It was the Root's Patent revolver the Colonel had given Lucas.

"Get up!"

"But what—what are you doing here?"

Lucas grinned, a mirthless twist with no amusement in it, but something of satisfaction. "It was a long chase, but I found you at last! You're coming home with me!"

"Home?" Martin tried to swallow. His mouth was dry and cottony.

"City Point, then! For a proper court-martial. No Sayre has ever run from the enemy, Martin. You're the first, and I damn well intend you to be the last!"

Martin stared at the cane. "Your leg—"

"The hell with the leg!"

"But—"

"I took a ball in the calf at Mill Springs, in Kentucky, if it's any of your damned business. Now get up!" Lucas pulled the pistol from his belt. "Don't try anything. You're a prisoner, I want you to understand that."

Martin was gripped by a sense of unreality. "Surely, Lucas, you—you—"

"Quick, now! I've already talked to the town constable. You're going into his jail till I can arrange transportation for the two of us." He gestured toward Martin's valise. "Pack whatever you want to take with you, and be quick about it!"

Mrs. Cates's voice trembled. "Please, Mr. Brown—do as he says! I don't want no trouble in my house." Behind her others, craning necks and murmuring, gathered in the dimly lit hall.

"No!"

Lucas frowned. "What do you mean, no?"

"I'll not go with you."

Lucas's dark eyes narrowed. He raised the muzzle of the pistol. "Martin, it doesn't make one iota of difference to me whether I shoot you here and now, as a prisoner making an escape, or let an Army firing squad do it later. But I warn you I'm deadly serious. It's a crime to desert from the Army and a heinous crime in wartime. You've got to be brought to account, not only for the Army's satisfaction but for my own—and Father's."

Shrugging, Martin turned and picked up the empty valise. Suddenly he threw it. The flying bag caught Lucas, still weak from his wound, in the face and he dropped the pistol. Staggering back, he brushed the lamp with his flailing arm. It fell to the floor, spilling oil, which blazed up and ran in fiery rivulets about the room. Like a cornered animal Martin sought a route of escape, but the hall was blocked with onlookers.

Lucas, dropping his cane, stumbled forward and managed to catch Martin about the ankles. Martin fell heavily on him and heard a muffled grunt of pain as Lucas's bad leg twisted. Someone brushed Mrs. Cates aside and plunged through the doorway after Martin. It was Lieutenant Phipps, grotesque in nightgown and nightcap. Martin floundered across the bed, poised for a moment in the open window, then threw himself into the blackness. Alighting in Mrs. Cates's roses, he tore himself clear of the thorny stalks and fled across the lawn, bounding over the white picket fence while cries of anger and frustration sounded from the window above.

Scratched and bleeding, his new clothing torn, he ran toward the river to swim across to safety. But a sentry challenged him.

"Who goes there?"

Gasping for breath, he paused in the shadows under a spreading oak. In the starshine he saw the pale face of the militiaman, searching the night, his piece at the ready.

"Who's there?" Uncertain, the man peered toward Martin. He raised the musket, cheek cradling the stock. "Stand where you are! Don't move!"

Martin ran again, this time toward the distant ridges. There was a blink of flame. Something exploded behind him. It was as if someone had clubbed him on the shoulder with a cudgel; the blow turned him, spun him. He dropped to one knee, a little giddy, then rose and plunged into the forest that bordered the town. He had been shot, he knew. Yet, strangely, it did not hurt; there was no pain at all.

The forest was dark. Neither starshine nor moonlight penetrated the gloom. Blindly he stumbled on, bumping into trees, falling headlong as his toe caught in matted roots, working his way deeper and deeper under the protecting canopy. Almost mechanically he veered this way and that, going slower and slower. Liquid was running down his back and into his boot. His sock was soaked with it, and his foot slipped about in the boot. *Blood!* he thought. *It must be blood. My own blood!* Still there was no pain.

The land seemed to rise before him. Was it imagination? No, there was stony rubble under his feet. He struggled up a gentle slope. Winded, he slumped on a rocky ledge. In a moment he would get up and run again, but for now he was tired, very tired. In the distance he thought he saw a rosy tinge to the sky and wondered if he had set Mrs. Cates's house afire. He regretted that; Mrs. Cates was a nice lady. Still, he could not let Lucas take him.

Closing his eyes, he lay down on the ledge, cheek against a blanket of moss. Once he had been willing to give himself up, to go back to face charges. Now things had changed. *Phronsie,* he thought. *I'm coming, Phronsie!* When he had rested he would find her. Somewhere beyond the ridge above, there was Phronsie.

"Phronsie," he muttered, and went to sleep, or swooned; he did not know which.

Floating in velvet blackness, he drifted here and there, at times conscious of murmurings, faint music, glimmerings of light. With a kind of wry humor he decided he had been misrouted. Heaven was not for him! Of course, this could be a kind of purgatory where unshriven souls waited for resolution of their fates. With nothing else to do he tried to remember church when he was a boy, to remember the mechanics of going to Hell.

The aimless drifting was pleasant. He relaxed, let his body slump. He could feel arms, hips, legs cradled in a soft substance. What did theology say about that? Well, he didn't care; his body was up to the Authorities. From somewhere he heard the music again and a soft voice. He strained to hear, but there was no more music, no more voice. Opening his eyes, he could see nothing. The clinging velvety blackness was all there was. Were his eyes all right? He wished he could see *something;* the thought of blindness bothered him. "I can't see anything!" he complained. When he struggled, twisting this way and that, the gentle voice spoke again, and pushed him down.

"What?" He was angry the voice did not speak more clearly. On the other hand, it might be a Heavenly dialect he was not familiar with. "All right," he agreed, and let himself sink again into the blackness.

Then he heard a voice—whose voice was it? A hand smoothed his brow.

"It's all right," she said.

She? Yes, of course; angels were feminine, or at least sexless.

"You're all right, Martin," Phronsie said. "You're with me, Martin. Everything's going to be fine."

In wonder he opened his eyes. It was morning, early morning. Shafts of sunlight filtered through the trees to cast a geometric pattern across the dew-wet grass of the clearing.

"Phronsie?"

"I'm here."

"Where—where . . . ?"

"You're right here, in my camp."

Closing his eyes, he sank back, puzzled, too tired to understand. She seemed to know what was on his mind. "You almost got here. I saw the crows circling when I was out gathering berries, and there you were!" Carefully she let him slip down into the fur robes and hovered above him. To his unaccustomed eyes her face was pale and indistinct. But it was Phronsie, no doubt about that. He felt satisfied. After a while he explained. "They shot me. A sentry shot me." Trying to shift his position, a fiery pain lanced his neck and shoulder. He winced, bit his lip.

"I know. The ball plowed through and then must have come out again, because I couldn't find it. But you lost a lot of blood." She made him drink a cup of hot meat-broth. "I—I was afraid, at first, you was— were—dead. You just laid there, on that rock. I dragged you to camp on a travois I made. You were so pale and still, bleeding like a stuck pig. The Sioux use *i ta so min* for bleeding so I roasted some seeds and ground them up and made a poultice. That helped, but finally I had to take Pa's shoemaker's thread and a big needle and sew you up proper. That did it."

He remembered devils pinching him, jabbing him, hurting his shoulder. That must have been the sewing. Something strange occurred to him; his lip curled in a grimace. *Saved. Saved by Sioux medicine!* It was ironic. When he started to laugh, she put a finger to his lips.

"Sleep, now, Martin! You need to gather your strength."

"But I want to tell you how it happened! Lucas came, you see, and—"

"No. Not now. Later."

He still protested. But when she put her cheek

against his, almost timidly, he felt a flush of pleasure, and became agreeable.

"All right," he consented, and slept.

After that there were times of lucidity and times when he drifted again into the somber blackness. Phronsie fed him, attended to his needs, brewed moldy-tasting potions he drank only at her urging, and changed the dressing of rags on his shoulder.

"Lucas!" he cried in delirium. "I hurt him! His leg was wounded, and I threw him down! Phronsie, I hurt Lucas!" Cradling him in her arms, she soothed him, sang to him—ballads, a scurrilous chant about an old boar and a sow. Under her ministrations the black mist faded, thinned. Finally he became lucid and clearheaded, though weak.

"You saved my life," he said. "I owe you my life, Phronsie. How will I ever make it up to you?"

She squatted before the fire, arranging skeins of thin-sliced venison to dry and smoke on a lattice of twigs. Her face was smudged with soot and the gingery hair was in disarray, appearing not to have known a comb for some time. Still wearing the greasy, smoke-blackened buckskins, she got to her feet. She was lank and lithe as ever.

"You don't have to make anything up to me, Martin. We're friends, aren't we?"

Friends. They were more than that. At least, he was!

Soon he could walk shakily about camp, leaning on a rude crutch she had cut. Now no dressings were needed on the deep shoulder wound; a puckered scar had appeared, a long furrow across the scapula almost to his neck. Now he could tell her about Lucas.

Gravely she listened. When he was done, she asked, "Why didn't you let him take you, then? Onct—once—I remember, you said you were tired of running. You said you were going to give out who you were, go back to face the music."

Leaning on the crutch, he looked at her for a long time. Under his gaze she became uneasy, plucked a stem of grass, worried it with her teeth.

"*You* know, Phronsie."

"I know what?"

"I came back because of you. That's why I came back. I—I love you, Phronsie!"

Agitated, she got to her feet, chewed viciously on the grass. "Foolishment! That's what it is! We're friends, that's all! I don't want to hear any more palavering about love, Martin Sayre!"

"I know. 'Get the hell out of my camp!' You've said that before, and didn't mean it any more than you do now. You're a big humbug, Sophronia Bettencourt!" Dropping the crutch, he tottered across to her, nearly falling in the process. Alarmed, she came to his aid with an arm under his shoulder. He was weak, but determined; wrapping his arms about her, he pressed his lips hard against hers.

"Martin!" For a moment she tore herself loose, hands flat against his chest. Then, seeing him sway, she caught him again, averting her face. "God damn it, Martin, stop it! I ain't no lovesick female like your damned Lavinia Greene or whatever her name was! I ain't no—"

As he pressed tighter against her, her voice trailed away. In his arms the slender body softened, lost its rigidity, molded to his. "Oh, lordy, lordy, lordy—" he heard her say. "Martin, please!"

He loved her, but his wound betrayed him. Suddenly everything went dim and shadowy again. He would have fallen had she not caught and almost carried him, ingloriously, to his furry bed in the lean-to. As he lay there, gasping for breath and embarrassed, she knelt above him, blue eyes malicious.

"Pilgrim, in your present condition, you ain't fit to make love to a flea."

"Well, it's not funny," he groaned, putting a hand over his eyes more to shield his red face than keep the sunlight out. "It shames a man, don't you see?"

Her voice turned tender. "There's no shame to it, Martin. You been through a lot. When your blood thickens up a little, maybe you can try it again."

Surprised, he tried to prop himself on his elbows. "Phronsie—you mean you—you're—"

But she was gone, dancing like a sprite into the woods, the woven berry basket over her arm. Her voice floated back to him:

> My days have been so wondrous free!
> The little birds that fly
> With careless ease from tree to tree
> Are not so blest as I!

The time was full summer, and their time was idyllic. As Martin's strength returned they lay together on the furs of the lean-to, swam naked in the rocky pool, two pale fish twisting and turning, at times coming together to warm their bodies with the fire that burned in them. Afterwards they lay, still naked, in the sun, on a granite ledge, looking with pleasure at each other. She was a virgin—had been a virgin. Still, she came to him almost like a courtesan, with an innate knowledge of what would please him and what would pleasure her.

Together they roamed the hills, burned in the sun.

Hand in hand they watched deer in the brakes, saw beavers building dams across the creek, started mutually as a long spotted snake looped down from a tree overhanging their path. Phronsie muttered something in Sioux, and he was curious.

"I told him I was sorry I scared him away from the bird eggs or whatever he was after. This is their land, they were here long before we were. So you got to be polite." She explained how a Sioux, before he shoots a deer for meat, asks first. "He will say 'Wo hi tka'—that means deer—'Wo hi tka, if you come into my lodge I will give you red paint.' The Sioux love red."

Sha, sha—he remembered the Sioux delegation grunting *sha, sha* in approval. *Sha* meant red, too. If something was red, it was good also, by definition.

Once he had been annoyed by her barbaric ways. Now he was fascinated; in this sylvan setting they seemed natural, appropriate. She taught him some of the graceful hand language, and a few Sioux words. Corn was *wa ka ma za*, potatoes *be lo*, beef *to lo*, sugar a jawbreaking *cha hum pi as ka*. He never did master the word for mushrooms, the succulent white morsels she gathered for his breakfast, sliced thin and fried crisp and toothsome. It was something like *ya ma nu mi in ni qua pa*. When he tried to say it she was overcome with laughter, lying flat on the grass in a paroxysm of mirth. In mock anger he spread himself over her. They wrestled together, crushing the wildflowers. Finally, breathing hard, she conceded defeat.

"You're pretty strong anymore," she gasped. "I can't hardly handle you these days!"

"That's because I love you," he murmured in her ear, "and I mean to marry you!"

That upset her. Turning her back, she sat in silence, hands clasped around buckskin knees.

THE SANTEE MASSACRE

"Did I say something . . . wrong?"

For a while she would not speak, only picked grass, sullenly.

"Tell me, then!"

Swinging round, she stared at him over her shoulder. "I don't want to hear no more talk about marrying, pilgrim! Marrying is for city folks, down there in New Ulm and Mankato and Fairmont and places like that!"

Free. Free as the little birds that fly! He thought he understood, yet their life together ought to be somehow sanctified.

"But—"

"I don't want to hear no more about it!"

Waking early one morning, before the sun was up, he slipped into the forest to relieve himself. It was then that he saw the Sioux. A file of warriors topped a ridge, slipped over like a serpent, and glided out of sight toward the valley below. In the clear light of dawn he could see they were heavily armed. Pennons fluttered from lances, many carried rifles. They were so silent and businesslike that he felt a chill. Hurrying back to camp, he woke Phronsie.

"I know," she said. "I been aware. Many have passed by, in the past week or so. They got black paint on their faces. That means war."

All this time, while he was living this rich, carefree life, Phronsie had been on the alert, looking, listening, aware of movement around the camp that he had been ignorant of! There was a lot for him to learn.

"War?"

She nodded, poking moodily at the ashes of the cookfire. "I expect they aim to get their brothers out of Fort Ridgely one way or the other."

He helped her start the fire, put the coffeepot on to

boil. "They don't stop to talk to you anymore? Like they did that time, Wolf Talker and Yellow Horse and the others?"

"I figure it's because they don't want to put me in a bad light. I mean, well, I'm white, spite of my Indian ways, and they know I don't hold with killing. So they just kind of slip by, and don't visit." In the morning cool she huddled in her blanket; he was suddenly struck by her vulnerability. "Guess I got to take sides one way or the other. They're my friends, and Mrs. Cates and a lot of the whites is my friends, too. Lordy, what can a poor girl do?"

This time it was his turn to say, "It'll be all right, Phronsie, it will work out. Don't worry."

She sighed, shook her head. "There'll be a lot of blood spilled before this is over, Martin. And I'm right smack in the middle!" She rose suddenly, distraught. "Martin, what can I do? Things are coming to an end for them, for Shakopee and Wolf Talker and all the rest! They can't fight the whole U. S. Army! What good is brave against cannons?"

He held her tight, not knowing what to say. Later, he comforted her in the only way he knew how.

CHAPTER EIGHT

"What day is this?" Martin asked.

"I don't keep much track of days."

"What date, then?"

Phronsie shrugged. "Well, it's August. Somewheres in the middle, I guess. Maybe tenth, twelfth—who cares?"

They lay on the ledge beside the forest pool, enjoying the healing warmth of the sun. Squinting upward, Martin remarked, "Must be noon or thereabouts. Probably Sunday, too."

Splitting a stem of grass and holding it delicately between her fingers, near her lips, Phronsie asked, "Why Sunday?"

"Peaceful. Like when I was a boy at home, in Jamaica Plain. After church things were always quiet and peaceful. After dinner, especially. The Colonel—Father—dozing in his chair with the *Globe* on his lap, Mother doing needlework, old Caesar—that was our dog—asleep, head between his paws . . ."

She blew softly at the split grass, nodding her head in approval of the flutelike sound. "You miss them, don't you?"

"I like it here—with you."

"Still and all, you miss them."

"I guess so."

"Tell me about it, then." Rolling next to him, she put her head in the crook of his bare arm, now as brown from the sun as her own.

He felt a kind of relief talking about Jamaica Plain, the big old house, mother's kitchen garden, their cook, Emma, who had been with the Sayre family for over forty years. "Indian pudding," he recalled. "Thick, with nutmeg and brown sugar, and then cream poured over it. My brother and I used to sneak into the kitchen when Emma wasn't looking and stick our fingers in it." At the thought of Lucas he became somber. "All in all, Lucas wasn't a bad brother. He taught me lots of things, and was very patient. He used to take me hunting and fishing. I wasn't a good shot, though. When it came to putting worms on my hook, I always worried whether it hurt them, and that made him cuss! But one time, when the Colonel made me go to bed without any supper because I plagued Emma so, Lucas—" Martin swallowed, plucked his own blade of grass to cover his emotion. "Lucas came up the back stairway and brought me his pork chop and some bread he'd saved from his own supper."

Phronsie was silent. After a while she murmured, "I never had no—had any brothers or sisters. Leastwise, not that I know of, though Pa was always kind of a roisterer, I heard."

Sitting up, chin resting on knees, he locked arms about his knees. Staring at the sunlight dimpling the pond, he did not see it. In his mind there formed a vision of Lucas with the Root's Patent pistol pointed, himself balancing precariously on the bed at the Widow Cates's, himself wrestling Lucas down and hearing the groan of pain as Lucas's bad leg twisted. "I didn't mean to do it, you understand! He got that wound at Mill Springs, in Kentucky. God, I didn't mean to do it!"

Phronsie sat up also and put her arm around him. "Of course you didn't, Martin! What else could you do?"

A wren fluttered from the trees overhead, cocked a wary eye, then drank from the pool. Its brown wings glowed in the sunlight, luminously.

"You love your brother, don't you?"

"I love my family, and Lucas is family."

Trying to change his mood, she went to her possibles bag and took out two tattered volumes. Squatting beside Martin, she opened one. "This here is a book I gave ten cents for in New Ulm. See—it's a primer. And the other is the Bible. I want you to help me with those squiggly *little* letters."

Relieved to abandon his dismal thoughts, he took up the book. For an hour he tutored her, explaining the reason for capitals and lower-case letters. Phronsie became exasperated at her slow progress, stating that she thought lower-case letters complicated and unnecessary.

"You want to learn, don't you?"

"Yes."

"Then pay attention and stop complaining!"

She was an attentive student, with native intelligence eager for knowledge. It was a pleasure to teach her. He thought of the tabula rasa old Professor Dakin had spoken of at college, the clean slate ready to take an impression. In ways she shamed him with her quickness. Finding her adding a sum quicker than he could, he laid down the scrap of hide he had been writing numbers on. "That's enough for today!"

"But I got to hurry! I wasted a lot of time! I—I don't really mean *wasted*, of course. But I want to learn to speak pretty, like you do!"

"Speaking pretty is all right, but I like you to *look* pretty!"

"What do you mean?"

He spoke of supper at Mrs. Cates's, Phronsie's appearance in the borrowed dress, the first time he had seen her in feminine apparel. "You were more than pretty, you were beautiful!"

"That wasn't me!"

"What does *that* mean, for Heaven's sake!"

"Lordy, I was just doing a turn! I mean, that was playacting. That wasn't *me*. Leastways, not the real me. This"—she touched her bosom—"this is *me*, Phronsie Bettencourt. Don't hornswoggle yourself, Martin Sayre, and be sorry about it afterward."

He took her in his arms; she bent to him. "I can't imagine ever being sorry," he murmured.

It was an idyllic existence but for one thing. Their camp was astride an old Sioux trail; more and more war parties, faces ominously painted, passed by. Phronsie thought some were Chippewas, come from the north to help their Santee Sioux brothers against the white settlers. It was obvious a great battle was forming. Phronsie said her pa used an Indian term. Her brow wrinkled in recollection. "Don't rightly recollect the word for it, but it means 'stirring gravy.' Thats what the Sioux call a big fight."

Though he had no paints and no brushes, Phronsie brought him wild berries and fruits, which he crushed and mixed with water to make reds, blues, and yellows. For canvas he used sun-dried squares of deerhide, for brushes willow twigs chewed on one end until they developed a silky tuft. The materials and tools were crude, but they gave fair results.

"Of course," Phronsie said, watching him do a creditable portrait of her friend Yellow Horse, "the Sioux has been painting things for hundreds of years, I guess." She squatted near, chewing her everlasting blade of grass. "They like round things to paint, mostly. Round is a big thing to a Sioux, The sun is round, the moon is round, a tipi is round. When they go hunting in the summer they pitch their lodges in a big circle. Their shields are always round." She frowned, searching for words. "I don't know actual how to say it, but Pa explained it to me. It's like, well, the edge of a circle don't—hasn't—got any end, see? It just keeps going round and round. And that's what the Sioux thinks. They get born. They grow and take a wife. Then they get old and die. But sons and grandsons are coming along all the time and life goes on, like a circle. You understand me, Martin?"

He laid down the willow-twig brush. "You said it better than I could have, Phronsie. You're practically a college graduate, right now."

She was suspicious. "You funning me?"

"Of course not. I meant it."

Content as he was, black moods came on him still at times. He could be silent, reflective, and sit for hours at the makeshift easel, staring, seeing nothing. One day Phronsie slipped up behind him and put her hands over his eyes. "Guess who!" Snatched suddenly from his thoughts, he jumped. "Don't do that! Don't ever do that, Phronsie!"

Hurt, she pouted. "My Lord, you're spooky today! Come to think of it, you been acting queer for a passel of days. Martin, what's wrong?"

Contrite, he sat again on the makeshift stool. "I'm sorry. I was just thinking."

"About what? You know you can tell me." She laughed. "After all, we been about as close—is that the word?—as a man and a woman can be."

He was in no mood for badinage. "Lucas," he sighed. "I was just thinking about Lucas."

"Lucas?"

"Him, and a lot more. Home—Jamaica Plain—the Army, you—a lot of things!"

Pulling him down to a grassy hillock, she lay against him. "You having a good time here? I mean . . . with me?"

"You know that."

"Still and all, you're unhappy."

"Yes."

"I know what's wrong."

She probably did. He had never known a female with her guileless prescience.

"Do you?"

"Well, you ran away from the Army. You hid out on your uncle's farm, and he was killed. Lucas tried to take you, and you hurt him and ran away. Now you figure you got to leave this garden place here, and go into the outside because of what you done."

"Did," he said absently. "It's the preterite tense."

She was impatient. "But isn't that the truth of it?"

For a moment he was silent. Then he admitted, "Of course, you're right. You're always right, Phronsie. You just keep on being right in your innocent way. Yes, I'm the one that sinned and I guess I've got to make up for it! I don't know if Lucas is still in New

Ulm, but anyway, I've made up my mind to go back and give myself up. This time I mean to do it. It's a penance."

She frowned at the new word.

"Don't bother," he said. "It's just a word. What counts in the book are deeds, not words." He pulled her to him, held her as if taking courage. "I love you, Phronsie, and I don't know what will happen to me, but I've got to go. Does that make any sense at all?"

She kissed his cheek. "Pa always said a man has got to do what a man has got to do. It never made much sense before, but I guess I understand now."

"I'll miss you," he said, and wished he had had grander, more passionate words to embroider his feelings. But she surprised him.

"I'm going with you."

"No! You can't do that! I can't ask you to do that!"

"You're not asking *me*," she declared. "I'm telling *you*! I'm going down to New Ulm with you, Martin. A lot of blood is going to be spilled pretty soon, and I been pondering too. Finally I made up *my* mind." Her face was serious. "They made me choose up sides, them whites down there and the Sioux. I got good friends both places, and I grieve to see them fight. There's probably right on both sides, and that's the hell of it! But it don't really signify that I love my Sioux brothers, because I'm not a Sioux. I'm white, I was born white, and I'll die white! If I got to make up my mind, and Lord knows I don't want to, then I guess I got to go down there and be with my own kind." Her eyes were edged with tears. "Does that make sense to *you*?"

He didn't answer. He didn't have to. Instead they lay together a long time in the sun-dappled glade, saying nothing, losing themselves in each other; there was a kind of instinctual understanding between them which did not need words.

The next day they prepared to leave for New Ulm. They traveled light. This time their whole baggage was a canvas sack Martin slung over his shoulder. Puzzled, he waved a hand around the camp; the lean-to with its furs, the oiled traps hanging on the trees, smoke-blackened coffeepot, the bullet mold, and the small pigs of lead.

"You're just going to leave all this again?"

Phronsie, picking up her possibles bag, said, "Don't matter. If I need it again, it'll be here. No one will touch it. They know it's mine. And if I don't need it again, why—" She broke off, shouldering her musket.

"Well," he said, "*hopo*, eh?"

"In a minute." She went to Jake Bettencourt's grave with a handful of wildflowers and put fresh blooms in the jar. For a long time she knelt, lips moving soundlessly. The tattered Bible had been heavy going for her, especially with the small print and archaic words, but with Martin's help she enjoyed it. Was she saying one of the prayers in the back, perhaps a psalm? Martin hoped, but was disappointed when she concluded with a thoroughly Sioux train of gestures which he recognized—a beseeching of the Sioux deity. Phronsie made the *medicine* sign, then raised her hands high over her head, index fingers pointing to the zenith. *Great Medicine Chief*, the Sioux chief god, supreme above Rock, Thunder, Buffalo, and the rest of the Sioux pantheon.

When she returned, she was weeping. Awkwardly Martin took her hand. "I wish I'd known your father. He must have been a great old man."

" 'Tisn't that." She scrubbed her eyes with a sleeve. "Pa's all right here—he's fine. When his time come, he was ready. He'd lived a good life, he said, and this is where he wanted to be buried, in the trees right where the old Sioux trail crossed. No, it isn't that."

He understood. It was not only her father she was leaving; it was a way of life. Certain forest flowers, he knew, withered and died when transplanted to clay pots in the town. He was so moved by her emotion that there was hardly a twinge from his own. After all, he thought, they were both going toward something that could change their lives completely—perhaps end his.

Together they started down the trail, she in her well-worn buckskins, he in the baggy and torn remnants of the expensive clothes bought in New Ulm. With a light load and Martin restored to health, they made good time. By noon they came out on the road to New Ulm, near where Martin had been challenged that first day by the two officious militiamen. "I'm getting to know the lay of the land pretty well," he said. "I—"

"Wait!" Phronsie snatched at his sleeve.

"What is it?"

Quickly she pulled him off the dusty road.

"Chippewas!"

He crouched beside her in the gloom, peering. "I don't see anyone."

"They're there, anyway. By the bend of the road. Scouts."

"I thought you and all Indians were brothers."

"I don't know anything about Chippewas! Pa always said a Chippewa was about as reliable as Minnesota weather—fair one day and blizzard the next."

There was a rustle of dead leaves behind them. Phronsie whirled, musket at the ready. A brown arm knocked it spinning. Someone caught Martin from behind in a viselike grip that hurt his chest, made him grasp for breath. Then they were both flung down, encircled by unfriendly faces.

The leader of the patrol, a burly bowlegged man in white man's jeans, a necklace of bear claws about his neck and hair cut in a high roach decorated with dyed porcupine quills, prowled about them. He carried a cavalry saber and prodded them with it.

"God damn it, stop that!" Martin protested, trying to sit up. "You'll hurt her!" Oddly, he felt no fear, only anger. A moccasined foot caught him in the face and he fell back, tasting blood in his mouth.

"Keep your mouth shut!" Phronsie warned. "Lay still!"

When Roach Head barked a command they were jerked to their feet. Their hands were tied behind their backs with rawhide thongs. Two braves were told to guard them. The rest of the scout group faded into the forest, probably to return to their ambush on the New Ulm road. At the same time Martin heard a faraway rattle of gunfire. The town could not be more than three or four miles distant. Sound carried far in the warm light air of summer.

One of the guards poked him in the ribs with a painted bow. Phronsie asked a question in Sioux, accompanying it with a gesture. The man only looked sullen and prodded them forward, up the rocky slope they had descended shortly before.

"Where are they taking us?" Martin muttered.

Phronsie, trudging beside him, shook her head. "Lord knows. Just be grateful they haven't stuck that yellow mop of hair of yours in their belt."

In about an hour they broke out into sunlight, far up the ridge in a meadow overlooking the river. "Look!" Martin said.

"What?"

"Nothing! Nothing on the river! No keel boats, no lumber barges, no ferries—nothing!"

From here they could see the town of New Ulm. The rattle of musketry was louder now. Over the town a pall of smoke loomed, fiery tongues licking at the base of sable plumes.

"Shakopee's done it!" Phronsie murmured. "Oh, Lord. The Sioux are burning the town, like they promised they'd do!"

Herded across the grassy plain, they came at last to a circle of lodges near the edge of the forest. Before the largest, on an old leather trunk half covered by a scarlet blanket, sat an impressive figure.

"Shakopee," Phronsie whispered.

Even seated, the chief was commanding. He wore a shirt of deerskin with trailing fringes and quillwork across the chest. The shirt was laced up the side, the sleeves also laced. His leggings were of buckskin with a broad stripe of colored beads down the side. From his neck dangled a small leather pouch decorated with an eagle feather, which Martin knew from Phronsie's tutelage was his own personal medicine. One hand held a pennoned lance, its shaft painted in red and white and yellow, and his plaited braids were wrapped in otter fur. Shakopee was a kingly figure, a middle-aged man accustomed to command. The face held Martin's gaze. Shakopee's cheekbones were high and prominent, the nose bold, hooked like the beak of a bird of prey. The forehead was high, overhanging the dark inscrutable eyes. His body was sharp planes and angles, deep shadows, patches of sunlit skin shining like a bronze sculpture burnished with the patina of age.

About the chief lounged what in Versailles or Vienna would have been imperial courtiers—broad-shouldered braves, wide of chest and shoulder, long bodied, bowed of leg, naked chests gleaming with oil. Some wore leather sashes over one shoulder, others carried painted war shields. Sable-black hairdos were ornamented with arrangements of eagle feathers. Martin remembered the slant of the feather was a code spelling out the warrior's coups.

Wrists chafed by the bonds, the two prisoners stood blinking in the sunlight. Except for the singing of birds and the distant sound of gunfire, the meadow was still. Sweating in the hot light, Martin muttered, "What are they going to do with us?"

"Be quiet. Don't talk. Hold your head up, and look him in the eye. That's what they respect."

Shakopee continued to regard them with a fathomless gaze. Finally one of the courtiers caught Shakopee's eyes. The chief nodded. The man spoke at length behind a cupped hand. Shakopee beckoned.

"He means us," Phronsie whispered.

Someone behind them untied their bonds. Martin's hands tingled from the flow of fresh blood; he clenched and unclenched his fists. Though they might both be in danger of their lives he felt a perverse elation. God, if only he could paint the colorful assembly! His eye was entranced by the savage scene, the brilliant colors, each face unique, a study deserving its own portrait.

"*Hie, hie,*" Phronsie said, rubbing her wrists. *Thanks.*

Leaning forward, Shakopee spoke to her, accompanying the words with quick flowing gestures. On the ground a dark facsimile of his hand talk danced about like the shadow plays Martin remembered Aunt Flossie used to entertain Lucas and him when they were tired from play.

Phronsie stepped forward. In her high, clear voice he recalled from that first meeting with Yellow Horse and the peace delegation, Phronsie spoke to the chief, accompanying her words with a fluttering of the brown fingers. She might have been an actress on the stage of a Boston theater, playing Portia. Martin caught a few words, understood some of the gestures. Hand in front of breast, first two fingers extended, the others curled in the fist, then the hand going upward and outward. That was *friend*. Phronsie was saying they came as friends. Hands clasped before her slender waist, back of right hand down; that meant *peace. We walk in peace.*

There was more, much more. Martin didn't follow it all; it was a long and impassioned statement. *I am white. I must go to my people.* Not likely; that would not be a popular statement. She tapped her right breast gently with the two first fingers of her hand. *Father.* He knew that one. *My father was your friend?* Possibly. His mouth was dry and cottony, his feet hurt from standing so long in one place. Uncle Alonzo had met these same Indians and died.

At last she finished. She stood motionless, as impassive as any of the Sioux warriors who watched. Shakopee took from a pouch a clay pipe, a white man's clay pipe, brown and cracked from long use. Carefully he tamped tobacco into it, bending forward as a warrior brought a coal from a small fire smoldering nearby. Puffing, he leaned back on the dais.

"What are they going to do?" Martin whispered.

Phronsie didn't answer, only continued to look straight ahead, arms folded. Sweat ran down Martin's chest, dripped over his loins. The long wait was beginning to fray his nerves.

At last Shakopee raised an index finger, sweeping it toward himself in a gesture that could only mean *come to me*.

"Don't move," Phronsie muttered. Edging forward, she stood before the great chief. Shakopee handed her the clay pipe. Gravely she accepted it, drew deep, blew ceremonial puffs to each of the four cardinal directions and a final shimmering circle upward to the Great Medicine Chief on the Starry Road. He heard her say, "*Hie, hie,*" again, handing the pipe back to Shakopee.

In response to his curt command, a burly warrior stepped forward, dragging his late-model Sharp's breech-loading rifle at the trail. He gestured to Martin and Phronsie, pointing down the trail they had followed to Shakopee's headquarters. They followed him into the sun-streaked gloom of the forest.

"Don't look back!" Phronsie muttered. "Don't do nothing! Anything, I mean. Don't do anything!" Together again, they traversed the narrow trail, the warrior's high feathered roach guiding them. "Shakopee let us go. He did it for Pa's sake. Only—" Her voice caught in what sounded like a small sob. "Only he said—don't come back!"

He took her hand, not knowing what to say.

"It's the end," she murmured. "How can they fight the whole damned U.S.? They don't understand how many millions of white people there are. This is the end, the damned end!" Her voice rose in anger; their escort turned, scowling. "I remember the lodges, the smoke coming from the cooking fires, dancing. They sang a lot. The women were always singing. There was the Fox Society, and the Silent Eaters, and the

Backwards Men. They gave away things to each other. The greatest was the one that gave away everything till he—he didn't have anything left." Her voice faltered, broke.

"It's all right," Martin said, and knew it would not be all right. "Anyway, I was proud of you, the way you acted."

"I'm glad Pa didn't live to see this day. He always said he'd been cheated by many a white man, but never by a Sioux. When he was dying they came to see him and made medicine. They sang and danced and drummed and stayed till the end. They wanted to put him up on kind of a pole scaffold, like they do their own dead, but I didn't want it that way, so they helped me dig the grave and stayed till they were sure I'd be all right."

From time to time painted faces loomed out of the green gloom, warrior sentinels guarding the trails. Bands of weary braves passed by, quivers empty of arrows and faces streaked with smoke and sweat; sometimes they carried wounded. Each time a word from the guide carried them safely past. Near sundown they approached New Ulm on a grassy rise, screened by scrub oak. The guide spoke a few guttural words, then disappeared into the forest.

"He said it's up to us, from here on in," Phronsie translated.

Though the Sioux had apparently delayed their attack for the night, there was scattered gunfire. Many of the houses on the west side of town were in flames, and a pall of smoke drifted low. The trees in North German Park had been cut down, probably to make barricades. On the high windmill the Stars and Stripes fluttered. In the golden light of late afternoon they saw that the Dakota House was no more; only a few blackened uprights still stood. The roof of the post office likewise was burned away. As they watched, a fire arrow soared into the sky and fell into a pile of lumber on a barge tied near the ferry landing. Moments later the wood was afire. Men with axes cut the lines and let the barge drift away so that it would not set fire to the landing.

Phronsie swallowed hard. "I hope Mrs. Cates is safe."

Taking advantage of what cover they could find on the grassy slope, they went furtively toward the town. "We come safe this far," Phronsie warned. "It won't do to get shot for an Indian. If we can get to Mrs. Cates's place, we'll be all right."

As they came closer they saw that rifle pits had been dug on the outskirts. From behind the cover of fan-shaped cedar leaves, Martin saw a head pop up. A rifle barrel emerged as the occupant looked out briefly, then withdrew.

"We'd best wait for dark," he advised. "Maybe then we can work our way in without getting killed."

As they came closer, even in the fading light they could see more destruction. Zook's store burned, and the warehouses behind were in danger. A volunteer brigade carried water from the river, but they were losing ground fast. Finally the defenders retreated from the scorching heat, abandoning the well-stocked buildings. Varicolored smoke curled into the dusky sky. There were muffled booms as powder barrels exploded. Burning fragments of beams, siding, and joists soared into the sky.

Phronsie shuddered. "Maybe we ought to go back."

"No."

"You sure?"

"I'm going to do what I have to do." He took her

hand. "And you've made your decision, Phronsie Bettencourt. You're going to do what you have to do. It's hard lines, as they say, but that's what's got to be."

"I guess so." She squeezed his hand. "Long as I'm with you, that is."

In full dark they dodged down Washington Street. Someone loosed a shot at them. There were hoarse cries. "I seen one of 'em!" "No, there was two!" "Where did they go?" "Damned red bastards!" They ran, stopping only when confronted by the raging flames enveloping Zook's store. In the firelit gloom Martin stumbled over something. Regaining his footing, he touched the soft bundle. It was Levi Zook.

"Don't look!" he said to Phronsie, his voice harsh.

"What is it?"

In spite of him she looked. When something, possibly a barrel of coal oil, flared up in the ruins of the store, she drew back, hand to her mouth. "Oh, Lord! I—I wouldn't have wished that on anyone, not even him!"

Zook's body was half burned away. The face was whole, however. The mouth was stuffed with grass. Martin remembered. *Let 'em eat grass!* One of the Sioux attackers had found Levi Zook and dealt with him in his own way.

In a shower of ashes they stumbled on, faces black with soot and burning with the heat from flaming buildings. The brick houses built by the government for the "cracker-and-molasses" Indians were untouched, but deserted. Had Governor Ramsey's civilized Indians joined their bloodthirsty brothers on the ridges above the town?

Nearing North German Park they were challenged. In the firelit darkness a fat man stood square and indomitable in their way, musket pointing.

"Don't shoot!" Martin cried, spreading his body before Phronsie. "We—we're white!"

The man hesitated, stepped forward. "Who are you?"

"Martin . . ." He hesitated. "Martin . . . Sayre. And this is—"

"I'm Phronsie Bettencourt," she said, "and put that damned thing down before you hurt someone!"

Warily the fat man prowled forward. Martin recognized him. It was the red-faced citizen Phronsie had argued with that day they returned for the first time to New Ulm, the man who was incensed when she defended the Sioux.

"I know you," he cried, "spite of all that black on your face! Ain't you the feller that jumped out of Mrs. Cates's window and got away last month? The one that's wanted for deserting from the Army? Martin Sayre?"

Martin nodded. "I'm that man."

The fat man prodded him with the barrel of the musket; his face shone with triumph. "Get goin' then, Sayre! The major will surely want to see *you*!"

CHAPTER NINE

In the grim light of dawn New Ulm reminded Martin of the Shiloh battlefield. Many structures along the river, including the ferry landing, were afire. In the town the Behnke Building had burned to the ground, along with the Dakota House. Rising sun filtered through the smoke, lighting the river with a bloody glow. The Sioux attackers had withdrawn, probably to mount a new and stronger attack with the assistance of their Chippewa allies. Except for the crackling of flames and the incongruous cheerful songs as birds wheeled and darted in the smoky sky, the August morning was quiet.

Manacles chafing his wrists, Martin waited for "the major" to return from a reconnaissance. Lieutenant Phipps, guarding his prize, scanned the river through a brass spyglass. "I'm second in command," he had let Martin know, importantly. Phronsie, waiting beside Martin, muttered, "Stuffed shirt!"

There was even a peach orchard, as there had been at Shiloh. Near the burned-out post office a citizen had planted a grassy plot with freestones. Heat from the burning structure had blistered them. Now withered leaves spun down in the morning breeze, and fruit still hung from bare and blackened limbs. The carmine glare on the river reminded Martin of the pool where the wounded Reb had lain—Bloody Pond, the men of Wallace's division had come to call it.

Since he had left New Ulm there had been built on a rise above the park a fort of saw logs, a rambling structure in which the townspeople huddled while militiamen manned the ramparts. The soldiers seemed more capable than Martin remembered, having a businesslike and military air. In the center of the compound civilians moved about under shelters of sheets and blankets rigged against the oncoming sun. More smoke arose from cooking fires. Men poured lead into molds and women smoothed and sacked musket balls. In a corner a hospital of sorts had been set up; wounded were being cared for by the women. In spite of the proximity of the river water was scarce, and several men labored at digging a well.

"Isn't any help coming from Fort Ridgely?" Phronsie asked.

Phipps shook his head.

"Isn't there a telegraph line?" Martin asked.

"Cut three days ago. Them damned coffee coolers are probably setting round reading the *Republican* while old Shakopee finishes us off and scoots into the woods again!" He tipped his battered shako. "Excuse the cuss words, but it don't look good."

"Can't you *send* someone to Fort Ridgely for help?"

Phipps grimaced. "Tried twice already. They never got there." He handed the spyglass to Phronsie. "Look down by the ferry landing, in that cottonwood with the double trunk."

Curious, she took the glass, twisted the barrel to focus. With a sharp intake of breath she handed the spyglass back to Phipps. Under the tan and soot her face was pale.

"What is it?" Martin asked.

"Shakopee's people caught them, and—" She broke off, biting her lip.

"Stuck 'em full of arrows like a porcupine," Phipps growled. "Then hung 'em up in a tree so's we could see 'em! A German named Nagel, and a feller worked for Levi Zook—I don't recall his name. Shakopee isn't about to let anyone out of here till they burn us out— kill every last critter in New Ulm: men and womenfolk, children, sheep, cattle, dogs and cats!" Closing the spyglass with a snap, he squared his shoulders and assumed a military bearing, hand on saber hilt. "Here comes the major."

The commanding officer was Lucas Sayre, U.S.A., retired. Followed by two riflemen, he limped along the parapet, cane under his arm. From their encounter in the bedroom at Mrs. Cates's, Martin remembered Lucas as thin, sallow, obviously ill. Now he looked renewed, vigorous, filled with determination.

"Good morning, Lucas," Martin said in a low voice.

Lieutenant Phipps hovered at the major's elbow. "Patrol caught him last night, Major, as he was trying to sneak into town."

Lucas's eyes narrowed. "It's you, eh?"

"I wasn't trying to sneak anywhere, Lucas. I came back to give myself up."

"That's true," Phronsie confirmed.

Lucas unlimbered his cane, leaned on it. "And who are you, ma'am?"

"Name's Phronsie Bettencourt. I and Martin— Martin and I—are friends."

Phipps spoke into Lucas's ear. "She's a renegade, Major! We'd best keep an eye on her too!"

Phronsie said something obscene to the militiaman. His face reddened.

"Well," Lucas murmured. Thoughtfully, he rubbed his chin. "Came back, eh?"

"I—I had to."

"You're the worse for wear."

"You look better than I remembered."

There was awkward silence.

"I *am* better. Hardly limp at all. I told them what I needed was an active duty assignment, and by God, I've got it now! Good thing I came when I did. These blockheaded farmers were milling around in circles. I've got 'em straightened out now, acting like soldiers!"

"I'm sorry I hurt your leg that night, but I was panicky, Lucas. I didn't have time to think things out. Now I know I was wrong."

Lucas nodded in satisfaction. Raising the cane like a baton, he pointed it at Martin. "Lieutenant, take this man and lock him up in that old shack at the edge of the compound. Put a guard on him till I can get around to dealing with his case."

"Wait a minute!" Martin held out manacled hands. "I'll give you my parole, Lucas. I mean"—he gestured—"you need help, that's plain to see. Don't keep me locked up!"

"You'd be one hell of a lot of help," Lucas sneered. "Can't shoot anyone, eh? Give you a gun—one of our scarce guns—you wouldn't even defend yourself, let alone these poor people cooped up in here."

Martin bit his lip; it was probably true.

"He's your own brother!" Phronsie protested.

Lucas stared at her, eyes iron-hard. "I've disowned him, ma'am, not that it's any of your business!"

"You can't disown your own kin!"

"This is a waste of time. Phipps, take him away and keep good watch on him. He escaped me once, and I'll not have it happen again!"

"Come on, Sayre," Phipps commanded, drawing his saber, "Off to jail!"

Phronsie linked her arm in Martin's.

"Get away from him!" Phipps ordered. "He's a prisoner."

This time she said something more obscene. The militia lieutenant flinched at the words and did not further object.

"You shouldn't talk like that," Martin muttered.

"But he's your own brother! How can he treat you this way?"

"Lucas has got strict ideas of duty. He's doing what he thinks is right."

At the heavy oaken door of the shed she took leave of him. "I'm going to find Mrs. Cates. Maybe I can help with the cooking and minding the children and with the wounded. Don't lose hope, Martin. It'll all come out fine, you'll see!"

Long ago he had abandoned hope, and thought now only in terms of expiation. For her he managed a smile. "Maybe you're right."

Phipps saw him chained to a heavy log in the shed. Fortunately, there was enough slack so he could stand on the log and manage a narrow view of a corner of the compound. There was no further attack by the Sioux that day. Martin could imagine fire arrows hitting the sun-warped boards of the roof, roasting him alive.

At noon the guard, a stocky Scandinavian, opened the door to hand him a plate of beans and a cup of water.

"What's happening?" Martin asked.

"Ain't nothing happening. That's what makes it fearsome. Them devils is up to something, you bet me!"

That afternoon Bishop Henry Whipple was let in by the guard with the permission of Colonel Sayre. Taking off his wide-brimmed clerical hat, he sat on the other end of Martin's log. "Well, young man, I have been talking to Major Sayre. You are his brother Martin, eh? Not Martin Brown?"

"Yes, sir."

It was hot in the dusty shack. Bishop Whipple fanned himself. His collar was wilted and there was a spattering of blood on his shirt. "Not mine," he said, seeing Martin's gaze fix on the stain. "Poor fellow was bleeding, and it couldn't be stopped. All I could do was commend him to the Lord's care." He shook his head, sighed. "Desperate circumstances we are in—desperate, indeed! Well"—he shook summer dust from the hat—"so you were actually Alonzo Tarrant's nephew, that day I met you at his farm."

"Yes, sir."

"I must say I noted a resemblance. Alonzo seemed fond of you."

"My uncle was a good man, Bishop. I owe a lot to him and Aunt Flossie. They always seemed to understand me, somehow, when others didn't." He swallowed hard, remembering that night at the farm, that horrible night. "I'd been plowing, you see. I heard uncle call and I ran to the chicken house. They'd killed him, the Sioux. I just caught sight of them disappearing into the forest. I was scared. I didn't know what to do. I buried him—I couldn't just leave him like that—and started off to New Ulm. Then I lost my way in the forest, and Phronsie found me. I guess you know the rest."

Bishop Whipple nodded.

"You didn't recognize me, that one time when you stopped Phronsie in town to talk to her. So I figured I could pass for Martin Brown, live down what—what I'd done in the Army. But my brother found me." He clasped his hands together, worked his fingers. "I love Phronsie, Bishop. But it's too late for that now." He hesitated, feeling awkward. "Will you pray for me—for me, and her?"

Kneeling beside him, the bishop sought divine help for two young people—for Phronsie Bettencourt, and for Martin Sayre, who had returned to accept his punishment.

Finishing, he got wearily to his feet. "No one knows what the Lord's will is, Martin. Trust in him."

"In the *Republican*," Martin said, "I read that you'd gone east to ask the President for help."

"Unfortunately, I didn't accomplish much. The President was sympathetic, but I suppose he was too busy with the war to trouble himself with Minnesota. God help us, Martin—the Santee Sioux have lived here for hundreds of years! What else can anyone expect from them but to defend their ancestral lands, the meadows and hills and forests where their sacred dead are buried? I'm sure it would be possible to work out an agreement with them to share the land with the whites. But when the farmers want it *all*, when rascally traders cheat and steal from them, when the government turns a blind eye to the problem—" He passed a nervous hand across a sweat-damp brow. "I—I can't help getting upset, Martin! Excuse me, please!"

"Sir," Martin said, wanting to change the subject, "the night I escaped—got away—I knocked over a lamp in Mrs. Cates's house. Something caught fire. I looked back and saw flames. I'm sorry if I set her house afire, because I—"

"You needn't worry, son. The fire brigade came quickly, although the back room *is* a little scorched."

"Have you seen Mrs. Cates? And Thad? Are they all right?"

"She is well—cooking up a mess of beans. I saw her only half an hour ago, working like a Trojan. And Thad is fine, helping pour lead for bullets. By the way, I helped carry things out of the house when you set the room afire. I saw your painting of Phronsie Bettencourt and your studies of the Santee warriors. I can tell you there was some fuss about wasting paint on pictures of Indians. But you have a great talent, Martin. May God grant it be preserved!" When the guard, musket poised, opened the door, the bishop nodded to Martin and walked out heavily, as if a great load were on his shoulders.

May God grant it be preserved! What talent Martin Sayre had would soon come to an end, he knew, under the guns of a firing squad. He was gloomy when Phronsie, disdaining the guard, called through the open window.

"Martin?"

"You git down there!" the guard complained. "Ain't no one allow to talk to prisoner without leave by the major!"

"Pooh!" Phronsie said. "Lars Sigurdsson, you mind your own business!"

"But—"

She ignored him, turned to speak to Martin.

"You all right?"

He hauled himself up to the window. "I'm all right—so far."

"Anything I can bring you?"

"A file, if you can find one, so I can get this damned chain off my ankle!"

"I kind of hurt, too, Martin, when you do. It's like I'm in here with you, like I feel your pain. Maybe I'm trying to share it, take some of it off you."

"Listen," he said. "Listen. I've been thinking."

"About what?"

As he grasped the ragged sill with both hands, splinters pricked his fingers. "Ask Lucas to come here to talk with me."

"He's awful busy, Martin. People gather round him all the time, yammering for this and that. Everyone's upset and excited. They think Shakopee's going to make a big run at the fort in the morning."

"I don't care! Make Lucas come here!" Martin looked at the sun falling down the western sky in a haze of smoke. "It's important."

"I'll do her, if that's what you want, Martin. Only why . . . ?"

"I'll tell you later."

She stepped down. Anxious, he called after her.

"For God's sake, now, don't swear at him! He's more stubborn than you are. Just *persuade* him. Do you understand me?"

"Of course! Think I'm dumb?"

Dusk came, then night, full night. Martin could hear the muffled sounds of a besieged camp: the bubbling of cooking pots, a wounded man in pain, infants fretting, a sentry's call. The only light in the shed came from firelight wavering through cracks in the door. Outside, Sigurdsson or whatever his name was clumped up and down, ten steps this way, then ten steps back. The smell of coffee came to Martin, and he wished he had a cup.

When the bar on the door rattled, he tensed. The door opened. Lars Sigurdsson was there, lantern raised. As the guard drew respectfully aside, Lucas Sayre brushed by him. Standing in the doorway, his lean figure was black against the rays of the lamp. Lucas carried his cane under one arm, jauntily, like a British Army observer Martin remembered seeing on the streets of Washington before Wallace's division had moved to that frightful place called Shiloh.

"I hear you wanted to talk, Martin. It had better be important. I'm late for a staff meeting."

"It is important."

Lucas remained unmoving in the doorway.

"I've learned a whole lot since I've been out here. Guess I've learned to think differently."

"From that girl, eh? That shameless female? I've heard about her!"

"She's a fine girl, Lucas, and I won't hear anything against her!" Martin rose; the restraining chain clinked. "She taught me a lot and I—"

"What Lavinia Greene would think of you now!" Lucas shook his head.

"Lavinia Greene! I don't care about her! I'm a different man now, Lucas. Maybe I've grown up. Put it any way you like. But I want to make you a proposition."

Lucas's eyes narrowed. "What kind of balderdash is this? Make a proposition? Blast it, you're not in a position to offer a proposition to *anyone*!"

"Nevertheless," Martin said, steadily. "Nevertheless,

Lucas. Listen to me! You're in great danger. *We're* in danger; New Ulm is likely to be overrun by Santee Sioux and their Chippewa friends. I know the Sioux, speak a little of their language. They've been mistreated, they've been tricked, they've seen white men eat up their land like a plague of locusts. They've seen their peace delegation thrown in jail as if they were common criminals!"

"Scoundrels! Murderers! Look at what they did to your own uncle!"

"There's evil on both sides, Lucas, but someone's got to stop this slaughter, get the Santee Sioux and the farmers together again. Let me try to reach Fort Ridgely. If I can bring help, maybe we can stave them off till reasonable men can talk."

Lucas grinned, a macabre grimace. He clutched the cane tighter under his arm. "Red irregulars. By God, we'll smash them when they come against my saw logs! I've got a powder train laid. If worst comes to worst, we'll blow up the fort and them with it!"

"You're insane!" Martin protested. "There are hundreds of Sioux in the forest—maybe thousands! They'll swarm over those logs like ants! You need help!"

Lucas scowled. "What kind of help are you offering, pray? The kind you gave poor old Uncle Alonzo?"

"He was already dead when I reached him, Lucas!" Martin reached out with manacled hands. "In God's name, listen to me, listen to sense! You've sent out two runners. They're both dangling from the cottonwood tree by the ferry landing."

Lucas's eyes gleamed sullenly.

"I know the way, I know the woods, I know the Sioux. Let me go to Fort Ridgely!"

Lucas's laugh was a sharp, high-pitched bark. "Do you think I'm crazy? After all these weeks of chasing you I've finally got you under lock and key! Let you go? Christ, no! Do you think I'm a fool?"

"You *are* a fool, Lucas! You and people like you never know how to settle anything except by force. You're fool enough to let West Point pride take over and kill you, with all the rest of the people!"

Lucas was silent, his face grim.

"Please, Lucas. If I can get through and bring help, we can avert a massacre. If I don't make it . . ." He paused. "Then you won't have to bother your head anymore. Martin Sayre won't be a living disgrace to the Sayre family."

Lucas's face was a study in uncertainty. He bit his lip, rubbed his palm with the handle of the cane. "You'd probably only run away."

"Run away? Damn it, Lucas, the woods are full of Sioux! You know what they did to your messengers!" Martin couldn't think of anything to add to his case.

Lucas remained in the doorway, chewing at his beard. Finally he slapped his palm with the cane. "I'll think on it."

"Think on it? Time is running out! There's no *time* to think on it!"

His brother shrugged, leaned down to pass under the low doorway, nodded curtly to Sigurdsson. "Lock him up again, Private. I'll send someone to relieve you at midnight."

Again in blackness, Martin dragged the chain after him toward the window. "Lucas!"

There was nothing but the soft murmurings of the camp, the prickling of steely white stars in a mantle of night. Disconsolate, Martin slumped on the log. He had become resigned to the thought of his own death. But

Mrs. Cates, Thad, that good man Bishop Whipple—
Phronsie! After a while he slept, miserable.

Near midnight he was awakened by the rattle of the bar on the door; probably Sigurdsson's relief coming on. Then it was Sigurdsson himself bending over, shaking him. "Mr. Sayre!"

Groggily he sat up, blinking in the rays of the lantern.

"What is it?"

"You'll find out soon enough. Major said for me to bring you."

Knuckling his eyes, Martin stumbled to his feet; he felt physically and emotionally drained. Perhaps Lucas had decided to institute his own firing squad for deserters. Shivering in the night cool, he looked up at an almost full moon, chilly also.

His brother stood beneath the parapet with a group of anxious men. Martin recognized merchants of the town: the drygoods clerk from whom he had bought canvas for his paintings, the carpenter, Mason, who wanted a portrait of his father, the burly proprietor of Farmer's Rest Saloon. Others crowded about; all the faces were strained and worried. Halting on the edge of the council, Martin listened to a bearded scout, face and hands carefully blackened with soot.

"Major, they're all along the river too! I never see so many damned Sioux! They're creepin' through the reeds, gettin' set for something." The man pointed with the barrel of his shotgun. "See them little sparks up there on the hills? Sioux campfires. There must be hundreds of the red bastards, just waitin' for morning!"

Another scout, face similarly blackened, reported, "I went by Peter Kleiber's place. Damn fool—he never left."

"Is—was he there?" a hesitant voice asked.

"Blood all over the parlor! I never seen no body, though. Not him, nor Bertha, nor none of the childer. Probably the Sioux hacked 'em to death and threw the bodies in the river."

Still slow-minded with sleep, Martin clutched arms about his thin shirt, by now only a dirty remnant of expensive broadcloth. The scene—the anxious men, the firelit circle, the drama of imminent attack—reminded him of a Rembrandt canvas. The thought vanished quickly when Lucas called "Martin!"

He pushed through the circle. "Yes."

In the dust of the compound had been drawn a crude map of the river valley, scrawled Xs marking Mankato, New Ulm, and Breckenridge. A wavering line indicated the river. Lucas jabbed the ferrule of his cane at the cross that was Fort Ridgely.

"Along the river, they tell me, it's about seventeen miles. Of course, no one can reach the fort along the river. Too many Sioux strung out along there, and not much cover. It would have to be mostly through the forest."

In the flickering shadows his brother's face was sharpcut, saturnine. "Can't spare any fighting men. Come morning, the devils will be trying to climb the parapet. We'll need everyone that can fire a gun or swing a club."

Caught by the drama, others joined the group: careworn women, hobbling wounded, small children with wide, fearful eyes clinging to skirts.

"Well, then," Lucas said, turning to Martin with an air of finality, "you can try to go to Fort Ridgely if you want to."

Martin felt a hand in his. Phronsie stood at his side. "Martin!"

He pressed her hand. "I'm going to Fort Ridgely tonight."

"You'll be killed!"

Probably he would be. Oddly, he felt little emotion. He would be killed, or he wouldn't be killed; it seemed simple. There were no heroics. It was not the time for heroics.

"Better get going," Lucas urged.

"I—I was just bathing one of the babies," Phronsie went on, as if not understanding. "Then I saw Major Sayre and the rest, and I wondered—"

Lucas drew the Root's Patent revolver from the holster at his hip and proffered it. "Better take this."

Martin looked at it, the blue steel gleaming dully in the fire's glow, the snub-nosed shells in the magazine, the checkerboard pattern of the grips. The gun was well oiled, smelled oily. It lay, deadly and well cared for, in Lucas's palm.

"No."

"But you—"

"I don't want the gun, Lucas," Martin said. Somehow it seemed as if all his life had come down to this. "I don't intend to kill anybody. I'm just going to Fort Ridgely, that's all."

Bishop Whipple was in the throng; he bent his head and started to pray. *"Lord, help this our messenger on his way to bring us salvation. Preserve and keep him on this perilous journey. Guard him from harm. Save this land and its people of all races to press forward anew in a spirit of brotherliness. Amen."*

There were few concurring amens. Some of the men scowled at the bishop for the oblique reference to their Sioux enemies.

"Martin," Phronsie pleaded. Her eyes were bright with unaccustomed tears.

"Hush!" he said. "It'll be fine." Lamely he added, "It's something I've got to do. You know that."

With all watching he kissed her hard on the mouth, then thrust her away as if the contact burned.

"I'm ready," he said.

Lucas gestured with the cane. Warily someone opened the high gate, portal to the beleaguered sawlog fortress. "Looks all right," a voice announced.

"Quick, now!" Lucas snapped.

Martin slipped into smoke-tinged moonlight. As he hurried past the log wall toward the forest he heard his brother's voice from the parapet.

"Remember—when you come back we've got a matter to settle with the Judge Advocate General!"

CHAPTER TEN

In moonlight the land resembled the woodcuts of Hell in Uncle Alonzo's big volume of Dante's *Inferno*. Everywhere fires smoldered. Occasionally one flared brightly, sputtering and crackling, only to burn down again. Smoke stung Martin's nostrils, made his eyes smart. Across his path lay a dead cow, belly torn by the crows, while a lone calf nuzzled her udder. To his right, dark and silent, the river was illuminated only occasionally by flames from the burning ferry landing. With a handkerchief over his face to ward off the stench of desolation and death, he moved stealthily in the shadows of the burned-out post office. Pausing, he looked ahead, where he would have to leave the last available cover and strike out across the plain to the forest, a good half mile distant. Crossing, he would easily be seen in the moonlight.

Somewhere, not too far distant, a shout rang out, followed by the blast of a musket. The sounds seemed to have come from the vicinity of the saw-log fort.

Could the Sioux already have begun a night attack on New Ulm? That was not likely. Phronsie had told him the Sioux believed evil spirits came after dark. They would not willingly leave the shelter of their tipis after sundown, fearing to be bewitched.

Taking a deep breath, he was about to start across the meadow formed by a loop of the river when he became aware of movement in the blackened ruins of the post office. Crouching, he whirled, eyes narrow and searching. He had no defense; if it was a Santee scout, he was dead.

Seeing nothing, hearing nothing more, he straightened gradually, feeling his heart slow its pounding. His mouth was dry and cottony and beads of sweat lined his forehead.

"Martin?"

"Who's there?"

"It's me."

"Phronsie?"

She stepped from behind a tangle of blackened beams. "Who the hell did you think it was?"

"You crazy woman! How—why—"

"I can't let you go wandering about, pilgrim, without someone to wipe your nose and change your didies."

"How did you get out of the fort?"

Leaning on the musket, she grinned, teeth bright in the moon's rays. "Over the back wall."

"But—"

"Scared the hell out of the guards on the parapet. They thought"—she indicated the deerskin shirt, heavy with beads, the long fringes—"they thought I was Shakopee himself, come to start a war!"

He remembered the cry of alarm, the shot.

"You might have been killed!"

"We might both be killed. But if it's time to cash in my chips I'd just as soon do it with you."

"Oh, Phronsie!" Taking her in his arms, he hugged her. "You damned fool!" Struggling for words, he finally blurted, "I love you!"

"Me, too." She kissed his cheek. "Oh, lordy, lordy, lordy, Martin! What have we got ourselves into?"

"It doesn't matter," he said, cheek pressed hard against hers. "We're together. We'll make it together, or we'll fail together. But it's together, that's what's important."

"*Hopo*, then! We got a long way to go!" Moving out of the shadows, musket charged and at the ready, she peered across the plain. "Go low, Martin—bend over and skulk close to the grass. We got to keep close together so's we only make one shadow."

"Makes sense," he agreed.

Leaving the river, they traversed the plain without incident. Once a low-flying owl swooped down to investigate the two hunched figures. Frightened by the brush of wings, the ghostly night cry, Martin sprawled flat in the grass. Phronsie jibed at him, "Just an old owl, that's all. You scared of an owl?"

"I didn't know what it was. Might have been a Sioux scalping knife that ruffled my hair!"

"No Sioux yet, but I'd bet two bits one is watching us from someplace, biding his time till he sees what we're up to."

The thought sobered him. "Do you think so?"

"Could be. Could well be!"

He rose from dew-wet grass; it smelled rich and green and damp, a smell of growing things, of life itself. Achingly, he did not want to die. Bending, he followed the dark trace in the grass where Phronsie's moccasins had trod. In a few minutes they reached the shelter of the forest and paused in the shadows to catch their breath.

"Always feel better in the woods," Phronsie remarked. She looked to her priming to insure the powder in the pan had not been wet by dew. "Woods is home!"

With their movements so exposed, the plain had been frightening. But the forest was equally bad. Gone with the idyllic summer were the green leaves, the remembered sun-dappled earth beneath spreading boughs, the songs of wren and chickadee, the rasping of jays. It was more like the entrance to a witch's cave, the jungle depths looming before him.

Gingerly he followed Phronsie through the underbrush. Snags caught at his clothing. At times he found himself slipping and sliding on the carpet of pine needles. Though he had been angry at her for following him, he was glad now. Plunging into the forest by himself, he would soon have lost his way. He would have had to make for the river to correct his course. With Phronsie as guide, they were saving time. Through a break in the trees he scanned the sky and finally picked out Orion's Belt. The Clock, it was called by the Sioux. The stars constituting the belt were near the celestial equator; their position in the sky gave a fairly accurate estimate of time. Two in the morning, more or less, maybe two thirty. They were still under a cover of night, although the moon was bright.

Phronsie paused before a rivulet, gurgling and burbling as it foamed luminously across rocks. "Eight Mile Creek. Feeds into Clear Lake, up north."

Winded, he sat on a fallen log. "How far have we gone, do you think?"

"Five miles, more or less."

"Then we've got another twelve, thirteen, to go." Legs cramping, Martin rose from the log and massaged his thighs. His wrists still burned from the chafing of the manacles. His head ached too, probably from breathing smoke. "Better get going again!"

Occasionally their path took them from the forest to the edge of the river. Hot and sweating in spite of night cool, they knelt at a graveled bar, scooped up water, and sluiced it over face and breast and arms. Startled, a beaver slapped its tail against the surface and dived for its brushy house. In the distance an animal howled. Her hand raised for silence, Phronsie listened. When the wild cry faded into silence, lost in the watery murmuring of the river, Martin whispered, "A wolf?"

"Sioux," she said, grasping the stock of the musket more tightly. "Let's get out of here, back into the woods!" As they left the river Martin heard another cry, a thin wavering wail. It seemed to come from farther down the river, between them and Fort Ridgely.

"Could be they got us bracketed," Phronsie muttered.

Parting the screen of willows, he followed her, as his boots squished in the mud bordering the river. "What had we best do?"

"Do? There ain't nothing to do but press on, I guess."

Moving ever more rapidly they loped through the woods, both breathing hard. Phronsie muttered curses at the brambles, the clawing underbrush, the fallen logs barring their way. They waded other tributaries of the Minnesota, some only muddy trickles, others several feet wide and waist deep. Holding the musket over her head, Phronsie shivered. "This here is what they call Little Rock Creek. Damn—how cold can water get in August?"

August nineteenth, Martin remembered. His birthday had passed a week ago, and he had not been aware of it. A week ago Phronsie and he had lazed through an afternoon in camp, the camp they might never see again. He imagined Phronsie baking a birthday cake, with pink icing and small fluted candy roses, as Aunt Flossie used to do in Braintree. He saw a knife in his hand and was about to cut the cake. Then—

"You all right?" Phronsie called.

With an effort he wrenched himself away from the pleasant vision. Brain woolly with tension and fatigue, he had been half dozing, struggling mechanically forward.

"I'm all right!" he gasped. "Keep—keep on."

Nearing dawn they crossed the New Ulm road, near his uncle's farm. As the eastern sky began to show a streaking of light, Pipestone Lake shimmered below them, dawn mist rising from its surface like wisps of steam.

"Let's stop there for a minute," Martin suggested. "I've got to rest a little or we'll never reach the fort at all!"

Phronsie agreed. "I never knew Pa's old musket weighed so much!"

In growing dawn they straggled down the cottonwood-bordered lane. "Don't hear nothing anymore," Phronsie said. "Maybe we outdistanced them." Together they stood silent before the deserted dwelling. Nothing appeared disturbed. The house still looked to Martin as it had that rainy afternoon when he first trudged the lane, wet to the skin, and knocked on the door. Then there had been a lamp in the window, a comforting yellow glow.

He opened the door and they went in. The parlor smelled damp and musty, smelled of dusty carpeting, faded flowers, decaying wood. Even, he thought, there lingered odors of frying mush, bacon, and beans boiling in an iron pot.

"He was a good old man," Phronsie murmured.

She was awed by the rugs, the oil paintings on the walls, the rosewood desk, Aunt Flossie's fine china in a glass-fronted cabinet, dimly visible in the moldy gloom.

"I never was in the parlor. Lordy, he must have been rich!"

"They were well-off," Martin admitted. "In money, I mean. But they were rich in other ways. Humanity, I guess you'd say. Humanity, and understanding. That was more than money."

Gingerly she sank into an upholstered rocker. "Hope he don't mind if'n I plank my weary carcass down on this fine chair!"

In the kitchen remnants of that last noon meal still lay on the two plates: pork chops, fried potatoes, and cream gravy. Flies buzzed up from the bones. The gravy had desiccated until it looked like river-bottom mud, crazed with cracks. Wincing when the pump creaked, Martin poured a tin cup of water and handed it to Phronsie. "I—I buried him, Uncle Alonzo, out in back. I want to be with him, there, for a minute."

On the kitchen stoop he paused and looked at a layer of red caught between sullen streamers of cloud. The sky looked threatening. Slowly he walked toward his uncle's grave. Now there was a border of whitewashed stones, and a wooden cross with a roughly carved inscription: Alonzo Tarrant Died June 1862—A Good Neighbor. Probably Kurt Sigafoos, down the road, had put the gentle old man back in the earth, tidied up, left his friend to dream the Tarrants' improbable dreams.

"Uncle," he murmured, "I've come a long way, done lots of things since you—" He broke off, took a deep breath. "I've changed a lot, I guess. I wanted you to know."

"Martin?" Alarm edged Phronsie's voice.

Startled, he stared at the open kitchen door.

"Martin!"

He ran to the stoop, vaulted up three steps, and rushed into the kitchen. "What is it?"

She pushed him ahead of her, back out the kitchen door. "I saw them, coming down the lane! Two of them, maybe three. They've found us! Hurry!"

Together they scurried for the willows bordering the water. Pipestone Lake gleamed leaden gray, pockmarked from rain that was beginning to fall. From far off they heard the distant boom of thunder. Slipping and falling in muck along the shore, they hid in the reeds and peered toward the farmhouse. In the gray light of dawn Martin saw a feathered brave standing on the back porch, drawn bow at the ready, eyes searching. Another prowled about the barnyard, into the chicken coop, came out again; he carried a rifle. The third—there had been a third—whooped suddenly at the others and started toward the lake, head down like a hound.

"Hurry!" Martin said, clutching Phronsie's arm. "They've cut our trail!"

She pulled her arm loose and dropped to one knee, aiming the musket.

"What are you doing? Good God, they'll find us for sure!"

"They'll find us anyway! Better to give 'em something to think about!"

She knew best, he thought, and dropped beside her, his knees sinking cold into the mud.

"Don't aim to hit anyone," Phronsie muttered. "Just part his hair a little."

She squeezed the trigger. The recoil pushed them both off balance and they sprawled in the ooze. Martin, struggling up, saw their tracker had dropped his lance and was dancing about, clutching a shoulder.

"You hit him!"

"Lordy, I didn't mean to! Drew the bead a little too fine, I guess."

Together they struggled through the reeds skirting the lake and finally reached the far side where the forest met the water. As they reached the cover of the trees lightning illumined the heavens; a barrage of thunder deafened them. The rain began to fall, harder now. Looking back, Martin saw the other pursuers had joined the wounded brave, were bending over him.

"That'll slow them up for a while."

Phronsie paused to recharge her musket.

"You're crying," he said, surprised.

She didn't answer, only rammed the patch down hard in the barrel. "I am not!"

"But you are."

"Shut your mouth!" When he started off into the gloom of the forest she yelled at him, fiercely. "Not that way! Over there, past that dead oak!" Following him, she muttered, "You'd have us in Canada instead of Fort Ridgely."

Sodden pine needles made for slippery footing. At times Martin caught a glimpse of the river on their right and knew they were progressing upstream, as they ought. But it was Phronsie who kept them on a beeline, saving time and energy.

"That way, Martin. No, over the fallen log and down that little path."

"Path?"

"Deer trail, then, hurry!"

From time to time they paused, listening, peering back. They saw nothing but moss-grown trees; they heard nothing but the drip of rain from branches. The forest smelled dead, musty. Martin's heart pounded.

"See anything?"

Phronsie shook her head. The ginger hair hung dankly; her face was pale in the steel-gray light.

"Move on! We got at least another four, five mile to go!"

Pressing ahead, he said over his shoulder, "Good God! I forgot!"

"What?"

"We've got to cross the river somehow!"

"We'll handle that when we get there," Phronsie said between set teeth as she shifted the musket from one hand to the other.

"That's heavy," he said. "Let me carry it for you."

Shouldering him aside, she padded down the trail before him. "Don't nobody carry this old gun but me."

By now they were both footsore. The air seemed heavy and moist and did not refresh their lungs. Martin was determined not to pause, at least until Phronsie did. His legs were cramped, breath came in tortured gasps, and he wavered from side to side as he jogged the narrow trail. Phronsie was tired, too.

"Let's stop a minute. Lordy, my lungs is wheezing like a blacksmith's bellows."

Grateful, he collapsed on a slab of granite, rain wet and cold but welcome. Phronsie propped the musket across her knees, sat beside him, and looked back at the trail they had followed.

"Can't be more than another two mile to the crossing!"

"Maybe there's a ferry there."

"Used to be, but the Army's got its own boats now. Drove old Luther Sparkman out of business."

"Maybe we can hail the far side, get them to send a boat for us."

"Maybe."

The onslaught came so quickly that it found them unprepared. Arrows hissed past Martin's ear; one thunked into a tree near him. Phronsie cried out in alarm as a rain-glistened brave pinioned Martin's arms and threw him to the ground. Snatching up the musket, Phronsie tried to fire. A brown forearm drove up under the barrel and knocked the weapon from her hand. The two pursuers had come from in front of them. Probably leaving the wounded man behind, they had hurried along the river and gotten between them and the fort. Martin and Phronsie had been watching in the wrong direction.

An iron-hard forearm locked around his throat. The scene darkened, began to lose detail. Desperately he struggled, hands ineffectually plucking at the stranglehold. Gradually he slumped, body hanging limp. For a moment, a brief moment, the Sioux forearm relaxed. Remembering an old wrestling trick from school, Martin dropped to his knees while pulling down hard with the last of his strength. The Sioux rolled across Martin's back, toppled, sprawled in the pine needles. With a screech Martin flung himself atop the slippery body, his hands seeking a throat. The Sioux rolled away, quickly regained his feet, and drew a knife from his belt. He slashed once, twice, three times, but Martin jumped aside and kicked at his groin. His flailing toe found its mark; the brave groaned and bent over, hands fondling his crotch. Snatching up a shard of granite, Martin drove it down like a hatchet. For a moment the brave remained crouched, his hands still guarding his injured privates. Then he toppled slowly, falling in that same curled position.

"Phronsie!" Martin called.

She struggled in the embrace of the other man, clawing at his eyes with fingernails, a rain-wet wildcat. Martin rushed to grapple and the three, tangled together, fell. *The knife!* Martin thought. *The knife! Where is that knife the other man had?* Rolling about in the pine needles, he managed to free an arm and groped out, thinking to find it. Instead, he felt the cold steel of Phronsie's musket. With one arm he pulled it to him. A sudden turn of battle dragged him over it. The lock bruised his ribs and pain lanced his side.

Rolling over and over, locked in combat, he still scrabbled for the musket. Phronsie's body seemed limp now, and he feared for her.

"Phronsie?"

He fought to get to his feet. Finally he tottered up, locked against his assailant's body. Brown arms pinioned his waist; the braided head pressed into his stomach with sickening force.

"Phronsie!"

Her body lay still, flung against a tree as if a child had thrown it there.

"Phronsie!"

Clutching his hands together, he drove the doubled fists down like a hammer on the Sioux skull. Howling, the brave loosened his grasp. Martin snatched up the musket and swung it like a club. The iron-shod butt caught the brave across the shoulders and flung him against a tree. He swayed for a moment, dropped to his knees. Martin swung again. The Sioux saw the blow coming, rolled aside, and managed to get to his feet. For a moment he stared at Martin with dazed black eyes. Then he stumbled away into the forest.

Fumbling with the lock, Martin tried to fire the musket at the retreating back but could not manage it. Frustrated, he dropped the gun to kneel beside Phronsie. Her eyes were open and her breast rose and fell, rapidly.

"Are you—are you all right? By God, if they did anything to you . . ." His eyes stared through a red curtain of rage.

Rubbing her throat, she sat up with the aid of his arm.

Her voice was husky. "He—he was choking me. I couldn't breathe! It was awful! I saw Pa, Martin! I tell you I saw Pa! I was that far gone!"

He cradled her in his arms. "It's all right now."

"Where's the other—the other—" She looked fearfully about.

"Over there." Martin rose, looking down at the crumpled body. The splinter of granite lay near and he picked it up. The sharp edge was stained with blood. Silent, he watched rain wash away the blood. It would never wash away what was in his brain. He had killed. Thoughts came to his fevered mind. *I couldn't kill anybody, Uncle Alonzo!* He had made his case to Phronsie, too. *Not even then, I guess. I mean—not even then, could I kill! I'd probably be like a damned sheep, just standing there, ready to die!* But he *had* killed. In spite of his pious protestations he had killed for the most primitive reason—his woman. He had killed for Phronsie Bettencourt, and he would kill again for her if necessary.

Hearing a twig crack, he whirled and dropped the splinter of granite. It was only Phronsie getting unsteadily to her feet, one hand rubbing her bruised throat. She looked pale, and swayed.

"Are you *sure* you're all right?"

She nodded. "Hand me my gun. Probably the priming powder got wet."

She dried the priming pan and poured in powder from the horn at her waist. The motions seemed slow and awkward.

"Hurry!"

"I *am!*"

"There'll probably be more of them coming after us!"

She snapped the lid shut. "Don't I know?"

The dead body lay across their path. Martin stepped gingerly across, trying not to look. Phronsie avoided it also, saying only, "I think I knew him," in a strained voice. Then she pressed after Martin. "We haven't got all day."

The dense forest began to thin. There were a few stumps, mute white-crowned relicts where far-ranging soldiers from the fort had cut wood.

"Can't be far," Phronsie said.

Now she lagged behind. "Let me carry that gun!" he commanded.

She resisted, managing a thin smile. "You'd shoot yourself in the foot."

At last they emerged on a sandy bar where the forest retreated, giving way to the muddy Minnesota. The rain poured in sheets, a wavering veil as wind drove it like curtains in an open window. On the bluff opposite, dimly visible, lay the scattered buildings of Fort Ridgely. At a wharf was a steamboat, wisps of black smoke curling from its fluted stacks. The only spark of color in the leaden scene was the post flag, flapping listlessly.

"We made it!" Martin exulted.

"If we can get across." Dropping the musket, Phronsie slumped in the grass.

How did you hail a fort? "Ahoy the fort!" he shouted through cupped hands, feeling foolish.

If there had been an answer—unlikely—the sound of the rain washed it away.

"Ahoy, damn it!"

The words were choked off, absorbed by the drumming rain as they left his lips. Eagerly Martin searched the bank, hoping some riverman had left a skiff tied there. He found nothing but water birds, which squawked hoarsely and flapped away. Angry, he picked up a flat rock and skipped it across. Fort Ridgely lay silent and unattainable as the mountains of the moon.

Dejected, he climbed the bank to where Phronsie huddled. "Only one way, I guess."

She looked at him, dumbly.

"Swim. We've got to swim."

Making a small muffled sound, she shook her head.

"What?"

"I—I don't think I can."

"We've got to, Phronsie! You're a good swimmer!"

Something in her awkward position made him suspicious. He dropped beside her. "What's wrong?"

Suddenly he saw. The thigh of her jeans was soaked with blood. Fearful, he put his hand there. It came away stained with red. Feeling again, he found the stub of an arrow shaft.

"I—I broke it off," she said, almost apologetically.

"Oh, you fool! Phronsie!" Anxious, he bent over her. "Why didn't you tell me? I didn't know."

Her voice was fainter. "I didn't feel it at first, but then—" Under his supporting arm her body trembled, sagged. "A black arrow. A war arrow."

Untoward movement caught his eye. Downstream along the sandy shore running figures stooped low. Four, five, six—more of Shakopee's Sioux, pursuing! He snatched her up in his arms. She lay against him like a small child with her arms about his neck. "What are you going to do, Martin?"

"No choice now." He did not mention the rapidly approaching Sioux. "We've *got* to swim for it!"

"But I can't—"

"We can do anything," he said. It was not a boast; it only marked his determination.

Staggering under the load, he floundered down the bank into the water, leaving the precious musket behind. It was no good now. Martin had always been a good swimmer. In summer the Colonel took him and Lucas to Nantasket Beach on the ocean. He and his brother had delighted in struggling around offshore islands in the teeth of whitecaps. Lucas had generally beaten him back to the rented cottage, though. Lucas was used to excelling.

"I'm going to swim on my back," he told Phronsie. "Just relax and let me pull you by the shoulders!"

"Martin—" Her voice was an empty husk.

"Yes." He paused, up to his thighs in chill water.

"Kiss me."

Her lips were thin and cold. Blood; she had lost a lot of blood while he stupidly urged her on.

"Ready?"

There was the faintest nod of the precious ginger head.

"Here we go!"

As he fell backward into the muddy current, towing her by the fringed shoulders of the bucksin jacket, he saw Sioux scouts dancing along the shore. Smoke bloomed from a musket, an arrow pierced the air but fell wide. Frantically he kicked onward. Phronsie's limp body tugged, her face was dead white before him, her eyes were closed. Was she dying? Good God, no—please! He kicked out again, and again, as the rain hid a hostile shore, gradually fading behind them.

CHAPTER ELEVEN

Martin had never been a strong swimmer like Lucas. Now his only ally was desperation. *Kick, breathe, kick, breathe, kick again, and again*—were they moving at all? Lightning split the dawn sky. Black clouds churned in heavy relief and a cannonade of thunder deafened him. *Kick, breathe, kick*— Seeing her white face sink into the waves, he loosed his grip on Phronsie's shoulder and grasped a handful of hair, pulling her along by that, free arm stroking the water to supplement the leg kick. *Kick, stroke, kick, breathe*—

A bolt of lightning hit the shore they had left. A great oak blasted apart in a rocket of flame, burning debris pinwheeling into the gray dawn.

"Phronsie?" He took a mouthful of muddy river water for that. "Can you hear me?"

No answer; the pale face bobbed, the hair trailed like seaweed. *Kick, breathe, stroke*—in a new flash of blue-white light he imagined he saw in the foam a tinge of red. Was she bleeding to death as he fought the current, staining the Minnesota with her blood?

Coughing from water he had swallowed, Martin rolled sidewise and caught a glimpse of the far shore—steamboat, the scattered buildings of Fort Ridgely misted in gunmetal gray. By God, he *was* making progress! He *would* make it, he *had* to make it!

Pain bit the calf of his leg—a cramp. Doggedly he kept on kicking, paddling, the niceties of swimming technique forgotten or impossible. Now he only thrashed, churning the water. *Kick, breathe, stroke*—

"Phronsie! It's getting nearer! Do you hear?"

Lungs laboring, a stitch now in his side, he finally touched bottom. Reeds brushed his cheek. Staggering to his feet, clutching Phronsie Bettencourt by the hair, he floundered through the mud. A grass-topped bank, undercut by the current, loomed above his head. Desperate, he caught an exposed root to stay him. Getting an arm about her waist, he pulled her to safety.

"We're there! By God, we're there, Phronsie!"

Buckskins dank and heavy, she lay limp across his arm, bent backward like a wilted flower. Desperate, he tried to scale the bank. Gravel gave way under his feet—he had lost his boots, or jettisoned them, he did not remember which—and together they sprawled again into the water.

He had not come this far to be balked by gravity. Wiping his eyes with the back of his hand, he got mud in them. Half blinded, he made out a gully splitting the obstinate bank. Crawling on hands and knees, pulling the helpless body after him, he struggled up the rocky cleft. Someone was talking; he could hear muffled and indistinct words. *That's it! Now you're on the right track! Only a little farther!* Knees bloody, free hand cut and bruised, he inched forward. *Near the top now!* In spite of pain he grinned wryly. Talking to himself! With a final surge, a convulsive extension of his body, he sprawled in deep wet grass.

"Who the hell are *you*?"

That was not Martin Sayre's voice, he knew for sure. A booted toe prodded his side. Rubbing a bleared eye, he saw the muzzle of a rifle near his face.

"I said, who in tarnation *are* you people?"

Phronsie's head in his lap, Martin tried to speak, but his voice was only a dismal croak.

"Cawpril of the guard!" the sentry roared against the hissing rain. "Post number three!"

Martin found his voice. "If you don't get that gun out of my face I'll take it away and wrap it around your goddamned neck!"

It was spoken with such savage intensity that the sentry blinked, swallowed hard, and laid down the rifle to squat beside them in a rain-glistened slicker. "For a minute I thought you was Sioux, coming across the river to sneak in the back way."

"Do we look like Sioux?" Martin struggled to his feet, cradling Phronsie in bone-weary arms.

"*She* does." Seeing his corporal approach, the sentry picked up the rifle. "You—" He scratched his chin. "*You* look like a nickel's worth of cat meat, mister!"

A yellow-chevroned noncom loomed out of the rain. "What's the trouble?"

"She's dying!" Martin answered. "Sioux arrow in the thigh, bleeding bad! Where's the post surgeon?"

"Now just a minute," the corporal cautioned, voice heavy with authority. "First, I got to know who you folks are, where you come from. We got a lot of refugees here, and it's important to keep a tally. Besides, the hospital is full of wounded anyway, and Major says—".

Martin's voice was angry.

"I don't give a damn what your major says! Help me get this lady to the hospital or I'll crawl down your windpipe and kick your insides out!"

He did not know where the surprising words came from; it was not like Martin Sayre to speak thus. Possibly it was something he had once heard Phronsie say.

"I've got an important message for the C.O., from New Ulm! They're in trouble there, bad trouble, with a Sioux attack underway right this minute!"

Impressed, the corporal blew a whistle. Men emerged from the sumac bushes that bordered the river.

"Jenson, run get a litter! Schmidt, tell Surgeon Vollmer we got a bad case coming in! Begley, look up the adjutant and tell him Shakopee's gone to New Ulm!"

Apologetic, the corporal paced beside Martin as the litter bearers carried Phronsie across the parade ground.

"Oh, ain't we had a time here! The red devils swarmed out of the ditch south of officers' quarters yesterday morning and practical overrun the post! Burned the horse shed and Sutler's store, busted into the guardhouse and let out them friends of theirs—"

"The peace delegation? Yellow Horse and Wolf Talker and Fool Dog and the rest?"

"Don't concern myself with names. They're all alike to me. Bloodthirsty vermin, all of 'em! Anyway, they got what they come for. Now they're going to wipe out New Ulm, I guess, like they promised." At a fork in the graveled path he took Martin's arm. "Post H.Q. is up this way."

"I'm going with her!"

"But—"

Martin wrested free of the corporal's grasp. "She—she may be dying!"

The post hospital was crowded with wounded, casualties from the previous day's raid. Martin smelled blood, chloroform, vomit. Female refugees pressed into service as nurses moved from bed to bed bathing fevered brows, changing dressings. As Phronsie's litter passed, one woman pulled a sheet over the waxen face of a soldier. Others carried basins, rolled bandages, fed wounded men.

"What's this?" His scalpel poised over a mangled arm, Surgeon Vollmer took off a blood-speckled pince-nez and stared at Martin.

Martin's voice trembled and he stopped, forcing himself to speak slowly and distinctly. "We were sent from New Ulm to get help, and on the way the Sioux caught up with us. I killed one, I guess, but the other one shot Phronsie in the leg, and she's bleeding, and she—she—" Choked with emotion, he broke off.

With quick skill Vollmer slit the water-soaked buckskin, touched the broken shaft of the arrow. "Still bleeding. *Ach*, a good sign, that." With finger and thumb he opened an eyelid, stared for a moment. "We see. Yes, we see." Sharpening the scalpel again on his boot sole, he called, "Mrs. Springer?"

A bun-haired matron in a lacy kitchen apron, incongruous with blood stains, appeared.

"Prepare the young lady. Soon as I cut this arm, I take out the Sioux arrowhead."

Martin grasped Vollmer's arm. "Will she live?"

"People live, people die." The surgeon turned back to the rude table on which lay the man with the injured arm.

"But—"

"I am not God! I do not know the future. We do what we can, *hein*? Go away, young man."

Under Mrs. Springer's direction, the litter bearers

carried Phronsie away. Martin started to follow but was brought up by an impatient bark.

"Now just where is this fellow from New Ulm, eh?"

In the doorway stood a whiskered little man with major's oak leaves on his shoulders, pouter-pigeon chest heavy with campaign ribbons and medals. Walrus mustaches and a shock of iron-gray hair made him look like a combative terrier.

"Where is he, damn it? Speak up!" Behind him was an officer from the regulars, a lean, loose-jointed captain with collar insignia of the regulars.

"I'm Martin Sayre."

The terrier pranced forward, circling Martin, almost seeming to sniff at a strange scent. "Major Keefe, C. O. Sayre eh? From New Ulm? What's all this about the Sioux in force?" Quickly Martin gave details. "The situation must be desperate by now. They were in the hills, gathering together. Even now it might be too late. There were hundreds of them. My brother had things pretty well organized, but the village can't stand a major attack."

"Your brother?"

"Lucas Sayre. He was a breveted major in the Twenty-second Massachusetts. He came out here when he was wounded, and—" Martin broke off, not wanting to explain.

"I was at Cerro Gordo in Mexico with a Sayre from Massachusetts. Gideon Sayre, in the old days."

"My father."

"Major Keefe," the regular captain said apologetically, "we'd best be getting upriver fast as we can!"

"Do that, Whitney," Major Keefe agreed. "Get up steam! I'll have my adjutant issue orders to all the militia I can spare. Don't imagine Shakopee wants anything more to do with us, now that he's got his emissaries back. New Ulm, eh? That's where we figured the old rascal'd hit next, but we didn't know for sure."

Martin looked anxiously at the door through which Phronsie had been taken. Major Keefe was still talking. Would he never stop?

"Lucky, very lucky."

"I beg your pardon, Major?"

"You're lucky the *General Scott* came in last week from Fort Snelling with three companies of conscripts. A hundred miles, under forced draft, in eighteen hours! If they can reach New Ulm in time maybe we can scotch the Sioux for once and for all!"

"Yes, sir," Martin agreed. "Please, I'd like to see if the lady I brought in—"

"Heard about her. Mrs. Sayre?"

"No, sir. That is—I mean—"

"Of course. Soon as you've seen to her, go aboard the *General Scott* with Captain Whitney. He'll need you when the vessel gets near New Ulm. Lay of the land, you know—that sort of thing."

"But—"

Major Keefe was gone, trotting down the path toward post headquarters. Martin rushed through the door, blundering into a lady carrying a tray. A pitcher sailed into the air, splattering the wall, to roll unbroken on the rude boards of the floor. Hastily he picked it up and handed it to the astonished female.

"Ma'am, I'm sorry! I didn't mean—"

Seeing an orderly, Martin clutched his sleeve. "Where is she?"

The orderly, a youth with a blond cowlick over one eye, only stared at him.

"Phronsie, damn it! Phronsie Bettencourt!"

At the lackluster gaze, Martin dropped the boy's

arm. The hospital was a rabbit warren of interconnecting rooms, laid out by a mad Army carpenter. He might already be too late to find her. Desperately he hurried through the halls, peering into rooms, calling, "Phronsie! Where are you?"

At the far end of the building was a stairwell. Starting to ascend, he put a hand on the banister, paused, Surgeon Vollmer was coming down.

"Where is she? How is she? Please, Doctor—"

Vollmer held up a bloody arrowhead. "I got a collection of these damned things! This one hammered out from iron skillet, I think." He dropped it into a pocket.

"How is she?" Martin insisted, pinioning the surgeon by the lapels. "Damn it, how *is* she? Tell me!"

Gently Vollmer disengaged him. "She live, all right. *Mein Gott*, what a brave girl! Never cry, never move when I cut! Like Indian, her!" He pointed upward. "Door on right."

Martin clattered up the stairs. In the darkened room lay Phronsie in a borrowed nightgown. Mrs. Springer was bathing her brow from a basin. When Martin clattered in, the nurse frowned, putting a finger to her lips.

"Young man! This is a hospital!"

He dropped to one knee beside the cot. "Phronsie! Are you—are you all right?"

The face was pale and colorless as the sheet drawn up under her chin; the ginger hair lay dank on the pillow. In the darkened room Phronsie's blue eyes were only dark smudges in the ghostlike face. When her hand moved toward his he caught it, pressing it to his lips.

"I'm . . ."

He bent forward to listen.

"I'm . . . all right." The voice seemed to come from far away—very far away. In a rustle of skirts Mrs. Springer moved to the doorway. "If you need anything, sir, I'll be in the hallway."

"I couldn't live without you," Martin whispered. "Phronsie, if anything happened to you . . ."

She was silent, exhausted from the effort to reach his hand, from her few words.

"They want me to go back with the troops to New Ulm. They're getting up steam now. They've got three companies of conscripts, and Major Keefe is putting aboard all the militia he can spare. I don't know if it will be enough or if it will be too late. But at least we got through, and help is on the way. But I won't leave you, Phronsie; I'm going to stay till I know you're out of danger!"

"No." The word was faint but clear.

"What do you mean?"

The draped breast heaved with emotion. "Go back! You've got to go back!"

"But I—"

"I—I want you to go back. You made a bargain with Lucas."

Fever, he thought, seeing her distraught. Of course he had made a bargain with Lucas. But that was not important now. "I'll go back when you're well."

"No!" Half rising on the pillow, she wept. "I want you to do it now! Please, Martin!"

He was holding her hand too hard, and laid it gently on the sheet and stroked it. "I can't leave you like this, Phronsie. You mean too much to me. Lie back, now, and rest. You mustn't get excited."

Mrs. Springer came in, alarmed. "What's the trouble here? My goodness, young man, what are you doing to her?" Pressing Phronsie back on the pillow, she touched the pale forehead with the hem of her apron to gather beaded drops of perspiration. "There, there, now, dear—rest. You *must* rest."

Feeling guilty, Martin rose. But Phronsie called to him, her eyes closed, lips scarcely moving.

"I'm here," he said.

"Don't worry about me." She paused for a moment, as if to gather strength. "Remember, I'm"—she took a deep breath—"I'm Iron Girl."

For a long time he stood in the doorway, hearing from outside the sounds of bugles, shouted commands, a deep-toned blast from the *General Scott*.

"She's sleeping," Mrs. Springer murmured. Putting a finger to her lips, she ushered him out. "Poor girl, it's a pity what she's gone through."

On the landing Martin paused, seeing an August day that had turned fair. Summer sun poured through the window; the storm was only a smudge on the horizon. Smoke rose from the stacks of the *General Scott*. Files of soldiers snaked along the wharf and onto the paddle-wheeler's decks. *Go back?* He bit his lip. A long time ago he had been a young man, a student, without care. He was happy in the academic life, music, painting, the arts that contented and fulfilled. Then the war had come and he became a prisoner of obligation. *Go back.* Even now he could run away again. No one was watching. The infantry captain would send someone to look for him. When they didn't find Martin Sayre, the *General Scott* would go upstream anyway to the relief of New Ulm. Hadn't he done his part? A pharmacist brushed by him with a rack of colored pills in bottles. "'Scuse me, mister." Martin didn't move, and heard again the deep music of the *General Scott*'s whistle. There was another restraint now, a stronger one. He looked toward Phronsie's room. He could not run away and leave Phronsie. Neither could he run away and renounce his vow to Lucas. But if he did not flee now, when he had the chance, he would lose Phronsie, and probably his life. In an agony of indecision he paced the landing. Finally, reluctantly, he made up his mind.

Hurrying across the parade ground, now steaming in the sun, Martin saw evidence of the Sioux attack that had escaped his notice when he carried Phronsie at dawn to the post hospital. The grassy plain was pocked with rifle pits, and more were being dug. Several buildings at the perimeter had burned to the ground; charred remains smoldered, sending wisps of smoke into a morning calm. A detail prepared graves in the moist loam for the dead, the white dead. Crumpled bodies of Sioux lay about in profusion, and flies already buzzed about the limp forms. The pole in the center of the compound had been broken off short, and a torn and bullet-holed flag hung from a peeled sapling that had been spliced on.

As he neared the wharf he saw further signs of violence on the *General Scott*. Her pilothouse had been reinforced with plates of sheet iron, and the metal was dimpled and scarred with the marks of bullets. Black smoke curled from holes in the high stacks with their curlicued spark arresters. Her railings and other woodwork were split and gouged. The paddle wheel had lost several blades, and the vessel listed slightly as conscripts labored at pumps, sending murky Minnesota River water over the side.

"Now who the hell are *you*?" A bulky sentry, musket at port, barred his way as he stepped on the gangplank.

"Martin Sayre. Major Keefe said I was to come aboard."

"You got a pass?"

"No, I haven't got a pass. What do I need a pass for?"

The sentry eyed him. "How do I know whether you got business aboard?" He stared at Martin's unshaven face, torn and muddy clothing, bare feet. "You smell like a damned Sioux!" He backed away, musket at the ready. "Get the hell off'n here!"

"Sayre?"

Martin glanced up at the boiler deck. Captain Whitney beckoned. "Where in hell have you been? I just sent a runner to locate you. Hurry up! We're ready to cast off!"

Brushing past the open-mouthed sentry, Martin climbed a ladder to the upper deck. "Follow me," Whitney commanded. Clambering up another ladder to the wheelhouse he banged open the door. "Hook her up," he ordered the pilot.

It was dim in the wheelhouse; only a narrow slit of daylight showed above the iron plates. The pilot, a bearded man in a felt hat who chewed on a stogie, nodded. "Hook her up!" he called into a brass speaking-tube. Going to a hinged window in the sheet iron, he bellowed below. "Cast off bowlines! Cast off stern lines!" Back to the speaking-tube he called, "Give me ten revolutions astern!"

The *General Scott* trembled as her paddles threshed. Martin was aware of movement. They backed away from the wharf into the mainstream. Smoke drifted into the wheelhouse and cinders rained down. The pilot peered ahead through the slit. "Now!" he called. "All ahead full!" Reaching overhead, he jerked a rope. The *General Scott*'s deep whistle set the iron plates vibrating and hurt Martin's ears.

"We're off," Captain Whitney noted, drawing a watch from an inner pocket. "Almost nine A.M. We ought to make New Ulm by eleven at the latest."

Eleven. Standing near the door, Martin tried to roll a small wooden keg near to sit on. *Eleven*. What would they find at New Ulm? All dead, scalped, the town burned? Captain Whitney grinned at his attempt to move the keg.

"Heavy, eh?"

"Seems filled with lead."

Whitney took a thumb and finger of chewing tobacco from a pouch. "Gold."

"What?"

"Seventeen thousand dollars in gold! Congress finally appropriated the money to pay the Sioux annuities. Delivered to Fort Snelling just before we left."

"Too late," Martin murmured.

Whitney spat into a brass cuspidor. "Too damned late! Fat-assed congressmen, sitting on their duffs and rolling logs while the country goes to pot!" He rose, buttoning his coat. "Never was much of a sailor. Being cooped up in here unsettles my stomach." He slung field glasses around his neck, and Martin followed him out on deck.

As she breasted the current, the *General Scott*'s paddles drove foam high into the air; it drifted back over them in muddy spray. Smoke boiled from the stacks. From below came the *ssooo—hah—ssooo—hah* of the straining low-pressure engine. Looking down, Martin saw muzzles of rifles poking outward like the quills of a porcupine. The conscripts, released from the drudgery of drilling and polishing brass at Fort Snelling, watched eagerly for a target. In the bows a crew trained a twelve-pounder cannon. Around it were stacked iron balls in pyramids.

"There!" Captain Whitney cried, semaphoring with a lean arm. "On the far shore!"

At first the greenery had seemed sylvan, innocent, almost benign with the sun dappling the lush growth. Now Martin saw Sioux scouts, many of them. Beyond rifle shot they thronged out on a sandbar and shook fists, brandished lances. One brave galloped a piebald horse chest deep into the water and fired into the air. From below decks answering shots sounded in a ragged volley. Captain Whitney folded his lean body over the rail, brandishing a clenched fist.

"God damn it, the next man that fires a weapon without my express order gets his balls cut off!"

As they churned upriver the Sioux followed, dancing along the shoreline, whooping and yelling, making obscene gestures. Captain Whitney took another pinch of tobacco.

"You and the gal—the two of you came through *that*?"

Martin shrugged. "There probably weren't that many last night."

Whitney chewed a while. "Civilians is mostly a bother to the Army," he said finally, "but that was a brave thing to do, Mr. Sayre."

As they approached New Ulm the number of Sioux along the river bank increased. Martin remembered the Sioux expression for battle—"gravy stirring." There was going to be a big gravy stirring. Captain Whitney realized it also. In response to his command a sergeant brought Martin a Henry repeating rifle and a pouch of cartridges. Whitney buckled on his saber and sidearms. "Good God, look at the red sons of bitches!"

He shook his head. "I've drilled the ass off my recruits but they're still pretty green."

Around the bend they saw smoke from the burning buildings of New Ulm drifting up from a screen of willows. "The other side of that sandy point," Martin told Whitney, "is the upper ferry landing. Last time I saw it, it was serviceable. Might be a good idea to cut the point short and slide in there."

Whitney nodded, calling instructions to the pilot. Gathering together his noncoms, an experienced cadre of veterans, the captain held a council of war.

"Can't see much till we round that point, but we've got to be ready for anything. Murphy, the bow gun ready?"

"Yes, sir."

"Goetz, Swenson, Fields, Bauer?"

"We're ready, Captain."

"Keep your men under control. No shooting unless fired on, and then only in volleys. Aim low, take time to get a proper bead—"

Scattered firing broke out from the main deck forward. Whitney bit off his words in mid-sentence and rushed to the rail. "Damn 'em, they're swarming aboard!"

In an instant all was pandemonium. Careful plans were abandoned in a melee of hoarse shouts, ragged volleys, sabers slicing through the sunlight. In the ship's close transit around the bend the Sioux had burst from the cover of the willows to attack the *General Scott*. Some whipped horses out to the vessel, a distance of only a hundred yards, and clambered aboard. Others poled a stolen flatboat. Many of the attackers swam with rifles held overhead, and gleaming with water and savage paint, pulled themselves on deck. Quickly Martin vaulted over the rail. After hanging for a moment with one hand, he dropped to the main deck into a maelstrom of struggling bodies, conscripts locked in hand-to-hand battle with the Sioux.

The foe was too close for anything but pistols and sabers, sometimes only fists and kicks. Swinging the Henry like a club, Martin felt it crash against the skull of a brave with a black-painted face. The man's features suddenly turned lopsided, a face seen in a distorting mirror at a carnival; the warrior loosed his grip on a fresh-faced recruit's throat, and the boy staggered vomiting to the rail.

Hit by a glancing blow on the shoulder, Martin sprawled across the bow gun, now useless in hand-to-hand fighting. Dazed, he rolled sidewise just as another blow of a feathered hatchet missed his neck and glanced off the brass barrel of the bow gun. Back arched against the twelve-pounder, he planted his feet in his assailant's belly and kicked out. For a moment the man teetered against the gunwale, then fell backward into the river.

Tottering to his feet, Martin felt warmth trickling down his arm. When he picked up the Henry rifle it fell from his bloody grasp. He grabbed it again only in time to be half deafened by a Sioux musket going off in his ear. A hot iron creased his cheek. Blindly he swung the Henry again, hearing the crunch of walnut butt against bone.

"Don't stop!" Captain Whitney bawled to the pilot, cupping hands to be heard above the din. "Make for the damned landing!"

Martin saw a fur-hatted brave kneeling across a prostrate soldier and taking aim at the officer. Poising his rifle like a javelin, Martin drove it through air with a grunt that wrenched his stomach. The iron-shod butt smashed the warrior's face. Dropping his musket, he staggered to his feet. One of the noncoms, screeching like a banshee, half severed the brave's head with a whistling arc of his saber.

Slowly the *General Scott* lurched toward the landing. A sergeant got to the brass cannon and managed to fire a few rounds into the densely packed Sioux along the shore. Martin caught a glimpse of the log barricade on the heights above the town. The flag still waved from the battered windmill. Gravy stirring was going on there, too. Gasping for breath, dripping with blood and sweat, he snatched up a saber from the deck to cut a swath through a knot of Sioux who were beating a conscript to his knees with knobbed war clubs. A brave caught his wrist in an iron grip and twisted; Martin's saber clattered to the deck. In desperation he bit the brown wrist, feeling his teeth come together through meat. The brave howled in pain, clutching a mangled wrist. Retrieving the saber, Martin ran it through the glistening chest. It cut the Indian easily, but then stuck in the siding of the engine room. He wrenched it out only in time to parry a blow from a Sioux lance, driven like a dagger.

"Look!" someone yelled.

His back against a cranny in the engine-room wall, Martin stared ashore. Men were running from the saw-log fort; white men, Lucas Sayre's men! With the Sioux drawn away to attack the paddle-wheeler, Lucas had seized on the moment to launch a counterattack. Above the din Martin could hear the music of a bugle as the defenders of New Ulm ran down the slope toward the ferry landing.

"Up the Eighth Minnesota Infantry!" Captain Whitney was yelling. "Show the bastards what you're made of, boys!" Tunic half torn from his back, he stood spraddle-legged by the hog chains, bereft of any weapon but his field glasses, which he spun by their strap like David's sling. They caught a Sioux skull, and the optics fell out in a shower of sun-glinting glass. Holding his head and grimacing, the Sioux staggered over the side and began to paddle uncertainly toward shore.

"They're coming from the fort!" a noncom yelled, pointing with a dripping saber. "We got 'em in a vise now, boys! Give 'em hell!"

Caught between the troops on the *General Scott* and the defenders from the saw-log fort, the Sioux wavered, became indecisive, finally broke. Leaving off the assault, they dove from the boat and struggled through reeds and muck to shore. Horses neighed, kicked, pranced about as Sioux tried to mount them. The sergeant at the bow gun steered frantically as the vessel approached the landing. The twelve-pounder boomed. Like a bloody blossom, a knot of warriors burst apart. Sioux galloped, ran, scattered in all directions as they were caught in a crossfire. Their training at Fort Snelling showing, the conscripts regrouped under the orders of their sergeants. In rank and file they loaded muskets in the prescribed nine steps of General Casey's *Infantry Tactics*, took aim, and fired; the retreat of the Sioux turned to panic. Fleeing toward the distant hills, they were harried by Lucas's men, many of whom pursued the foe on horses, screaming with long pent-up emotion.

Knees shaky, Martin sagged down on a bollard. The paddle-wheeler's bows rumbled against the pilings of the wharf, and he had to put out a hand to keep from falling off the bollard. As Lucas's men swarmed aboard, a cheer broke out. They laughed and shook hands with the men of the *General Scott*. Martin was sick. His shoulder felt numb. Dumbly he gazed down at the puddle of blood—his blood—soaking into the weather-worn boards of the deck. In the other hand he still held what was left of the saber, blade broken off near the hilt so the weapon was a caricature of its former self.

"Here he is!" someone said. "Right here, Major!"

Martin looked up. His brother stood beside Captain Whitney. With cane no longer, and looking very military, Lucas stared at Martin.

"Hello," Martin murmured. "Hello, Lucas."

CHAPTER TWELVE

The battle of New Ulm broke the back of the Santee Sioux rebellion. In the valley of the Minnesota River it was estimated that six hundred and forty-four white men, women, and children were killed. Ninety-three soldiers, many of them young conscripts only recently mustered into Federal service, were also killed. The depredations of the angered Sioux, denied their yearly annuity, smarting from being cheated by rascally traders, and sustaining the loss of their lands to encroaching settlers, covered an area fifty miles wide and two hundred miles long. Many citizens, frightened by the massacre if not actually harmed, left the state to settle elsewhere; Governor Ramsey was furious. In a public statement he cried, "Execute the Sioux! Private revenge will otherwise take the place of official judgment!" In partial compliance with his wishes the Minnesota Legislature passed a law saying "All rights and claims of the Sioux tribes are annulled. Their reservations are to be denied, and the tribes deported beyond the boundaries of the state."

Newspapers echoed the governor's sentiments. The St. Paul *Press* fumed: "They have not been born than lift a hostile hand against a citizen of Minnesota!" When General Sibley pursued the fleeing Indians and captured several hundred who were later imprisoned at Fort Ridgely, the *Minnesota Republican* complained, "The Indians are called by some 'prisoners of war.' There was no war about it! It was wholesale robbery, rape, and murder!"

The only dissenting voice was that of Bishop Whipple. He was quoted as saying, "I ask that the people shall lay the blame of this great crime where it belongs, and rise up to demand the reform of an atrocious Indian system, which has always garnered for us the same fruit of anguish and blood." But no one listened.

Martin's own wounds had healed, and he felt fine. Through the courtesy of Major Keefe he had brought Phronsie back in an Army wagon train carrying supplies to the hungry refugees at New Ulm. In bed at Mrs. Cates's Phronsie was still thin and pale, but with the aid of a cane managed to walk a little in the September sunlight. Looking very frail, she sat in a borrowed gingham dress on a rocker on the front porch.

"Have you talked to Lucas yet?" she asked.

"Not since the day of the fight. I hear he's been back and forth to Fort Ridgely, making depositions to the military commission that's being set up by General Pope to try the Indians and finishing up his business here."

She said nothing, only stared at the river, looking across the burned buildings and debris of battle: the windmill and the tattered and bullet-pierced flag that still fluttered, the leafless skeletons in North German Park where trees had been immolated.

"Everything will be all right soon, Phronsie," he said, squeezing her hand.

Surgeon Vollmer had done a good job. But with Phronsie's animal health and spirit he thought she would be completely recovered by now. Still, it had been a shocking experience for anyone. Phronsie was thinking also, he knew, of her Sioux friends. Many had been killed. Many were in prison at Camp Ridgely. Shakopee, Fool Dog, Medicine Bottle and others had escaped, making for Canada and refuge with cavalry in pursuit lead by Lieutenant Phipps.

He kissed her and rose. "I promised Mrs. Cates I'd rebuild her chicken coop that burned. The chickens are wandering all over the place, and she's afraid coyotes will get them."

In new shirt and jeans he was hammering boards together when a shadow fell across his rough carpentry. It was Lucas Sayre. Lucas wore a proper saber and side arms, and from someone at the post had borrowed a well-tailored frock coat of dark blue with shining brass buttons belted by the buff-colored sash appropriate for an infantry officer of field grade. The silver eagles of a Regular Army Major glittered on his epaulets.

"Hello, Lucas, " Martin said again, laying down the hammer.

"You're still here."

"I don't intend to run away."

"Good."

Lucas sat on the sawhorse, flipping the tails of the coat aside. He rested hands on the pommel of his sword. "I want to talk to you."

Martin waited. His brother's bearded face was inscrutable. Lucas looked brown and fit. There was no evidence of the pale and wan cripple who had confronted Martin that night in the bedroom at Mrs. Cates's.

"I've cleared up most of my affairs here. Nothing more to keep me in this damned frontier village with a bunch of numbskulled Dutchmen and Swedes."

Martin said nothing. Lucas had always been pontifical.

"I've talked to Major Keefe at Fort Ridgely. I've talked to Captain Whitney. There's been an opportunity for me to think a lot about your—well, damn it, your case!"

Your case. Martin nodded.

"It was a brave thing you and that strange girl did. I don't mind telling you it saved us here. We'd just about run out of cartridges, food, water—everything. I guess you could say you saved New Ulm. Maybe you put the quietus on the whole damned Sioux uprising, though I hear they're still chasing some of them."

Martin nodded, wiped his brow with a bandanna. The sun was hot. Pulse pounded heavily in his temple. This was it. *Case. His case.*

"So I'll tell you what I'm willing to do. You're a hero around here, it seems. There's talk of the governor striking off a medal for you." Lucas grimaced and fingered his beard. "Heroes are always a lot of trouble to the Army. They have to be handled differently, it seems."

Lucas's beard, Martin noticed, was flecked with gray; he had not noticed it before. He remembered his brother's new beard when Lucas was seventeen, and Lucas joking when Martin felt his own chin for the reassuring fuzz. All in all, Lucas hadn't been too bad. Or was it just that Martin remembered things differently now?

"I'm going to leave it up to you, brother." It had

THE SANTEE MASSACRE

been a long time since Lucas called him that. "Make up your own mind. I can have Major Keefe put you in irons at Fort Ridgely and taken back under guard for court-martial, but I don't want to do that. You've distinguished yourself, you see."

For the first time Martin spoke. His voice was dry and husky. "Your leg—"

Lucas slapped his boot. "Good as new! All this action has been a tonic! They can't deny my application for active duty now!"

"I'm glad."

Gravely Lucas went on. "On the other hand, if you come with me on the cars, and pledge not to try to escape, we can handle the whole thing very quietly. I'll be your witness at the court-martial. With all you've done out here, and Kit Burke and my friends in high places in the War Department helping, I swear you'll be let off with a reprimand!"

Martin swallowed hard; his throat was constricted, as dry and dusty as the burned landscape.

"I don't want to go back, Lucas."

The bushy brows drew together. "Why, for God's sake? It's the honorable thing to do! You stand a good chance of having your name cleared—*our* name: Sayre!"

Martin picked up the hammer and looked at the grain of the wood of the handle, the shine on the head where it had struck legions of nails. "This is my country out here. I've grown to admire it—and the people. This is where I want to stay." He looked his brother in the eye. "This is where I think I've earned the *right* to stay!"

Lucas scowled, held the saber on his lap like a weapon at the ready. "You make things very difficult, Martin."

"That's what I'm obliged to do."

"But you don't *belong*, Martin! You're a Sayre, a Massachusetts Sayre! Our people have been around since the Mayflower docked! What in hell can there be for you here? Indians, floods, storms, crude people, no manners, tobacco spit and horse manure! You're a cultured person, Martin, with your painting and music and languages." Lucas's eyes narrowed. "It's that damned female, isn't it? What's her name—Phronsie?"

"Yes."

"Does she even have a last name?"

"Phronsie Bettencourt. Her father was a trapper."

Lucas snorted. "A woods colt! Half savage she is, with those indecent skin pants and rough talk. Martin, listen to me. I can't let you do it. Forget her! When you get home Lavinia Greene will be waiting for you." Laying the saber aside, he fumbled in an inner pocket. "I'd already written to Lavinia to prepare her. This morning the mail from Fort Snelling brought this." He handed Martin an envelope. It was post marked Dedham and smelled of French scent. "Read it, Martin, and consider. Damn it, *consider!*"

Martin read the letter. It meant nothing to him. "It doesn't change my mind, Lucas. I intend to stay here."

Lucas took back the letter, folded it. "I—I don't know what to say."

"You don't have to say anything."

"I came all the way out here to find you!"

Martin had never seen his brother defeated. There was a puzzled look on Lucas's face.

"I swore to take you back."

Now Martin felt the stronger. "You found me," he admitted. "But you found something else, too, Lucas. You found a new Martin Sayre, someone who feels at home here."

Lucas chewed at a corner of his mustache, spat into the sawdust, rubbed at the leather sling of the saber. "Damn all heroes!"

Martin touched his brother's blue-clad arm, a gesture unfamiliar to him. Lucas had always abhorred sentiment, as had the Colonel. "I—I love her, you see."

Lucas nodded almost absently, staring into the dust. "You'll still be a fugitive. You'll have to take your chances with that. I won't offer help again."

"I understand that. It's worth the risk."

"Well, if you make your bed, you have to lie in it! That's what Father always said."

"If you see Father and Mother—"

"I don't know what to tell them," Lucas muttered.

"Tell them I love them, that's all. But I have to make my own way *in* my own way, Lucas."

His brother's eyes searched his. "Are you sure? I mean—is this really what you want, Martin?"

"Yes."

Lucas stared a long time, teeth gnawing the grizzled mustache. Finally he said, "All right, damn it!"

Martin put out his hand. Lucas's face was a study. Finally he shook hands, curtly, and turned on his heel. At the back stoop he paused. "But you're bound to come to your senses soon and do the right thing, the Sayre thing—I believe that."

Thrilled by freedom, even a restricted freedom where he might one day have to reckon with a formal charge of desertion, Martin abandoned his carpentry and vaulted up the back stoop. He ran through the kitchen, where the astonished Mrs. Cates, hands and arms white with flour, was making noodles, and mounted the stairs to Phronsie's room. She was combing out her hair, grown long during her convalescence. She had not yet had the opportunity to trim it short.

"Can I come in?"

She nodded, looking again into the mirror.

"Good news, Phronsie! Wonderful news!"

Carefully she laid the brush on the bureau. In spite of his protests, she had salvaged her worn and ragged buckskins and hung them in the clothespress.

"I just had a talk with Lucas! He left it up to me! It seems . . ." He was awkward, talking about it. "I guess in some way people consider me—and you, of course—kind of heroes. I think Lucas figures I've paid my debt, at least part of it. He wanted me to go back to the Army, and promised he'd help get me off with some kind of minimum sentence. But I told him I was going to stay here and marry you!"

She slumped in the rocker but did not rock, only sat quietly, fingering the eagle-bone whistle. "That's good news. I'm real happy for you, Martin."

Pacing about the room, he ran hands through sun-bleached hair. "Uncle Alonzo spoke once of leaving me the farm. We can take over the farm, Phronsie, you and me! I've gotten good with my hands, and I can paint to bring in extra money! We'll watch things grow, and have children, and—"

Seeing the lack of emotion in her face, he broke off. "Phronsie, what's the matter?"

"Nothing. I said it was wonderful news."

"But you seem so strange!"

Mrs. Cates called up the stairway. "Phronsie! Mr. Sayre? Supper's on! Sauerkraut and pork, with dumplings!"

He took her hand in his; it was cold. "Are you feeling ill?"

She nodded. "Still a little weak, I suppose."

"I can bring something to eat to you, if you want."

She shook her head. "I can't eat, not right now."

"Maybe tea, and a slice of bread and butter?"

She seemed almost annoyed. "No, Martin! Nothing! You go on down and eat. You've been working hard."

"But—"

"Please!"

"All right. But get better fast, will you, Phronsie? There's so much we've got to do."

She managed a small smile and patted his hand. "I'll try. I'll give it all I've got. Now you go."

More of the defeated Sioux straggled in to be confined at Fort Ridgely. There were so many that hundreds, with their women and children, were allowed to stay encamped on the parade ground, their tipis overflowing the huge grassy square. It was a difficult logistical problem for the Army. Most of the Indians seemed chastened and peaceful and were thus permitted, for the time at least, to retain their weapons. Lieutenant Phipps had been successful in his pursuit; Shakopee, Medicine Bottle, and other leaders had been caught. Drugged with opium, they were brought back and jailed in the post stockade. It was estimated that several hundred warriors had participated in the Santee Massacre. Most had by now been accounted for, although a few diehards were still being pursued west of the James River by General Sibley's militia.

Sibley, the Baron of the Border, had been heavily criticized for inaction and dilatoriness during the campaign. One newspaper called him "a snail who falls back on his authority and refuses to march." Now, however, he took a leading role in the prosecution of the Sioux, organizing the military commission from his own staff: five field-grade officers headed by a Major James McBee, a gray-headed artilleryman with long experience at fighting the Sioux on the Platte River. McBee had been a military delegate to the Treaty of 1858, by which the Sioux had lost much of their ancestral lands to the whites for ten cents an acre and the promise of perpetual annuity—the treaty now abrogated by the Legislature.

At the end of September the trial of the Sioux warriors began at Fort Ridgely in a barracks prepared for the occasion. In an elaborate ruse most of the Sioux men were enticed into a storeroom on the promise of blankets, sugar, and coffee. On entering, they were seized and their weapons confiscated. They were then chained by the ankles two by two. Now the commission was prepared to act.

"What will they do with them?" Phronsie asked. Feeling better, but still leaning on the cane she walked along the lead-gray river with him.

"I don't know," he confessed. "Bishop Whipple is coming back from Washington next week; maybe that will help." The newspapers had reported President Lincoln, confronted by the bishop, as saying, "He came here the other day and talked with me about the rascality of this Indian business until I felt it down to my boots!" Martin gazed at the evening sky. The sunset was red, streaked with streamers of wind-driven cloud. Autumn came early to Minnesota. "They'll try to be fair, but there's public pressure to hang the whole lot."

One of the difficulties the military commission soon encountered was the matter of suitable interpreters. Few of the Sioux knew any English. The Army knew even less of the complexities of Sioux grammar. Many Santee Sioux had the same names. A man charged by a witness with a particular crime might not even be the actual miscreant. Bishop Whipple, returned from

Washington and an observer at the trials, was vehement in denouncing the unfairness. On a weekend he came down the river on the steam packet *Aurora* and knocked at Mrs. Cates's door.

"Well, Thad. It's a real nice to see you again. Is Miss Phronsie here?"

"I'll call her, sir," the boy said.

Martin was sitting in the parlor; Phronsie was upstairs, intently writing a letter. Bishop Whipple shook hands.

"Pleased to see you again, Martin. A lot of people hereabouts have you and Phronsie to thank for their lives."

Phronsie came down the stairs then. Together the three sat in the parlor. Mrs. Cates brought cookies and a pot of tea, then withdrew. Bishop Whipple stirred sugar into his tea.

"No, thank you, Phronsie. None of Mrs. Cates's oatmeal cookies tonight. I'm afraid I participated too freely in the fleshpots of Washington. Crab cakes, lobster, steamed clams—after so much wild meat I couldn't resist the temptation." Quickly he became serious. "As you no doubt know, these Indian trials are becoming a farce. They're not fair. The Sioux came in, so they thought, as prisoners of war. Now they're being tried as criminals thirteen to the dozen, without any regard to their true culpability. Why, that jackleg commission tries twenty in less time than we spend on one white man accused of murder!" Face somber, he rose to pace the floor, hands clasped behind his back. "Of course, many *are* guilty of murder, rape, theft—the whole gamut of crimes. So are a lot of white men. But at least the Sioux deserve an articulate spokesman. They need someone who understands them, their language." He paused. "Phronsie, Fool Dog and Shakopee and the rest are asking for Iron Girl. They say she is the only person who can—" The bishop made an awkward gesture across the black clerical frock. "Shakopee did thus; I think it means 'speak from the heart.'"

In the yellow glow of the oil lamp Phronsie's face was troubled. "That's right. *Truth.* Speak from the heart, not from the mouth."

"Will you come with me to Fort Ridgely and serve as my interpreter? As *amicus curiae*—friend of the court. Although I am not too popular with the judges, I have some influence. Besides, the Army will pay you three dollars a day and expenses."

Phronsie was surprised. "Me? Up in front of all those shoulderstraps? Why, I wouldn't know what to do, what to say!"

"You're all they've got, Phronsie," the bishop urged. "Their hope is in you to state their case accurately, render it in good English so that it can be understood by the commission."

She shook her head, looked dismal. Her hands worked at the borrowed gingham, smoothing imaginary wrinkles. "Good English? Jesus, Bishop, I—" She broke off, face red. "I didn't aim to say that! It just kind of popped out!"

Bishop Whipple smiled. "Child, I'll take that as meaning you're asking for divine guidance. I hope our Lord will move you to help these unfortunate people, more sinned against than sinning."

"Well"—she took a deep breath—"if I can help—"

"You sure can!"

"Then I'll do her, Bishop. I'll try."

Martin was not so confident. "Sir, she's still recovering from her wound. Do you think it's wise?"

Before the bishop could answer Phronsie interrupted, indignant. "I am *not* weak! I'm fit as a fiddle, leastways I'm almost."

"But—"

Phronsie rose. Spirit suffused her, brightened the once dull eyes, pinked her cheeks with new blood. "They're my friends! Of course I'll go, Martin! What kind of a person do you think I am?"

When the *Aurora* came downstream from Breckenridge, the three took passage to Fort Ridgely. Phronsie stayed with Surgeon Vollmer and his family, Martin and Bishop Whipple with the post chaplain. From the start Phronsie was plunged into long and tedious sessions of the military commission. Now the season was October, with first snowfall not far away. In the mornings ice had formed on the branches that fed the Minnesota. Grass not worn away by the moccasined tread of hundreds of Sioux women and children frosted white. In the bare and austere room where the Indians were being tried, a soldier was detailed to stoke the big iron stove with firewood. It glowed red, but the chill winds sifted in through cracks in the warped siding and around the windowsills. Wrapped in a comforter supplied by Mrs. Vollmer, Phronsie sat at a table with Bishop Whipple. Martin sat beyond the rail, in a row of benches supplied for newspaper correspondents, sketching the defendants as they took the stand. The papers were all represented: the *Republican*, the *Press*, the *Pioneer and Democrat*, even the Chicago *Times* and San Francisco *Call*, which bought several of Martin's sketches.

Many of the correspondents, bored by the routine operations of the military commission, became interested in Phronsie Bettencourt, the female interpreter.

They queried Martin on his relationship to her; he did not give them much. Phronsie was good copy. Several reporters featured articles on her. She was variously described as the daughter of a Winnebago chief, a daring female who once slew a bear with a carving knife, and the illegitimate offspring of a famous Minnesota politician. Phronsie did not speak to the importunate newsmen. Busy all day at the trials, she collapsed into bed each night, hoarse from speaking. The motherly Frau Vollmer kept the newsmen at bay with a broom and a guttural tirade of *Plattdeutsch*. Martin worried Phronsie was overtaxing herself. But there was nothing he could do.

Each day was a replica of the previous day. Early in the morning a new batch of Sioux, chained by leg irons, was herded into the courtroom to sit on benches under the watchful eyes of armed soldiers. Called to defend himself, a shabby blanket-wrapped Indian would rise, be escorted to the box, and give his name. Even this procedure was fraught with difficulty; Indian names were hard for the officers of the commission to understand.

"Wa—Day—Du—Ta?" Major McBee asked, scanning the roster.

Phronsie repeated the name, slowly.

"Hmmm," McBee scanned a roster. "That sounds like one we had the other day." The others joined him in examining the roster.

"Means high walker," Phronsie explained.

McBee was puzzled. "But here is a Wa—Day—something or other on October third, just last week!" He instructed an aide to carry the roster to Bishop Whipple's table. Together the bishop and Phronsie looked at it and talked in low tones. Finally Phronsie said, "That's his brother, Major."

McBee was confused. "Did we try his brother yet?"

Again there was searching of the roster. Some of the commission officers joined Bishop Whipple, pointing at entries and arguing. Finally Major McBee, impatient, rapped his gavel.

"Let us continue with Wa Pay whatever his name is. We can't waste time on trivialities like this!"

Looking angry, Phronsie muttered, "Trivialities!" under her breath. Martin heard her; apparently, so did Major McBee. The major glowered. Bishop Whipple whispered a warning in her ear. Phronsie bit her lip, drew the folds of the blanket more closely about her, and resumed translating.

"Were you present at the battle of Birch Coulee?"

High Walker, little more than a youth, shook his head.

"Have you borne arms against the state?"

"Sometimes, maybe."

"What does that mean, young man?"

"I don't think he understands the question," Phronsie interrupted.

"Well, state it again, then."

Signing and talking at the same time, Phronsie tried to explain. Finally High Walker admitted, "I shot a soldier, once."

Major McBee's brows twitched. "Aha!"

"He says," Phronsie reported after further questioning, "that a soldier from Fort Ridgely tried to—to—" She blushed, resorted to a graphic Sioux hand sign.

"What does that mean?" McBee demanded.

"The soldier wanted his sister to—to sleep with him."

"Oh!" McBee consulted the other officers, turned back. "Does he have any witnesses to this alleged rape? I suppose that is what he means."

High Walker shook his head. "Alone. Only my sister and me."

McBee adjusted his spectacles. "Hardly pertinent, I'd say." He consulted a sheaf of documents. "Corporal Hardy?"

"Yes, sir." A lank noncom, bandaged arm in a sling, rose and saluted smartly with his left hand.

"Charges against this man state that you observed him at the battle of Birch Coulee last August, when Captain Joseph Anderson of the Sixth Minnesota Infantry and his detail were attempting to bury the bodies of murdered settlers. You were a member of Captain Anderson's command?"

"I was, sir."

"Describe briefly what happened."

"Just after dawn the murdering brutes attacked us where we were camped at the edge of the woods. Seven of my company were killed, and I think twelve—maybe thirteen—wounded. It was touch and go till two companies of the Eighth came up to help us."

McBee pointed to High Walker.

"You saw this Indian there?"

"Yes, sir."

"Are you sure?"

"Yes, sir."

"Actively participating?"

The corporal was puzzled.

"I mean—was he—well, hostile?"

"Damn right!" Corporal Hardy licked his lips. " 'Scuse me. Anyway, he give me this!" He held out the bandaged arm. "Cut me with his hatchet! Next swing would have lopped off my head, I guess. Sergeant Schiefer knocked him down with the butt of his rifle and he got away, someplace. Anyway, I saw him then, and I see him now! I'm sure it's him!"

"Dismissed, Corporal," McBee said. He gestured to a guard. "Take the prisoner back, lock him up."

It was an unvarying ritual; prisoner after prisoner was brought to the box, identified, asked a few questions, led away. Sitting in Surgeon Vollmer's parlor with Martin and the bishop, Phronsie stormed and railed.

"Half the time they don't even know who they're trying! I never saw anything so miserable, so unfair!"

Bishop Whipple sighed. "Forty cases in six hours! I've written to the President again, but don't expect a reply. He's busy with the war."

Suddenly Phronsie began to weep. With a clenched fist she beat on the arm of the sofa. "Why does it have to be this way?"

Martin attempted to comfort her, but she would have no part of him; instead she rushed from the room. Surgeon Vollmer, hearing the commotion, came from the kitchen in carpet slippers; he was smoking his pipe.

"*Was ist los?*"

"Phronsie's a little upset," Martin said.

"*Ach*, I shouldn't wonder." Vollmer laid down his newspaper and joined them. "Poor girl, she has been through much. Now she works so hard, too."

"She's worn out," Martin sighed.

Vollmer puffed on the pipe. "*Ja*. But there is something more."

"Something more?"

"A kind of—I do not know what to call it. Maybe a kind of . . . maybe *weltschmerz*."

Martin did not know that word but Bishop Whipple

did. "It's a sort of hopelessness, a weariness with the world. Something beyond mere personal grief."

"That is what she has! Bishop, you say it good."

"But why . . ."

Bishop Whipple examined his folded hands. "I don't know, Martin. But I will pray for her and hope she may continue to do the Lord's work. She is needed."

Relentlessly the military commission proceeded, a complicated machine that frequently broke down in confusion and disarray. Nevertheless, by the middle of October three hundred and ninety prisoners had been processed. Three hundred and seven were sentenced to death by hanging. Wolf Talker, Fool Dog, Yellow Horse, and others were exonerated when it was proved they were in the guardhouse at Fort Ridgely during the fighting.

Shakopee was the last to be examined. Though his blanket was shabby and moccasins tattered, he bore himself proudly, refusing to answer questions. Through Phronsie he told the court, "It is no good to talk. You robbed and cheated us, molested our women, pushed us away from the land where the ancestors are buried. It is no good to talk anymore. Now you can kill us. That is all I am going to say."

As chief of the rebellious Sioux, he was condemned also. At the President's request, transcripts of the trials were forwarded to Washington. When the sentences were reviewed President Lincoln commuted the death sentences of most but let stand the sentencing of thirty-eight, including Shakopee and Medicine Bottle. In Mankato a special gallows was erected for the simultaneous execution of all thirty-eight. To guard against any possible outbreak from the other prisoners, a force of militia was assigned to keep order.

THE SANTEE MASSACRE

The thirty-eight, many of whom had accepted Christian baptism, were hanged quickly. A reporter from the *Call* filed an interesting story. As the black hoods were placed over the heads of the condemned Sioux, Shakopee heard a train whistle in the distance. Although it was not known whether the reporter knew Sioux, or had hired an interpreter to record the chief's words, he wrote that Shakopee then said, "As the white man comes in, the Indian goes out."

In a telegram to the President General Sibley reported, "Everything went off quietly."

CHAPTER THIRTEEN

After the chill of autumn a spell of clear warm weather lay on Minnesota. The Sioux had an expression for it: the Moon of Smokes. The air was hazy, the dry forest smelled of distant fires. Now that the Sioux had been defeated and their leaders hanged, the mood of the settlers quickened. Fugitives returned to the state. There was a spate of construction in New Ulm as gutted stores and houses were torn down and replaced by new structures smelling of raw wood and fresh paint. Commerce quickened; the river teemed with flatboats and paddle-wheelers. Zook's burned-out store was replaced with a new and larger one owned by an eastern entrepreneur, anxious to share in a new and booming economy. There was even good news from the war. The dilatory Ambrose Burnside had resigned the command of the Army of the Potomac and was replaced by Fighting Joe Hooker, whom the President counseled to "go forward with energy and sleepless vigilance and give us victories."

Day by day bands of the defeated Sioux under mili-

THE SANTEE MASSACRE

tary escort passed New Ulm on their way to a new reservation far to the west. Because of instances when indignant citizens had attacked them, jeering and throwing stones, the files kept to the foothills above the town, bright with autumn red and gold. Back in his old room at Mrs. Cates's boarding house Martin sat again at his easel, working on a portrait of Shakopee as the Santee chief stood in the dock—proud, serene, dignified even in ragged blanket and worn moccasins. From time to time he went to the window, where he could see the Sioux moving silently up the river toward Pipestone Lake. The sight depressed him. Anxious to share his melancholy, he paused at Phronsie's door. He heard her voice, infinitely sad and longing. She was singing.

"*My days have been so wondrous free*—Who is it?"

"Martin. Just Martin, Phronsie."

"Wait a minute." Opening the door, she put something quickly into her bosom.

He sat on the bed. "Were you writing? Did I disturb you? I didn't mean to."

She shook her head. "No. Just—nothing."

Sitting on the bed, hands locked about his knee, he looked out to the river, remembering the summer night he sat with her on the front porch roof and proposed marriage. Now he approached the subject again, but obliquely.

"Yesterday I rode out to Uncle Alonzo's place. It doesn't look too bad. Of course, everything is pretty well run down. The fields are full of weeds and grass, and rain has leaked in and spoiled some of Aunt Flossie's things. Most of the windows are broken out. The whole place smells foul and musty. But when it's opened up and the sun let in, that will pass."

She said nothing, only looked down at her folded

hands. He realized with a pang they had lost much of their nut-brown vigor; now they were pale, and certainly thinner—even blue-veined.

"Maybe . . ." He hesitated. "Maybe we can rent a trap and ride out there someday soon. Would you like that?"

"All right. It might do me good to get out more in the sun." She smiled, faintly. "Winter's coming. Winter was one of their gods, you know."

He took her hand. "Phronsie, you're going to get a lot better now that this nightmare is over! We'll go tomorrow. Let tomorrow be the beginning of something new!"

She nodded, bowed her head, still clasping his hand. He bent to kiss the straight clean part in the midst of the ginger locks, now long and luxuriant.

"All right, then. I'll walk down to the livery stable and make arrangements."

That night he slept better, feeling she was on the road to recovery. When they rode out to the farm he would talk further about marriage, press his suit—but again, he cautioned himself, diplomatically. He must not try too hard, not yet. Women were complex creatures. Phronsie Bettencourt was certainly one of the most complex.

Some time during the night the Moon of Smokes came to an end. A light snow began to fall. Feeling the room grow cold, Martin went to the window in his nightshirt to watch the falling flakes, large and fleecy, melting almost as soon as they touched the shed roof in the backyard. Back in bed under the goose-down comforter, he felt serene and untroubled. Everything, at long last, was going to work out.

Half asleep he thought—or dreamed—that his door opened. Phronsie stood in the light of the oil lamp

Mrs. Cates kept burning of nights in the hallway. "Phronsie?" he called, peering from under the comforter. There was no answer; his door was still closed. A dream. Again he closed his eyes, and was soon asleep.

In the morning one or two inches of new snow lay on the ground. Winter, the Santee god, was still powerful in spite of the defeat of his children. Shed roofs were pristine under the new fall. Below his window urchins on their way to school shouted, pranced about, and threw snowballs. A new school by North German Park had replaced the old one Lucas ordered destroyed to clear a field of fire.

Going down to breakfast, he did not see Phronsie. He had slept soundly and was late; all the other boarders had left for the sawmill, the ferry, the cobbler's shop, or the stores where they clerked. Biscuits, fried ham, and red-eye gravy awaited him, along with a pot of coffee.

"Where's Phronsie?" he asked Mrs. Cates, who was washing dishes in the kitchen.

She emerged slowly, wiping reddened hands on her apron.

"Gone."

He stared in disbelief. "Gone? Where? What—"

"I don't know." Carrying a cup of tea, she sat opposite him, one hand brushing crumbs from the table. "Only the Lord knows, I guess."

"But—"

"I was making coffee this morning—'twasn't light yet—when she come down the stairs in that outlandish outfit of hers, them old skins and fur hat. I don't think she wanted me to see her, kind of slunk by the dining-room door. But I seen her and called out. 'I can't explain,' she said, 'but I've got to go, Mrs. Cates.' Well, I was that flabbergasted I couldn't tell you! She thrown her arms around me and kissed me. I run after her but she was gone, around the corner and into the snow."

Phronsie. Gone! Martin was stunned. "But only yesterday she and I—"

"I went up to her room. I remembered last night she asked for the loan of a sadiron, said she wanted to press out a dress I'd loaned her. Well this morning she'd hung up all the clothes I give her, washed and ironed, neat as a pin. There was money on the bureau, too—all that money, I guess, she was paid from speaking for the Indians at Fort Ridgely." Mrs. Cates reached in an apron pocket to draw out a sheaf of bills. "She didn't owe me all this, Mr. Sayre! I don't know what to with it!"

Martin jumped up, spilling his coffee. "I—I've got to find her! Do you have any idea—"

Seeing the dazed look on Mrs. Cates's face as she stared at the money, he shook his head. "Of course not. You told me that already." At the stairs he paused. "Have you got a heavy coat I can borrow?"

"There's that old buffalo coat on the hall tree used to belong to my husband, Elmer."

Wriggling into the furry, malodorous thing, he ran out to the porch. The urchins were still throwing snowballs. One hit him on the cheek and burst into powder that drifted icily down his neck. Uncaring, he rounded the house, past the snow-steepled outbuildings, to trudge up the hill. Hatless, hands jammed into pockets, he felt his cheeks and ears tingling from the cold. Above the town, at the edge of the forest, he looked back. A paddle-wheeler lay at the dock, black smoke curling from her funnel. Soon the river would ice over and there would be no more river traffic until spring. He heard a distant sound of saws and hammers, a clanging bell from the schoolhouse. Abruptly he turned his back and plunged into the trees, now knowledgeably following an ancient trail where the deer came down from the heights to drink.

At noon the sun was only a red ball without warmth in the smoky sky. The temperature had dropped. In their new boots his feet were cold and blistered, but he pressed on. Thorns tore his jeans; his fingers were scratched from the occasional thickets of winter-killed vines through which he threaded his way. By now ears and cheeks were numb. He clapped ungloved hands together to urge the circulation.

He knew where he was going but several times lost his way and had to retrace his steps. By now the sun was only a few degrees above the horizon. The new fall of snow rimed his hair and beard; he did not mind that so much except that it melted and ran down his neck onto his chest and belly.

"Phronsie!" he called. "Where are you? Do you hear me?"

No one had heard. Skirting an intertwined grove of burr oaks, he caught sight in the distance of the little pond.

"Phronsie!"

The camp lay as they had left it so long ago. Snow covered the iron traps, softening their cruel outline. The lean-to sagged where one of the posts had collapsed. There was a thin crust of ice at the edges of the pond where they had laughed, bathed, and been happy.

"Phronsie?"

Again no answer; bleak forest stared back at him.

Disconsolate, he walked to the cross-marked mound where Jake Bettencourt lay. Jake, he thought, would not like to see what had happened to his Santee friends.

A thought came to him. In fading light he hurried up a familiar trail. In a few minutes he found her on the hump of rock where he had first seen her that day when, frightened and desperate, he mistook her for an Indian brave. Phronsie Bettencourt sat wrapped in her blanket. Remembering woodsmanship, he approached, careful to make no noise. There was no wind; he had always suspected she could scent approaching things like a deer. He clenched his fists in an effort to stifle the joy that surged within his breast.

"Hello, pilgrim," he said, softly.

She jerked into awareness, ready for flight.

"It's me—Martin."

Swathed in the snow-dusted blanket, she looked small and vulnerable.

"It's me," he repeated.

She nodded, noncommittal. "Lordy, don't you suppose I got ears? I know it's you. Didn't I hear you bumbling down that trail like a bull moose."

"You did not!"

"Well, I *did*!" Taking off her snow-mounded fur hat, she shook out a cloud of white flakes.

"You cut your hair!"

"It was too long. Bothered me, washing and combing and all."

As a hunter stalks a wary animal, he approached her. Sitting down on a fallen log, he asked casually, "What are you doing up here anyway?"

She nodded toward the valley of the Minnesota. In the snow mist he could just make out a file of Sioux winding in and out of the leafless willows along its banks. Cavalrymen edged the procession, urging the Indians along to make camp before nightfall.

Picking up a twig, he traced a pattern in the snow. "Why did you run away, Phronsie?"

Her eyes widened. "Didn't you find my letter?"

"Letter?" He remembered her working at something.

"I left it on your easel."

"Well, I didn't see it. When Mrs. Cates told me you were gone I got into such a state I didn't notice any letter. What did it say?"

She looked back at the file of Sioux, fading from view as the sun dimmed and the fall of snow increased. "What you already knew, I reckon. Martin, I can't marry up with you. I'm not any damned housewife, to make beds and sweep floors and wash clothes. I don't belong in a house. I'm a—a—well, I guess I'm a woods colt, that's all."

"You're a woman," he said soberly, staring at the pattern in the snow. He had traced a rough approximation of the Sioux sign for *love*, two wrists crossed over a sketchy breast. She saw it, too, and looked quickly away. "And I love you."

She shook her head. "I'm going with them. The Santee people. That's where I belong." Her voice caught in a small sob. "Damn it all, they're driving them farther and farther out of the country! People like Ramsey and Sibley won't be satisfied till they herd them over the cliffs into the salt sea!"

"Nevertheless," he insisted, "where you go, I go!"

"What kind of foolishness is that, anyway?"

Squatting in the bulky buffalo coat, he embellished his drawing. "If you don't want to be a housewife, I don't want to be a farmer. It's simple as that. But no matter what happens, I'm going to stay with you."

She burst into tears. "You can't do that! It's going to be hard times for them from now on. They need someone to speak for them, haggle for the best deal they can get, and that's what I can do. But you . . ."

With satisfaction he looked down at the completed snow picture. "I'll take along my paints and paint them! You're right; some day they'll be gone. They need a record of what they were, their great days, before the white men came."

Frustrated, she slid off the boulder and faced him. "God damn it, no! I won't have it!"

"Didn't I tell you a hundred times I don't like to hear you swear like that?"

"I'll swear all I damned please!"

Taking her in his arms he held her tight. "Ah, Phronsie! You can't lose me! You're my woman, you stubborn thing, even if you don't know it!"

She fought him, pressing forearms against the furry pelt of his coat. "No! No, Martin!"

He released her enough to look into her eyes. "You don't mean that, Phronsie. You love me too, I *know*!"

"Why do you make it so rough for me, Martin?" Shaking, she slumped on the boulder, clenched fist to her mouth. "I tell you—it isn't to be! You're not my kind and I'm not your kind! It won't work! Some day you'd come to your senses and—and—" She broke off, weeping.

Woods. colt.. Half. Indian. He remembered the words. They were those his brother Lucas had used when he tried to persuade Martin to go back. *You're not my kind and I'm not your kind! Bound to come to your senses.*

"Listen to me," he said, his voice almost harsh. "Phronsie Bettencourt, look me in the eye!"

Unwillingly she looked up, face tear stained.

THE SANTEE MASSACRE

"Did Lucas—my brother Lucas—did he talk to you?"

"About what?"

"You know damned well! He talked to you, didn't he? He told you all these things you're saying like a silly parrot! *Woods colt! You're not my kind! Come to your senses!* All that rubbish!"

Her voice was low. "What if he did?"

"What if he did? Good God, Phronsie, why didn't you listen to me instead of Lucas?"

Her eyes were dim with tears. "It was *my* idea, not his, anyway! All Lucas did was help me with some of the words. I knew a long time ago I wasn't for you." She wiped her eyes with a sleeve. "Martin, you're educated, and cult—" She paused. "Cult—ured. You talk all kinds of languages and play music and know about poets and things like that. God damn it—I can swear if I want—go back and marry that Lavinia Greene or whatever her name is and have pretty children and live in a big house and do whatever city folks do! *I don't care!*"

"Why, you great ninny. I'd die back there now in all that hustle-bustle and noise and dirt! Horsecars clanging, streets full of unhappy people, Lavinia Greene and her prinking and posing and tea drinking with her little finger cocked up in the air. I belong *here*, with you"— he gestured toward the retreating Sioux—"with you, and them. I love you, Phronsie Bettencourt! We're together like cottonwood and bark, and not to be separated till we die. If you'll marry me, I'd be satisfied to have old Wolf Talker do it, however the Sioux manage it. In any case, you're not going to be rid of me, ever!" Pulling her to him, he tilted her chin back and kissed her hard on the lips.

She gasped, trying to push him away, and swore fluently. He kissed her harder, smothering the flood of invective. "You can't fool me acting like that! I know you better! You're just putting on a performance!"

Suddenly she ceased her struggles as if exhausted, gave herself to him. "Oh, Martin! God help me! It's not right, but—"

"The rightest thing in the world, Phronsie. If everything was as right as this, the world wouldn't be in such trouble."

"You—you sure you're not just sorry for me?"

"Sorry for you?" Amused, he clasped her tighter, pressed his bearded cheek against hers. "Phronsie, I wish I was one half the man you are."

Again she flared up. "I ain't no man!"

"Figure of speech," he apologized.

"Well—" Picking up the possibles bag, she threw it over her shoulder. "Which way does our stick float now?"

"We'll stop by Mrs. Cates's. For the last time. I'll pick up my paints and brushes and some other things. Tomorrow we'll follow them, wherever they go." He took her hand *"Hopo!"*

Under the few crimson streaks in the evening sky the Santee Sioux toiled westward, into exile. He could no longer see Shakopee's people. Hand in hand Martin and Phronsie descended the long hill toward the town. Lights were beginning to blink on, yellow pinpricks against the new snow.

> "A hard, cruel, cynical novel—
> and a good one."—
> *The Washington Post Book World*

HORN OF AFRICA

by Philip Caputo

author of *A Rumor of War*

Three mercenaries embark on a reckless mission to turn a tribe of warriors into a modern army. Caught in the fanaticism of mad war, thrust beyond the reach of civilization, they crossed the boundaries of conscience and confronted war's bottomless capacity for violence and evil.

"Shades of Joseph Conrad and Graham Greene."—*Booklist*

A Dell Book $3.95   (13675-X)

At your local bookstore or use this handy coupon for ordering:

| DELL BOOKS   HORN OF AFRICA $3.95   (13675-X)
| P.O. BOX 1000, PINE BROOK, N.J. 07058-1000

Please send me the above title. I am enclosing $_____ (please add 75c per copy to cover postage and handling). Send check or money order—no cash or C.O.D.'s. Please allow up to 8 weeks for shipment.

Mr./Mrs./Miss_____

Address_____

City_____ State/Zip_____

The National Bestseller!

GOODBYE, DARKNESS

by WILLIAM MANCHESTER
author of *American Caesar*

The riveting, factual memoir of WW II battle in the Pacific—and of an idealistic ex-marine's personal struggle to understand its significance 35 years later.

"A strong and honest account, and it ends with a clash of cymbals."—*The New York Times Book Review*

"The most moving memoir of combat in World War II that I have read. A testimony to the fortitude of man. A gripping, haunting book."—William L. Shirer

A Dell Book $3.95   (13110-3)

At your local bookstore or use this handy coupon for ordering:

| DELL BOOKS   GOODBYE, DARKNESS $3.95   (13110-3)
P.O. BOX 1000, PINE BROOK, N.J. 07058-1000

Please send me the above title. I am enclosing $_____ (please add 75c per copy to cover postage and handling). Send check or money order—no cash or C.O.D.'s. Please allow up to 8 weeks for shipment.

Mr./Mrs./Miss_____

Address_____

City_____ State/Zip_____